Midnight Wine

Jan McDonald

Raven Crest Books

Cover Design by www.StunningBookCovers.com

ISBN-13: 978-0-9931909-4-0
ISBN-10: 0-99-319094-4

**"There from thy daughter, sister, wife
At midnight drain the stream of life."**

Lord Byron. (The Giaour.)

CHAPTER ONE

It was four in the morning and Beckett was still awake, insomnia developed into an art form. He lay on his bed charting the progress of a spider as it made its way across the cracked ceiling, grateful for the diversion from images that made nightmares seem like fairy stories designed to lull the innocent to sleep.

It was ten years since his life had been turned inside out and every which way, and ten years since all that he held dear had been snatched from him. Then, vampires were simply a product of Bram Stoker's imagination as far as he knew; now it was different. Now he knew the truth.

They existed and they were out there.

That night he had walked away from the priesthood, away from his life and away from God. Father Paul Beckett was now just Beckett. Dr Beckett to be strictly accurate; a PhD in Psychology was the result of his search for his own sanity.

The telephone at his bedside shrilled, jerking him upright as he made a grab at the receiver. It was the call he'd been dreading. There was a gut-wrenching sob in his ear then a pitiful, "Help me, Beckett."

He was out of bed the instant he heard her voice, the telephone cradled between his shoulder and his ear, while he dragged on jeans. He hopped from foot to foot, wrestling with socks, and lost his balance, kicking the empty Jack Daniels bottle which earlier that night had been half full.

"Stay where you are, Kat. I'm coming. Understand? Stay put."

He pushed his fingers through his shoulder length hair; prematurely silver, it was a defiant reminder of things he'd

1

rather forget.

"Kat?"

He grabbed the roll-neck sweater that he'd tossed onto a chair earlier and pulled it roughly over his head, phone still in place. The soft light illuminated a livid, jagged scar that ran diagonally across the left side of his chest between two of his ribs, drawing the attention to his lean musculature. His slate grey-eyes betrayed the panic that surged through him, and those that knew him would see the old pain reflected in them.

"I'm sorry Beckett," she whispered.

He heard a soft thud as her telephone hit the floor, accompanied by muffled sobbing. Tossing the phone onto a chair he snatched his keys from the side table as he wrenched open the door, mentally crossing his fingers that this wouldn't be one of the times his old jeep refused to start.

After a couple of graveyard coughs, the dilapidated four-by-four juddered into life and climbed the narrow road over the mountain from the Welsh market town of Abergavenny to the old mining community of Blaenavon, more by Beckett's will than the power of its old engine. Kat was on the edge and he knew that minutes could make a difference. He floored the accelerator, ignoring the plume of smoke that emerged from the exhaust pipe along with the smell of burning clutch. He also realised that he was probably still over the limit, but at that time of day he'd risk it. He had to.

He slowed down as he turned into the unmade road that wound itself back down from the top of the mountain to her cottage. The whole place was in darkness and the front door stood wide open. Beckett felt his chest tighten.

No. Please don't have gone out. Not like that. He daren't think about what may have happened if she had. Not again. Not this time.

He stepped inside, not breathing, past images melding with present cold dread.

"Kat?"

There was momentary silence before he heard the soft whimper coming from the darkened interior of her sitting room. He exhaled all the air in his lungs in one hit. She was still home. Allowing himself to breathe normally again he stepped softly into the room and over to her side.

She was sitting on the floor, hunched against the far wall, hugging her knees and rocking slowly back and forth. He didn't speak or move, allowing her to become aware of his presence without startling her. She suddenly stopped rocking and became very still. She was in pyjamas and a fleece jacket and Beckett guessed - from the spoiled make-up and her usually immaculate, short dark hair standing in chaotic clumps - that she'd been this way for some time. He picked up the telephone from the floor, put it back on the receiver and switched on the lamp beside it on an old sideboard. She still didn't move or speak.

"Kat, look at me," he said, his voice almost a whisper.

He didn't touch her, knowing that to do so could send her over the edge of her own abyss; he needed to bring her back from her inner world slowly.

Squatting beside her, he said gently, "Kat, it's me, Beckett. Let me help you up."

He held out his hand but still he didn't touch her. She lifted her gaunt face to him, her eyes unable to contain the pool of tears that blurred the amethyst dazzle which had once lived there. Her cheekbones were more prominent and she looked even thinner than when he'd seen her last, barely three days ago. His gut twisted at the sight of her, his worst fears manifest. It was happening again.

"Kat," he said softly.

She peered at him, struggling to focus and it was several moments before he saw recognition dawning slowly.

"I had the dream again," she said, "but this time I could taste it. I tasted the blood. I can still taste it. The things I did ..." Her voice was trembling and she balled her hands into fists, pushing her knuckles hard into her temples, as if to block the images that only she could see.

"Make it stop, Beckett. Oh, God, please make it stop," she begged as she reached out for him.

He took her arm gently, blanching as his fingers felt bone through skin. "There's no blood, Kat. It was a bad dream - just a nightmare."

And he knew all about nightmares.

Kat shook her head vigorously. "It's more. I don't know how or why, but I know it's more than that. And I can't take it any longer. You have to help me, I'm going crazy." Her eyes pleaded with him.

He pulled her to him gently, still careful not to send her back into her own hell. "It will be okay. I promise."

She allowed herself to rest her head against him and he sensed her panic begin to subside.

"You're sweet Beckett. Are you this good with all your patients that call you in the middle of the night?"

He smiled and the storm in his eyes dissipated. "Absolutely. Especially the beautiful ones. I always do house calls." He lifted her to her feet and guided her to the old sofa. "Come and sit down."

Her weak smile didn't fool him as she closed her eyes on the fragments of the dream that so obviously still lingered.

"I need a drink," she said. "There's brandy in the kitchen."

It was the last thing she needed but he said, "Stay there, I'll get it for you."

In her kitchen, he sighed as he poured brandy into a small tumbler. He wanted to put his arms around her and tell her it didn't matter; that he'd take care of her, no matter what. But that wasn't about to happen now that she was this far gone nor, for that matter, while she was his patient. He felt as if he'd failed her. Just like he'd failed Grace.

Not for the first time, he faced the possibility that his

feelings for Kat had more to do with wanting to save her when he'd been unable to save his own sister, than with anything else. He shook his head in an effort to dispel the carousel of thoughts. It was way past time he sent her to Lane.

Dr Lane Dearing was the best in their field and if anyone could help Kat now, it was Lane. For too long he'd blocked out the possibilities of her condition, refusing to believe it could happen again. She was vulnerable and so thin that he felt even a hug could snap her in two. Now he had no choice. If he was right, then only Lane could help her.

He closed his eyes to the memories that came unbidden, not daring to give them access, but the familiar story clamoured in his brain refusing to be hushed; the anaemia, the wasting away, and the blood dreams. History was inexorably repeating itself. Grace had gone through it all before the end.

He turned as he sensed her behind him.

Kat stood limply in the open doorway clutching a newspaper. "Have you seen this?"

"What is it?" he asked quietly.

Her tears found their own way onto her chin and dripped onto a darkening patch on her T-shirt. She dropped the newspaper and returned to her sofa, saying nothing.

He grabbed at the fallen newspaper. *What the hell ...?*

His answer grinned from the middle of the page. Dr Greg 'I love me' Randall, the egotistical son-of-a-bitch behind the guilt that haunted her, the father of the child she given up for adoption a lifetime ago. He ground his teeth, wanting to pull the face out of the newsprint and smash his fist into it.

"You have to let go of the past, Kat," he said, "Let yourself live now and start to think of the future." It was inadequate and he knew it.

She didn't answer him; just stared straight ahead.

Eventually she said, "I'm finished, Beckett. I can't pretend any more. My practice has dwindled down to next to nothing, and the ones that do still come look at me with a mixture of pity and curiosity. I mean who wants to go see a herbalist that's messed up in the head? *Look at me.* I'm a goddamn skeleton. How can I help anyone else when I can't help myself?"

"The way you always do. By caring."

"Maybe that's it; maybe I don't care anymore."

He smiled at her, "I don't believe that and neither do you. Any way, your messed up head is my territory, so hands off. Stick to your herbs and magic potions."

He watched as a hint of a smile flickered weakly around her mouth but didn't quite make it to her eyes.

"Kat, I want you to listen to me. I want you to see a friend of mine, Dr Lane Dearing. She can help you better than I can."

Despair etched her thin features. "You too, Beckett? I guess I should have known that even you'd give up on me in the end. I must be a real drag."

He put his hands on her shoulders, careful not to hold her too tightly, but couldn't stop himself raising his voice. "Listen to me dammit. I want you to see Lane because I think I know what's wrong with you and if I'm right she's the one who can help you through this."

She looked shocked. "What do you think is wrong with me? *What?*" she demanded.

Beckett closed his eyes. He'd lost sight of professionalism; bungled it because of his intense feelings. Her spiralling anxiety was totally his fault and he was losing control of the situation. He took a deep breath.

"I'm not certain." He hesitated. "But I may have seen something similar before. And it was Lane that helped."

"Am I going to die? ... Beckett?"

"No. You aren't going to die. I can't say any more until you've seen Lane. Let's get you fixed up to see her."

He was falling for her and he knew he'd crossed the

line.

"I'm sorry Kat, I can't be your therapist feeling the way I do. I'm falling for you and that's why I have to pass you on to Lane. You can't remain my patient. It would be unethical and unfair to you."

He sighed. This wasn't the way he'd planned on telling her. *I've blown it. Just look at her; she can't handle this. Bloody fool!*

"Beckett, I ..."

He placed his finger on her lips. "Don't. I'm sorry. I shouldn't have said anything. I don't expect you to feel the same, I know how much you're hurting and I just want you to know that you aren't going to do this alone. Understand? I'm not going to let you go through this without me. But you have to see that I can't think clearly around you, and you deserve much more. Lane is the best. Hell, she's even better than me."

His effort to bring a smile, no matter how fleeting, failed. It was as though she hadn't heard him as she leaned forward and picked up the discarded newspaper. "I always knew he'd do well. Anything else wasn't an option with him."

"Kat, listen to me. You *have* to let him go. It's over. It's been over for eighteen years. Let it go before it eats you away."

"Graduated top of his year; youngest consultant to be appointed at the University Hospital; his own private clinic where he does research into AIDS as well as his hospital work ..." she paused, "... I don't love him, if that's what you think. I thought I did a million years ago, but he never loved me. I wouldn't have given up my baby if there had been a chance. I'd have hung on somehow, hoping that one day ... but I did what I thought was best for my son. I listened to everyone else instead of my heart. I should have told Greg; he had a right to know. He never married you know. Oh ... I don't know what's wrong with me ... it's like an obsession; a sore place I have to pick at - it's like he's haunting me."

Beckett didn't comment on the fact that he thought that a girl dropping out of medical school because she was pregnant and ill would stab the conscience of any guy, especially one that had been her lover for most of the previous summer. Greg had to have wondered if the child was his and the fact he never even enquired about Kat spoke volumes. Dr Greg Randall was an asshole.

"Will you see Lane?" he asked quietly.

"Yes." The sadness in the amethyst eyes hit him hard. *You failed me,* they said. *Even you won't stay the distance. Even you, Beckett.*

"Today?" he ventured.

She sighed. "Why not? If I'm going to be sectioned it might as well be today. Thanks for coming to my rescue; I'll be OK now ..., look it's getting light. I need to take a bath and change before clinic. If anyone comes, that is."

She managed a half smile and reached for the glass of brandy. As she raised it to her lips, a wave of revulsion swept over her and she let the glass fall to the floor, her hand flying to cover her mouth as she saw the amber liquid turn into a dark pool of blood.

CHAPTER TWO

Beckett dialled Lane's Dearing's private number from memory. She answered straight away and he smiled at the sound of her smoky voice.

"Hi, it's Beckett. How're you doing?"

"That would be the Beckett that bailed on me half way through a high profile charity gala, would it? Or maybe it's the Beckett who keeps promising me dinner then cancelling at the last minute? Oh I know! It's the Beckett that doesn't call for over six months then out of the blue ..."

He interrupted her. "Cheap shot, but deadly accurate. I'm mortally wounded. How are you, Legs?" he asked, calling her by the affectionate name he had for her.

"Barely coping without you. You?"

"So, so. Listen, I need your help."

"Of course you do, why else would you call me? I gave up on dinner long ago. What's up Handsome?"

"I need to refer a patient to you."

"Out of your depth? Not like you."

"No. Look, it's urgent. Can you see her today? Her name's Katerini Pappas." His tone was enough.

Lane dropped their customary easy banter born of their more than comfortable friendship, switching easily into professional colleague mode. "Of course, hold on a tick."

He heard her flicking through her diary. "How about five o'clock. My last appointment's at four so I can give her as long as you like. Care to enlighten me?"

"I'd rather you made up your own mind, free and clear of my opinion."

"I see. Like that is it? Why me?"

"Because you're the best, and don't go all coy on me,

we both know it. And because I trust you."

Lane laughed. "What I mean is, why hand her over?" She paused, then, "Oh, I get it. You've got the hots for her, right?"

"God, you can be so basic when you want to be. If you must know, I do find her attractive, but she is my client and it has gone no further. And, it's for the best."

"Best for your career or best for her?"

"Her, of course," he replied.

"In that case, it would be a pleasure to help. Sure you can't tell me anything?"

Beckett hesitated; he didn't want to colour her judgement.

Eventually he said, "She's extremely fragile, right on the edge. One push …"

"Oh, that's a great help. Come on, Handsome. Give me more."

"Okay. She has a long history, eighteen years of it."

Lane gave a low whistle. "Miracles take a little longer, honey. And?"

"*And* she's anaemic. *And* she's plagued by dreams."

"Dreams?" she queried, though Beckett knew from the edge in her voice that she was already aware of their nature.

"Blood dreams."

"Oh, God."

"I'm afraid for her, Lane."

"In that case, so am I. Thanks, Handsome. Do the same for you one day."

"Lane?"

"Yes?"

"You have to help her."

"I'll do my best. Am I to keep you informed? Are we sending ethics right down the tubes?"

"Don't know, I'll ask her. Appreciate it. So long, Legs."

Lane put the telephone down in slow motion. Her pale auburn hair, the shade of warm honey, fell from behind her shoulder as her thoughts raced ahead, building a mental picture that she had no desire to look on but one that was all too familiar. She felt the tell-tale crawling in the pit of her stomach that warned of impending trouble as surely as the seaweed on her secretary's door told of approaching bad weather.

She reached into the drawer of her mahogany desk for a cigarette, lit it thoughtfully, leaned back in her chair and crossed the long elegant legs that had earned her the affectionate name that Beckett always used for her. She held her cigarette between the first and middle finger of her right hand and clicked the nails of her thumb and fourth finger together. Becket would recognise the sign. It meant she was deeply worried. And she didn't worry easily.

***

Kat scanned the mail on her doormat. It was mostly junk or advertising material from herbal suppliers, along with two more cancellation notes. *Great. Well, keep them coming. Soon there will be no appointments to cancel.*

A cursory flick through her diary showed just two entries. Mrs Davies, who would just want a repeat prescription of her nerve tonic that would take her only a few minutes to dispense, then it would be Mr Khan with his multitude of non-existent aches and pains. He would have a cup of herbal tea with her and take home a bottle of placebo 'medicine' that was little more than herbal tonic. Then he would telephone her the following day to say he felt so much better, that she was truly a miracle worker and next time she really must charge him something. She smiled. She liked Mr Khan who came to her simply because he was lonely and she wondered where he would go when she shut her doors for the last time.

The morning followed its expected course, broken only by the telephone call from Beckett saying that Lane was expecting her at five and did she want him to go with her?

No, she didn't.

He seemed disappointed and she could imagine the frown lines deepening on his attractive, if care worn, face. He asked if Lane could keep him informed of her progress.

Of course.

Did she mind if he called her from time to time, just to see how she was?

No, that would be fine.

She was deeply disturbed at Beckett's passing her onto someone else. She'd have to go through it all again; relive the sordid details of it all; relive the pain, the sickness, everything. She couldn't bring herself to consider his reasons. Not while she was like this. *Damn you, Beckett.*

She slammed the diary shut.

Well, this would be the last time she put herself through it. If this Dr Dearing couldn't help her, then she may as well ... what? Be dead? It was a reasonable assumption given her rapidly deteriorating condition. There would be no one to miss her except maybe Beckett, and he'd get over her. *So, Lane Dearing, give it your best shot.*

Her anxiety levels hiked up as the time came closer for her to see Lane. By the time she left the cottage she was riding high on surging waves of panic, caught between the urge to run far away and just keep on going, or to see it through.

At the bottom of the mountain she stopped at the junction, swallowed hard and pressed her dry lips together then, before she could change her mind, turned right and headed for Lane's consulting room in Abergavenny.

Inside her room Lane looked at her wristwatch. Almost five o'clock. She opened the door to the outer office.

"Lucy, I've fitted in a new patient. You can go early. I'll lock up."

Her secretary narrowed her heavily kohl-lined eyes. "I haven't prepared any files for you, Doctor."

Lane made a mock grimace. "Now I know I'm in

trouble. You only call me 'Doctor' when I've done something you disapprove of. I know, I know, I'm sorry. I should have let the appointment come through you. Trust me on this one?"

Lucy persisted, "I've been worried about you, Lane. Your aura is all fuzzy. I looked at your cards last night, and they weren't at all reassuring."

"Lucy, I *wish* you'd quit messing with tarot cards and looking at my goddamn aura. We really need to talk about your obsession with all this stuff. Really, I'll be fine, so go home and have a nice evening with that man of yours. Don't lock the door on your way out."

"But, it's what I saw, a stranger coming and ..."

"And that's all I want to hear about cards and auras tonight thanks, Lucy. I'll see you in the morning." She smiled and nodded towards the door.

In the ten years that Lucy had worked for Lane, their relationship had evolved from employer and employee to an easy friendship that existed solely at work and neither of their lives outside impinged on the other. Lane was careful never to upset that arrangement. Lucy had also learned when not ask questions about after hours appointments, the files for which would always be locked in Lane's private drawer. She nodded back at Lane in a gesture of understanding.

Lane cared about Lucy and indulged her eccentricities - her love of crystals and her tarot cards, her gypsy skirts and conspiracy theories - and she regularly rebuked Beckett when he referred to her as Loopy Lucy, but she was in no mood for gypsy warnings and omens as she contemplated the enormity of what Kat was probably about to face.

"Good night, then." Lucy hesitated at the door. "Be careful, Lane."

Lane had already disappeared into her room.

As she opened the door Lucy walked straight into Kat who was standing motionless in the hallway. She smiled encouragingly.

"Hi," she said, "You must be the five o'clock. Go on in, Dr Dearing is expecting you."

Kat stepped inside and the door closed behind her.

The door to the inner office stood ajar and she could see a warm light from the lamp on the mahogany desk straight ahead. Panic rose in her like a hot tide. At this time of year the daylight would be fading soon. Before long it would be dark and she dreaded the night. Why had she agreed to this? This was her last chance and she knew it. It was fight or flight time.

Before it could be flight, she heard movement in the consulting room and sucking in air, she tapped on the door. "Hello?"

The door was pulled open from the inside and Kat faced a beautiful woman whose smile made her feel better even before she spoke. Lane was dressed in an elegant dark suit, the tight-fitting skirt fashionably above her knee, with rich gold lights shining in her hair that hung loose in a silk curtain. She held out a hand and locked her tranquil gaze into Kat's frightened eyes.

"Hello, you must be Katerini. I'm Dr Dearing; Lane if you'd prefer."

Kat took the hand, it was warm and somehow comforting; a capable hand, a hand you could trust. "Yes, um, I came in as someone else left, your secretary I think, she let me in. I'm Katerini Pappas."

Lane smiled at her. "Come on in and sit down." She indicated a large comfortable looking armchair facing its twin into which Lane sank easily, crossing her elegant legs.

"Katerini Pappas. That's an interesting name. Greek?"

"My father was Greek. I was named after the small village where I was born, but I'm mostly called Kat."

"Kat it is then." Lane picked up a silver box from the coffee table between them. "Smoke?"

"No. Thanks."

"Coffee?"

"No, nothing thanks ... really."

"Okay then, let's get started. I don't have any of your history, but Beckett has told me that your problems are long standing. Take your time and tell me."

Kat began slowly. "I was treated for haemolytic anaemia as a child, regular blood transfusions, liver biopsies, the works. Apparently it's something that's prevalent among Mediterranean people and with my Greek heritage, well, it fitted. It went on for years then they decided it was pernicious anaemia although they never did really confirm it. I still get anaemic from time to time. I know my blood count is in my boots right now. It'll work out. I manage it myself."

She saw Lane's raised eyebrow and questioning glance but chose to ignore it.

"When was the last relapse?" Lane continued.

"About six months ago."

"I understand you don't sleep well, that you're troubled by bad dreams. Can you tell me about them?"

"*No,*" she said, too quickly. "No. not yet. I'm sorry... do you think I could have that cigarette now, please?"

Lane passed the silver box to her and slipped a slim, gold lighter out of her jacket pocket, flicked it into life and waited as Kat inhaled and coughed, betraying her non-smoker status and her anxiety state orbiting in outer space.

"Do you work, Kat?"

"I'm a herbalist. I have ... had ... a practice."

"Married?"

"No, nor likely to be."

Lane didn't take her up on the remark but Kat had no doubt that she'd mentally filed it for later.

"Do you have any children?" she continued.

Kat stiffened visibly. "Beckett didn't tell you? No ... why would he?"

"Tell me what?"

"That I have a son somewhere. I got pregnant while I was in medical school – another student – he's ... well, he

15

doesn't matter. Anyway, I thought I was in love with him but he sure as hell wasn't in love with me. So what was I to do? I don't agree with abortion so I decided on adoption. It was all nice and neat and clinical and discreet with no time to form any kind of bond with the son. This way he would have what I couldn't give him as a penniless student, I could carry on with my medical career and at least not lose everything. Well, that's what I thought anyway."

"What happened?"

"The anaemia flared right up during my pregnancy and after my baby was born it got out of control, I got really sick. I lost too much time and couldn't make it up, so I quit. End of story. End of career."

"Not quite," Lane said quietly, throwing a deep, warm smile at Kat..

"I'm sorry?"

"Not quite the end of your career. You said you were a herbalist. That must have taken a great deal of study and effort."

Kat smiled and visibly relaxed, on safe ground discussing anything but the reason she was there. "The exams were tough. It felt like medical school all over again and, in a way, I had to prove myself more; not everyone understands that a herbalist isn't a quack. It took a few years to build up the practice."

"Well then, we'd better get you well again so that you can keep that practice of yours. What about your social life? Relationships?"

"If you're asking if there's a man in my life, then the answer is no. I ... there hasn't been anyone for several years now."

Lane appeared to let it go. "Can we talk about the dreams now?" she ventured.

Kat remained didn't move, seeming hardly to breathe. The heavy silence in the room was fractured only by the steady tick of the beautifully ornate grandfather clock in the corner, and eventually by her harsh sigh as she exhaled the unfamiliar blue smoke that ripped into her throat. Only she saw the instant replay of the worst of the dreams; the one where she tore the flesh from the throat of a lover with her teeth, where she ripped and cut into his flesh in search of the crimson elixir; relishing the warmth and taste of the blood, drinking and sucking, becoming more and more sexually charged as she drank.

Knowing it hadn't really been a dream.

She came to a sudden decision, stubbed out the cigarette and stood up quickly. "It's late. I have to go. I'm really sorry for wasting your time."

Lane stood up and put her hand on Kat's emaciated arm. "There's no hurry. Stay and talk. We can talk about something else. Stay for a while, at least have a cup of tea."

Kat pulled away from her and headed for the door. "I'm sorry. You don't understand. Can't you see? It's almost dark. I need to get home. I have to."

CHAPTER THREE

Kat's heart rate was off the chart, the offending muscle pounding painfully against her ribs. She was barely breathing and her throat was dry as the panic attack took hold. She'd been stupid and naïve to think she could get away with being out in the dark.

The traffic had come to a standstill and flashing blue lights up ahead gave the reason. She swerved out of the motionless line of vehicles that were blocking the mountain road and into a lay-by, prompting the blaring of several horns. She was out of the car in seconds, not even taking time to lock it; not caring for the consequences of this open invitation - let them take it, she didn't care.

She was only minutes away from the safe haven of her cottage if she ran. The last remaining threads of composure went into freefall as the twilight conceded to darkness and rational thought took flight. She ran blindly past the line of cars, ignoring the voice in the fluorescent yellow jacket calling to her, asking if she was all right, pushing herself to run faster and faster down the lane to where her cottage waited to give her refuge.

Out of breath and trembling, she stopped at her gate and bent forwards, hands on her thighs and lungs heaving painfully. She leaned on the gatepost as her breathing gradually became steadier and the sharp pain in her chest began to subside before she attempted to walk to her front door. It was over, enough was enough, she'd resign herself to the fact she was going to die and just stay the hell away from everyone while she did so.

He stepped from out of the deepening darkness and grabbed at her hair from behind before she even saw or heard him. His knee thumped into the middle of her back, pushing her hard against the wall, grazing her cheek against the brickwork.

She felt the cold of a steel blade at her throat.

Sickened and winded her mind raced, yanked into the present, self preservation expelling previous thoughts and bringing rationality into sharp focus. *Humour him*, she thought. *That's the only way to stay alive.*

He hadn't spoken and she frantically searched for words that would come to her aid. "I don't have much money, but you can have what I've got. Let me just get my purse from my bag. I won't scream, just don't cut me. Please."

*Don't cut me, don't cut me, **please** don't cut me*, she thought. *I can't deal with blood.*

The cold steel pressed against her throat.

"I don't want your money. I want you to come with me."

Lava streams of panic erupted in her chest until she felt she would explode. *What was this? Rape? Kidnap?*

His voice sounded young, probably in his late-teens, and he was strong. She was no match for him.

"What do you want? I told you I don't have much money. Let me go, please."

"And *I* told *you*, you're coming with me." He pressed the steel blade harder against her throat. "You are going to do just what I tell you. Aren't you?"

She managed a weak "Yes."

His free hand pulled her left arm roughly behind her as he moved his knee to hold it against her back and grabbed the other with a savage force that sent flames of pain searing into her shoulder and fireworks flaring in her head. She felt metal tightening around her wrists and biting into her flesh as she tried to relax her arms, desperate to prevent being cut.

He spun her around and pushed her down the path and into the lane, prodding her towards to the car that loomed out of the darkness, previously unnoticed in the shadows

She was trembling as he shoved her into the passenger seat, slamming the door with enough violence to shake the car, but nevertheless, she managed to dredge up enough courage to take a good look at him.

She'd been right: he was probably eighteen or nineteen, good looking from what she could see in the dim glow from the lit dashboard. He was dressed completely in black and affected dark glasses in blatant disregard for the fact that it was night.

Let him stay in control, don't freak him out. Try and talk your way out of it. "What do you want?" she whispered hoarsely.

"I want you to help me. You *are* the quack that lives here?"

She nodded and immediately jumped to the wrong conclusion. "I don't keep any drugs on the premises if that's what you want."

"I don't want drugs," he spat. "Enough talking 'til we get where we're going." He flashed the steel blade at her.

Kat shook as her imagination took hold; she could practically feel the steel blade slicing through her skin and cartilage. Through veins and arteries.

She could see the blood. She could taste it.

Her heart lurched and she felt as though she would faint. She bit into her lip to try and stay with it ... not too hard - she couldn't afford to break the skin. No blood. There mustn't be blood.

Especially in her mouth.

She leaned back into the seat, breathing through the torrent of emotions that blitzed her. One thing was for sure. She knew now that she didn't want to die. If she could get out of this, she would go straight back to Lane and do whatever it took to be well again.

***

Beckett's answering machine kicked in at the third ring. Lane swore under her breath with accustomed flair.

21

"Beckett, where the hell are you? Ring me," she snapped into the machine.

She put the phone down and reached for the directory. Kat was a practising herbalist so she should be listed. She was. Lane wrote down her address and made for the door.

She was only minutes behind Kat and could possibly catch up with her. If not she could be at Kat's home very soon after her. She diverted her incoming calls to her cell phone and slammed the door behind her.

Kat had to be heading for home; she was seriously freaked about being out in the dark. Lane knew what she was afraid of and it did nothing to reassure her.

Her cell phone rang and she pulled her car over, took out her cigarettes and lit one as she answered the call.

"Dr Dearing," she said.

"Lane? It's me", Beckett's state of high anxiety was carried on his voice. "So, tell me. What do you think?"

She exhaled smoke. "Beckett, I blew it. She bailed on me. I wish to God you'd told me how sick she was, that lady is in a whole lot of trouble. Why the hell did you wait so long?"

"You let her leave? Jesus, Lane! I trusted you with her, what did you say to her? You frighten the crap out of her or something? If ..."

"Calm down, Beckett. I didn't say anything. I asked her about the dreams and she was off like a rabbit. What do you want me to do? Section her? I can't. You never said she was scared of the dark ... I mean, really, Handsome, the woman is petrified. I could have seen her earlier, cancelled someone else, anything."

Beckett moaned softly, "Okay, okay, look this is getting us nowhere, where are you?"

"On my way to her place, I'm about ten minutes away normally, but at this time of night ..."

"I'll meet you there. Wait for me."

Fifteen minutes later Beckett pulled up behind Lane outside Kat's cottage and slammed his brakes on. His old jeep came to a stop less than an inch from Lane's bumper. She frowned at him.

"Still a careful driver, I see. Cool it, Handsome. There's nobody home. Wherever she is, it's not here."

"Shit!"

"Nice."

"Goddamn it Lane, if you were thinking what I'm thinking …"

"Actually, I am."

Beckett leaned against her vintage E-Type Jaguar. "So what now? I don't even begin to know where to look. She's almost a recluse, doesn't date and she has no friends that I know of."

"Well, we can wait it out until she comes home and pray we're wrong or we can drive around in the hope of finding her."

He turned and kicked out at her bumper.

"Hey! Kick your own damn car. Second thoughts it probably wouldn't survive it. Why do you drive such a heap of junk?"

"Probably because I don't have the stock portfolio and the antique collection that you have. You wait here. I'm going to drive around, you never know," he muttered. "If she comes back, try not to make her run again. I'll call you."

"Can't wait. Oh, and Beckett?"

"Yeah?"

"Drive carefully. I don't suit black."

Despite his anxiety, he grinned at her. "That's what you think, kiddo."

CHAPTER FOUR

Kat remained silent as they drove through the back streets of Newport. She didn't recognise the road but instinctively felt that they were heading towards the most dilapidated area of the city's dockland.

He stopped the car outside what looked like an old warehouse and was out of the car and yanking open her door with swift easy movements. Before she had time to think, he was manhandling her onto the pavement. She could see the reflected lights from the city and the nearer streetlights glinting on the knife. The pain in her shoulder had dulled to a deep ache, which instantly reverted to searing pain when she tried to move it.

She looked around her; the only other buildings nearby looked set for demolition.

He pushed her roughly through a side door. It was, as she thought, a disused warehouse, though from the stench it had been a refuge and toilet for every desperate, homeless person in the city. She saw a camping stove and a sleeping bag bundled untidily in a corner. Used syringes and crumpled pieces of silver foil littered the filthy floor. Her heart went out to the boy.

He seemed to read her and pushed her roughly onto the floor. "They're not mine," he said. "I don't. Now I have your attention, you are going to help me."

She didn't know why she felt such overwhelming relief but suddenly there was only compassion for him.

"Are you sick?" she asked.

"Sick? Yes, I'm sick and there's no doctor out there that can fix it."

"What makes you think I can?"

"You want to hope you can. You really do."

Kat looked up at him. "If you want me to help you, you need to let me out of these damn handcuffs."

He was silent for a minute or two. "And then what? You try and run off and I'll have to stop you."

"I won't be able to help you if you don't. I think you dislocated my shoulder and the pain is so bad I may pass out on you. How much help will I be to you then?"

Her words were brave, but she was shaking inside. *Keep reasoning with him*, she thought. *He doesn't sound stupid. Desperate maybe, but not stupid.*

He bent down to her, put the point of his knife under her chin and pressed upwards.

"No funny stuff, right?"

Every sinew strained as she nodded at him. "Right," she agreed.

He stepped behind her, unlocked the handcuffs and tugged her hands free. She sat breathless, eyes closed, waiting for the pain to subside. When she opened her eyes again he had lit a paraffin lamp.

"Is this where you live?" she asked.

He shook his head. "I stay here sometimes that's all. What's it to you?"

"Nothing, I just wondered. Don't you have any family?"

"They're dead."

"I'm sorry."

"You're sorry, I'm sorry, everyone's sorry! Doesn't make it right though, does it? Drunk driver saw them both off when I was five."

"And that makes it all right for you to go around abducting people at knife-point does it?"

He laughed, "You've got balls lady, I'll give you that. Do us both a favour and lose the social worker act, I've heard it all before. So, are you going to help me or not? You should know I can't pay, not like the others."

"Just for the record, several of my patients can't pay. One man keeps my garden tidy in exchange for his medicine and another patient brings me home-made jam and eggs from her chickens, so before you start judging me by other people standards check out the facts. If you *had* just come and asked me for help I would have given it. There was no need for all this."

She'd gone too far, she knew it, but he'd touched a raw nerve. He slapped her hard across the mouth, leaving a red weal and a blood trail at the corner of her mouth.

She spat hard onto the floor, again and again, spitting and retching, but couldn't rid herself of the taste of blood. It was too late. She wiped her mouth on the bottom of her sleeve as her amethyst eyes shifted hue into the darkest violet of midnight. Her vision swam and she saw everything through a crimson veil. Volcanic rage welled up inside as she tasted the blood in her mouth again. This time she swallowed it; there was no turning back.

"You bastard!" she screamed as she threw herself at him, pounding his face, all her pain lost in the scarlet haze. He fell to the ground, his dark glasses skidding across the filthy floor. Surprise had been on her side and he lay beneath her as she brought her knee crashing into his groin.

He was powerless as she kicked into him repeatedly with a savage intensity and strength that belied her spare frame. She couldn't remember picking it up, but all of a sudden his knife was in her hand and she pressed the glinting blade to his throat.

"So how do you like it? I can kill you with one cut. Do you hear me?"

The images conjured up by her own words made her feel sick and yet powerful in the same moment.

He lay on the floor at her feet in obvious agony, fire in his groin and unspeakable pain in his chest. He was nursing more than one broken rib and a suspect lump was rising on the bridge of his nose. Amazement spread, along with the blood, across his face at the savagery with which she'd attacked him - the thin, pale, weakling woman who'd gone with him so quietly, transformed in an instant into a raving madwoman with the strength of three men.

She bent down and took his keys from his pocket then took a step back and dropped the knife onto the soiled floor.

"I'd say that makes us even. Get up, before I change my mind."

"Can't," he gasped.

"Stay there, then. Oh, and by the way, I'm taking your car, though I doubt very much that it is *your* car. You can come and get the keys tomorrow if it is, if not then I'll leave it where it can be found and returned to its owner. If you can walk, that is." Then, almost as an afterthought, "Don't worry there'll be no police."

"Why?"

I don't know, she thought. *I really don't.*

"Don't push it. And before I go, let's have a good look at you. Just in case I change my mind."

She reached down and pulled him into the dim light.

Her breath caught in her throat and she stumbled backwards as she stared into his rare amethyst eyes. Eyes that were identical to her own.

Shock made her fall to her knees and she crawled to his side just as he momentarily lost consciousness. Jagged thoughts sliced her mind as she knelt there shaking her head. *It couldn't be. Not possible. No. No. No!* But she recognised the truth as surely as recognised her own son as he slid into unconsciousness.

"No," she whispered. "Oh, God. No."

The amethyst eyes were a family trait, and he had the same lean face as her father. More than that, she knew with the instincts of a mother that she knelt over her son.

CHAPTER FIVE

Tears fell onto the back of her hand as she reached forwards and gently stroked the unconscious face. Her own son had kidnapped her at knife-point. And she'd attacked him like a wild animal.

"Nikolos?" She barely whispered the name she had given him before they had taken him away; her father's name, unable to resist the parting gift.

The boy lay motionless and his breathing was laboured, courtesy of the broken ribs. She didn't dare call an ambulance - it would be too hard to explain - and a taxi driver would probably call the police.

Beckett? Yes, Beckett would come and she could probably persuade him to ask no questions.

While she was contemplating the alternatives he stirred. "Nikolos?"

He put his hand to his chest. "You've broken my ribs, you bitch."

"Can you stand?"

He fended her reaching arms away. "Get away from me."

"Try and stand, I'll help you."

She pushed her good arm under his back and tried to gently lift him.

He stood with less of a problem than she'd anticipated.

"Can you walk?" she ventured.

He nodded and glanced down at the knife.

"Don't even think about it, Nikolos. I don't know what the hell happened here tonight, but we can't stay here like this."

"It's Nik now," he snarled. "Just, Nik."

Fresh tears spilled over her lashes and she swallowed

hard. "All right Nik. I don't know how you found me, but thank God you did. Let's get out of here and make some sense out of this, okay?"

"Don't you dare try to act the caring mother. And don't flatter yourself that I came looking for you because of who you were once. For how long? A day? Two? Before you dumped me like a sack of rubbish. I found out about you by accident and it so happens that you may be able to help fix me. That's all I want from you. I figure you owe me that much."

She couldn't speak as pain and sadness washed over her in dreadful waves.

He snatched the keys from her hands. "I'll drive. You're a freakin' nut case. Get in." He spat on the ground as though to underline his contempt.

They drove in silence to her cottage where she led him into her warm kitchen, busying herself with bottles of dark liquid. Neither spoke until she offered him a glass of strong smelling brown fluid.

"Here drink this. It'll ease the pain."

He looked down at the dark brown liquid suspiciously. "What is it? It smells like shit."

She smiled involuntarily. "It doesn't taste too good either, but it will ease the pain. Promise. Here, look, I've got a cup myself. It's not poison, it's tincture of willow bark. Nature's aspirin, mixed with some other painkilling herbs."

He took a sip and pulled a face. "You got no proper pills?"

"Just drink it. I'll see to your bruises in a minute. Just think yourself lucky it's not the police that are looking after you."

Her face softened as she looked at him closely, the previous hours lost in the revelation that blotted all else from her mind, even her own pain. He was so much like her father, his hair falling in the same dark waves that her father's did. The resemblance was incredible, except for the hardness around the mouth. *A gift from Greg*, she thought.

"What's wrong with you Nik? What do the doctors say?" she asked gently, although fearing that she knew the answer.

"What do you care? You gave that responsibility away when you gave me away. Anyway, by the look of you, you can't help me." He was sullen, remaining silent for several minutes and then he carried on reluctantly, "Something hereditary. Some disease that you gave to me, I guess. Thanks."

She went cold. He continued, his voice bitter with resentment.

"A recessive gene, whatever that is, some doctor tried to explain it to me, but what it comes down to is that you or my father passed this on to me. Did you know that when you dumped me? Is that why you did it? Didn't want the hassle? Or was it just guilt?"

She closed her eyes and shook her head. "No," she whispered.

"I assume it's from you and not my father? That's if you know who my father is."

Greg didn't know about his son. She'd known back then what his reaction would have been so she'd said nothing, not even when she'd been so ill. He wouldn't have wanted anything to do with a baby. It would have got in the way of his career then, and now - at the top of his field - he would welcome it even less. Besides, she knew the boy's sickness had come from her; it was all too familiar. She simply shook her head.

"I'm sorry."

"Then that makes you a whore as well as a bitch."

She turned away from him, desperate that he shouldn't see the old hurt back again. Better he think her a slut than open that can of worms.

"They said it was probably because of the Greek blood. Oh yes, they knew that much about you. It's all in my records. "

She nodded. "Haemolytic anaemia is common among the people of the Mediterranean countries, especially Italy and Greece. I think what you have is something similar. And yes, I have it too."

He stood quickly, and she frowned at his ability to move so freely with

his injuries. *The resilience of youth*, she thought.

"Then I guess I'm wasting my time. If you have it and can't cure it, how the hell are you going to fix me up?"

"I can maybe help you cope with it and I believe there may be someone who can help us both. Come with me?"

"I've seen 'em all, doctors *and* shrinks."

She blanched at the thought of Beckett that his words had conjured. She should call him.

"Why?" she ventured.

"Because of how I used to get; prowling around all hours of the night, and dreams that would scare the crap out of Freddie Kruger."

"I know," she whispered.

He looked at her strangely. "Then you'll also know what blood does to me?"

She nodded again.

"And what I had to do to quench the thirst?"

The horror in her eyes stopped him dead.

He leered at her. "What? Not been there yet? Of course you haven't, that's why you're so bloody pale and thin. Oh, then you'll enjoy hearing this. One night I went to a club with some friends of mine, a Goth club called Danse Macabre, and I met someone who showed me what I am. The club's a place where people like us go to hang out, along with all the other punters like the Lifestylers, Role Players and Goths. Oh, and then there's the wannabes."

"I don't understand you," she whispered, shaking her head.

"Then let me explain. Lifestylers are the ones that adopt the dress and posture of the romantic Gothic, like

Byron. They live in the past. The Role Players are the losers that pretend they are something they're not, playing at being vampires and slayers instead of getting a life. Then the wannabes, well, they just live for the day when someone like me will come along and feed off them, hoping that they'll get lucky and be turned into this living hell. The Goths are okay; they just adopt the dress and listen to the hardcore house music, using the clothes and the black makeup and music to express their own darkness. But there are others there too. Some just like us, you know the real ones."

"Real ones?" Her mind was racing.

He threw his head back and laughed. The bitterness of it lodged deep inside her like a poisoned bullet and she felt his anger and his pain. She had the urge to comfort him but not the right. She was a stranger to her own son.

"You don't know, do you? You really don't. Look in the goddamn mirror. Apart from how thin you are, you don't look above twenty-five, and how old are you? Thirty-five? Six? Thirty-seven? And the blood, think about that for a minute. You're terrified of it because deep down inside you know you need it. You want it. And what about the dark? Like what that does to you? No, I guess not, you're terrified because of what it does to you. And what about men? Now that's an interesting one, isn't it? I'll bet you're an animal when you're aroused. But I guess they don't stay around too long."

Kat clamped her hands over her ears, her eyes squeezed shut, desperate to block him out as his intensity shook her again. She was pale, almost translucent, and her voice trembled.

"How dare you? How *dare* you? Get out. I can't help you. God knows if anybody can. Go before I call the police."

"I'm going, but this isn't the last time you've seen me. I guarantee it."

He stood directly in front of her and thumped on his

chest. "*Look* at me. No broken ribs here; not even a bruise. Oh, and the nose is just fine. How's that? Let me explain to you. Ultra- rapid healing is one of the advantages of this shit. Forget haemolytic or any other kind of anaemia. Do I have to spell it out? I'm a vampire. And so, Mother dearest, are you."

CHAPTER SIX

Time slid backwards in her mind as she sat shivering in her kitchen, despite the warmth of the range that did nothing to comfort her, as memories of a summer of love turned sour, swiftly followed by her own sickness and the heart break of parting with her child, overwhelmed her. Numb to her surroundings, she sat motionless while the events of the night replayed in her mind and random images of the past bled into the present and the memory of Nik striding down her path on an obvious high of rage and hunger.

Despite her efforts to control her thoughts, they spiralled in reverse to the time when her life had been changed forever.

To a summer when she was in love and nothing else mattered. When the days were heady with sun and wine and Greg's passionate love-making, and how it had all turned sour.

Greg had turned out to be nothing more or less than an egocentric asshole who had quickly bored of her and lost no time in letting her know it. She craved nothing more than to extricate herself from the situation and retain some dignity at least.

And then had come the knowledge that she was pregnant. And what followed was too painful to relive.

The memories were still raw, even after eighteen years and in the warmth and safety of her kitchen Kat closed her eyes, exhausted and undone.

The telephone rang, catapulting her back to the present. She let it ring until her answering machine kicked in automatically and she heard Beckett's voice.

"Kat? Kat if you're there pick the phone up honey. It's

35

me, Beckett."

She picked up the phone and held it to her ear. She didn't speak.

"Kat, is that you? Where the hell have you been? I've been worried sick. I'm coming over."

"No!" she snapped.

"Kat, listen. I'm sorry if you think I let you down, let me try and fix it? At least let me explain my reasons for sending you to Lane."

"I don't care. I don't care about anything any more. Don't waste your time on me Beckett. Find yourself another lost cause."

"Kat, don't do this."

"Go away, Beckett. It's too late."

Her doorbell rang and she laid the phone down and went to answer it, half-hoping, half-knowing, that it would be Lane, and with that came a glimmer of hope. For her and for Nik.

Lane met Kat's eyes with her own, portraying understanding and behind it a quiet authority. She gazed past her to the telephone hanging by its cord.

"Let's go and calm Beckett down," she said, nodding towards the sitting room. "He's a bit tightly wound."

Lane stepped inside the cottage and closed the door behind her, followed Kat into the sitting room and picked up the phone.

"Kat! Kat, are you still there?" Beckett's voice was laden with panic.

"Relax Beckett, it's me, I've just arrived. Just stay where you are for a while. Kat and I have some things to talk about. I'll call you later." She didn't wait for his reply before she hung up on him.

Lane took in Kat's haggard appearance. "Rough night?"

She nodded, unsure of why she trusted Lane yet knowing instinctively that she could and that she should.

"Where did you go? Beckett and I looked all over for

you. He's very worried about you. We both are."

"Save it for someone else. I'll be okay."

Lane frowned and shook her head. "You are going to need someone to trust sooner or later, so it may as well be sooner and it may as well be me."

Kat hesitated for a moment then said, "I saw my son last night," her voice subdued.

Lane's expression didn't alter and she remained silent.

Kat's voice trembled. "He's eighteen now. Oh God, I wish I hadn't listened to them all, I wish I'd kept him. I could have managed somehow. I could have. Now it's too late. He said his parents, his adoptive parents, had been killed in a road accident when he was five. You should have seen him, he was so angry and so ... hopeless. He's sick, Lane. Sick like me, but it's worse with him, he's really confused. It almost seems as if he's ... psychotic."

Lane raised an eyebrow. "What makes you say that?"

"Apart from the fact that he kidnapped me at knife-point, he's delusional."

"Delusional?"

"He actually believes he's a vampire for God's sake, and he tried hard to convince me that I'm one too. That's hardly sane, is it? Can you help him? Whatever it takes, please help him."

"Do you have any alcohol anywhere?" Lane asked.

"What?" Kat was perplexed.

"Alcohol. Sherry, whisky, brandy?"

Kat frowned. "In the cupboard to your left."

Lane grabbed the cheap bottle of brandy from the shelf where Beckett had replaced it the night before and immediately poured two hefty measures into tumblers from the shelf below.

"Here, drink this."

Kat shook her head. "No. No thanks. I told you I'll be okay."

"And I'm telling you that you are going to need this. Drink it. Or do I have to hold your nose?"

Kat shook her head. "You're a strange one," she said.

"I'll take it as a compliment." She nodded towards the glass. "Finish it."

Kat drank it down and Lane promptly refilled the glass.

"Are you trying to get me drunk?"

"Just enough to help you cope with what I have to say."

Kat looked grave, but drank the brandy down as Lane immediately refilled the empty glass. She could feel the warm spirit coursing through her body as Lane's voice became softer, muffled and a little distant.

Lane smiled warmly at Kat, she liked her and that wasn't going to make what she had to say any easier. She laid her hand over Kat's. "I want you to listen to me very carefully. Okay?"

Kat nodded and almost lost her balance.

"Good, I think you're drunk enough, so here goes. Most myths and legends have their roots in truth. The older the myth, usually the truer it is in my experience. Vampires are no exception."

Kat looked at Lane her understanding lost again. "I'm sorry. What did you say? Vampires?"

Everything became surreal as Lane continued, "Vampires exist, and it is very likely from what you have told me that your son is one, though hopefully not beyond help. There are different types of vampire; the Inheritors, or the Born, as their name suggests, are those who are born vampire. The Classic vampire, or the Created, are the ones who are turned, but they have to carry a recessive gene to enable this to happen. The Latents are the vampires who have the recessive gene but have not yet been turned, and there are the Psi vampires, which feed on energy not blood. I believe that you have been surviving this way, though only just, for several years without realising it. Then of course there are the Undead. They're ... well ... they're something else. Kat, I'm certain that you're a Latent vampire.

Kat stared at her in disbelief, shaking her head, unable to accept what she was hearing and feeling like Alice at the bottom of the rabbit-hole.

"Kat, do you understand what I am saying to you? I believe that you are a Latent vampire and are, in fact, on the verge of giving in to the lust for blood. If you feed, just once, then you will fulfil the blueprint of your DNA and become a vampire and I won't be able to help you."

Lane took the glass from Kat's white-knuckled grip and set it on the table.

"Kat, look at me. How old do you think I am? Thirty? In fact, I was born into the Florentine court in 1553 and my name is Leonora di Toledo and I grew up in the care of my aunt and uncle, Eleanora and Cossimo de Medici, while my own father was in Spain as commander in chief of the navy. While I was under his care, my uncle, shall we say, became too fond of me. He couldn't bear the thought of me eventually leaving his court and so he married me off to his son, Don Pietro. He believed that he could make it all right by settling a massive dowry, around thirty million in today's terms, along with several estates in Tuscany. He had in fact married me to a violent bully who delighted in beating me senseless. My dear husband was also more interested in squandering the Medici fortune on his whores than taking care of our estates. My life was made more bearable for a while by my cousin Isabella. She too was trapped in a loveless marriage and her husband was constantly away in Rome. She was fun and threw great parties and whilst Pietro was away from home philandering, I was able to enjoy my life. I fell in love with a young poet and we had an affair. Whilst my uncle was alive I was under his protection but when he died, that protection died with it. My lover was thrown into a dungeon and Pietro was given the thumbs up to 'take care' of his wayward wife. History tells that he strangled me with a dog chain and that I bit him before dying. In fact he presented me to a vampire for my punishment.

Unfortunately the vampire didn't kill me, but turned me and left me to live by feeding or die. History was right in the fact that I did bite Pietro, actually it was more that I tore out his throat and fed on him. I had my revenge for all the beatings and I allowed him to bleed to his death.

"My name isn't Lane Dearing; Lane is a contraction of Leonora and over the past centuries I have needed to change my identity for reasons which you will come to understand. Dearing is the name of one of my more recent husbands that I have outlived by over a century. I'm just about to celebrate my four hundred and fifty-sixth birthday. And, as much as I wish that all this wasn't true, it is - and you are going to have to face it."

Kat leaped up and instantly fell back onto the sofa; the alcohol, fatigue and shock inevitably blending into a cocktail of delirium.

"What kind of sick joke is this?" she slurred. "Why're you telling me these lies? Does Beckett know what you're doing to me?" She tried unsuccessfully to stand again.

Lane sighed. "I was afraid you'd take that view. Okay, let's see if this helps." She picked up her empty glass and smashed it against the edge of the table, then without a pause drew the jagged edges across her wrist.

Kate's arm flew up to her face, shielding her eyes from the sight of the flowing dark red blood. She began to cry softly.

"Kat, look. It's all right. I promise. Look."

She could feel Lane's hand on her arm, gently prising it away from her face. Eventually she looked at the jagged wound on Lane's wrist. There was just a faint red line where there should have been a fountain of dark red blood. The cut had already closed and almost healed. Images of Nik with no apparent injuries where he should have been nursing at least one fracture came unbidden. Lane let go of her arm.

"I apologise for the theatrics, but Hollywood did get that bit right, well for some of us anyway."

Kat shook her head, her disbelief written on her face as if carved in stone. "I don't know how you did that, but I refuse to believe in vampires. They're fiction, a figment of Bram Stoker's imagination. Not real. Do you hear me? Not real!"

"I assure you I'm very real, and I *am* a vampire and have been for almost four and a half centuries. You are going to have to accept this Kat, because it is the truth. If you want me to help you then you must start trusting me. I am telling you the complete and utter truth. Vampires have been documented throughout history many, many hundreds of years before Mr. Stoker dipped his nib into the inkwell. We believe that the first of our kind was born in Ancient Egypt, the son of a pharaoh, a product of their incestuous practices and their powerful magic that somehow distorted his DNA to make it receptive to the infection by a virus that we now call the Human Vampiric Virus, or HVV. Our line has continued throughout the centuries, unbroken but not unadulterated. It soon became evident that this one vampire's offspring carried the DNA - the blueprint of the vampire - and from that time on, the virus has mutated until now we are either born like this or were turned by others merely needing to feed and not understanding how to control their hunger. The virus cannot be spread by any means other than ingesting the blood of an infected vampire, but it can and sometimes does kill.

"Our history has been fairly well hidden over time, we have the ability to cloud minds, but there have always been those who were determined to discover the truth that was buried in myth. I'm afraid that Hollywood has somewhat glamorised and at the same time demonised our condition, helped along in good measure by modern literature. It's of no matter. I mean ... who would believe it?"

"I want Beckett," Kat said in a small voice.

Lane shook her head. "Not yet. Not until you understand that I am trying to help you and that you *need* my help. There are more like you out there, believe me, and it's my job to take care of you, or as many of you as I can. Besides, Beckett can't help you. Not in the way I can."

"I won't listen to all this. I must be going mad." Her voice rose, "Is that it? Is it me that's insane?" she demanded.

Lane's heart ached for her; there was nothing she could say or do to take away the disbelief and, eventually, the misery of the acceptance. She could only be there when the truth hit home and help her deal with it.

"Do you know how long you have been this way?" asked Lane.

"If you mean how long have I been sick, then that should prove you wrong. I was fine until I was pregnant. Don't ask me why. So you see I'm not, what did you call it, a Latent? And I sure as hell would know if I'd been bitten by a goddamn vampire. You're way off the mark. I wasn't born sick."

"You don't have to be. If you were born a latent, then your condition will have lain dormant until such time that something triggered a reaction in you and your DNA profile actually began to change," replied Lane.

Kat shook her head vigorously, "DNA can't change. That is not possible. This conversation is over, I'm calling Beckett."

Lane picked up the phone and handed it to her. "Go ahead, call him - but trust me, he's not going to tell you anything you want to hear."

Kat's hand shook as she dialled the number. She fumbled it three times before it rang at the other end.

Beckett's voice filled her with some comfort, but this quickly turned to dismay as she realised she was listening to his answering machine. "Hi, this is Paul Beckett. Sorry I'm not at home. Leave a message. Bye."

"He's not there," she said dismally.

"That's because, if I know Beckett, he's on his way here, even though I told him to stay away – or, should I say, *especially* as I told him to stay away."

"I can't listen to you any more." She put her head in her hands. "I don't understand. This is all lies! Why are you lying to me like this?"

Lane persisted. "How else do you explain your fear of the night and blood? Why do you react the way you do when you see blood? Or worse, taste it? It's the craving, Kat. You crave it and therefore you fear it. You fear the loss of control that comes with the lust. Am I right? ... And what about Beckett?"

"What about him?"

"He's falling for you. How long have you known him? Have you slept with him? Because, quite frankly, he's sex walking and I can't see any reason why not, unless of course you don't trust yourself with him? Is that it?"

"It's none of your damn business, but no, I haven't slept with him, it's not like that, Beckett's ... too nice, I guess."

Lane gave a half smile, "Yes, he is, isn't he? Look, I can help you but you have to listen to me."

Kat shook her head. "No. Lots of people have phobias; it doesn't make them vampires, even *if* there were such things. You won't stop will you? Well, I'm not buying into it. Not any of it. Understand?"

Lane settled back in the chair and stretched out her long shapely legs sipping at the brandy still in her glass. It wasn't the vintage Armagnac that she was used to but right then she didn't care. Over the centuries, born into the Medici family, a pampered favourite of Cossimo Medici, the powerful Grand Duke of Tuscany, she had acquired great wealth and the taste for all things refined; after all, she'd had the luxury of time. Despite its harshness the spirit failed to warm her or to override the cold dread that was building inside her.

They sat in silence, their situation not conducive to small talk and Lane knew she'd need Beckett behind her if she were ever going to get Kat to even begin to understand what was happening to her. Because however much she denied it, sooner or later she would have to face the truth.

She was a vampire.

CHAPTER SEVEN

Nik was strung out on hunger and rage. He needed to feed. Kat had taken him to the edge. He knew he could go back and feed on her then cast her aside to either drink or die. He didn't care which.

He had the psychological advantage; she knew he was her son now, and so she wouldn't want to hurt him. It would be instinctive, despite the fact she'd turned her back on him all those years ago, and there would be guilt too, which would make her want to help, not injure him. No. It wouldn't be much fun, no challenge in that. He'd save her for another night.

The club would be different, packed with Goths and Lifestylers, and wannabe vampires. He grinned; maybe he'd oblige one of them. Besides, after the blood he'd be horny as hell and spoilt for choice at the club. It was a gathering place for kids with no place else to go, kids that nobody would miss, or be forgotten after a week or so, drifters, prostitutes, teenagers that had left homes where no-one cared, drawn to the excitement and darkness of the club and his world or taken there by others of his kind to toy with until the time they would feed on them.

Man, he had the power; he was practically a god. What the hell was he thinking about trying to get her to cure him? He didn't want that now, he had what he wanted. He was calling the shots now, no longer at the mercy of the system that had failed him. He would turn against them all and then they would see how powerful he was.

The club was bouncing. Strobe lights throbbed in time with the dark rhythm of the music and the only other lights were red and deliberately dim. It excited the wannabes and was easy on the eyes of the real vampire's

45

whose sight could cut through the darkest night but whose retinas could be damaged by the glare of bright light, especially sunlight or any other form of ultra-violet light.

He was charged; he could feel his blood pumping through the walls of his arteries and veins, his heart racing as it always did before he fed. He was wired now and oblivious to everything except his need for blood, remaining oblivious to the conversation taking place on the sofa right next to him.

Andrei Marinescu, the suave club owner was in deep conversation with a senior member of the Vampire High Council. Talk had been heated and although it had become relatively quiet, tension still crackled between them as Andrei's easy arrogance was matched by the other's clear authority.

The elder man spoke in a refined voice that still bore a hint of his Eastern European origins. "So I can count on your support, Andrei? When the time comes?"

Andrei had worked hard to eradicate the sound of his origins and spoke now with a cultured voice. "Yes, Sir. Without question. I and my house are loyal to you and always will be." Andrei's tawny eyes darkened momentarily, it wouldn't do for his guest to see the resentment behind the lie.

"That is good to know. And in return your business enterprises, including this one, shall remain under my protection. It would of course, be prudent to avoid any clashes with my junior members, they do get somewhat carried away with enthusiasm for things which they don't understand or appreciate. There are too many do-gooders on the Council these days who see humans as more than food. It comes from allowing other than pure blood as members. The Code has to be revised before we all end up feeding from plastic bags in sterile clinics, and when I am elected Patriarch we shall soon be free to enjoy our predatory instincts to the full. Make no mistake, Andrei, you will not regret your loyalty." He stood to leave, nodding dismissal to his host.

Ignorant of what was playing out beside him, Nik allowed his sharp eyes to play with several possible prey, finally settling on a young girl sitting alone in a corner who looked as though she would give him a good time. He hoped she hadn't been taking drugs; he'd leave her there if so, he didn't want any of that inside him to take the edge off. He smiled at her and focused his will across the club, drawing her eyes.

She put down her drink and looked around, aware of him yet not seeing him. *Not yet*, he was in the mood to savour his bloodlust and play with her mind. He deepened his concentration and smiled as she looked around again.

Stand up, he thought. *Stand up, leave your drink and come over here.*

The girl picked up her drink then put it back on the table and looked around her again before standing uncertainly. She walked towards him. *That's right sweetheart, this way. Keep coming. Come to Nik.*

She was half way across the room when she saw him. She found his eyes, stopped and smiled at him. *Easy.*

He sensed the presence a split second before he felt the vice-like grip on his shoulder. Andrei Marinescu loomed behind him, dwarfing his own six feet, his grasp defying Nik to move. He lost his telepathic hold over the girl.

"Good Evening Nik. Having a good time? You're hungry, oh, and angry, I can feel it. You wouldn't have your eye on her now would you?" He nodded his ebony-crowned head towards the girl who still stood close by but appearing not to see either of them.

Nik shook his head. Not a god after all. Not while Andrei Marinescu was around. He was just a young punk on the prowl compared to this tall sophisticated man who had power even over his own kind. The vice didn't slacken.

"There are certain things that you must learn, Nik, if you are to remain safe here. There are rules. I know you know that, because I'm the one who explained them to you, but I'll remind you. Rule number one is, that you don't take prey without permission. You have to be selective. No loose ends. We don't want police poking around here because some young tart hasn't shown up at home and Daddy has called them, do we? And we don't want the Council down on our backs. Find your prey and then check with Luke, the Head of Security. It's easy.

"The second rule is that you don't take prey that is already spoken for. Understand? And she is spoken for. I have a taking for her myself. I had some business to take care of first and now … well, who knows? But one thing I do know is that she's full of promise. And she's promised to me. If you had obeyed the first rule you would have been aware of that. Look elsewhere. "And Nik, rule three. Don't take more than you need, we don't want any unexplained mishaps, do we? Are we clear?"

Nik was sullen and unresponsive.

The grip on his shoulder increased. "Are we clear?" Andrei persisted.

Nik nodded.

Andrei's eyes flashed crimson at Nik; there would be no further warning. The grip slackened, Andrei was gone and so was the girl.

Directly above him on the viewing balcony a man stood in shadow, from where he had watched the exchange. Behind a black silk mask, his ice blue eyes danced with pleasure at Nik's discomfort. Here was a young man with a chip on his shoulder the size of the Everest, and he was angry. Anger was such a powerful emotion, possessing the energy and power of a volcano, both of them ignited by heat and fire. The boy had potential. More than he'd seen in a long time.

He motioned to one of the security team and spoke quietly in his ear. The club's tough guy nodded briefly and disappeared into the darkness of the upstairs rooms.

In a single fluid movement he emerged from shadow to

stand at the edge of the balcony. The glow of the red lamps cast eerie lights across the black silk mask that covered the top half of his face.

He affected the dress of a Gothic, and his mask left only his thin, sensuous mouth and eyes visible. There was an air about him, something in his bearing that made it obvious that he was no ordinary patron of the club. The iceberg eyes flashed behind the black silk, the lazy lids closed and when they opened again those same eyes were aflame with crimson light as they followed Nik below.

Music pounded the walls, bounced off floor and ceiling, but Nik was in no mood to stay any longer. Andrei had made him feel like an insolent schoolboy caught playing truant. No longer a god. One day he'd show him, one day he'd get even with him.

His hunger was driving him now, fuelled by anger, humiliation and frustration. He needed to feed, and feed soon. Already he knew that he wouldn't be able to control himself once the blood was flowing. He knew he wouldn't stop at just enough to satisfy his hunger.

He knew he would gorge himself until the veins that fed him bled dry. And he didn't care about the implications of it.

Now he had to hunt out in the open and risk being caught. There was always the Sanctuary, but he was reluctant to go there unless he had no alternative. In his eyes it was nothing more than a Council-run feeding station. He despised the Council and all it stood for, with its Codes and restrictive rules. He wouldn't be able to satisfy his savage needs there, even though he could guarantee a supply of fresh blood. Besides, he enjoyed the hunt.

At the door, their voices drowned by music, Luke, the Head of Security, and a pretty young Goth girl were arguing. He wasn't allowing her in but she was being persistent.

"Problem?" Nik asked the girl.

"Yeah. Dickweed won't let me in. You gonna get me in?"

He took in her heavy boots over fishnet tights, the straining black satin corset top and black leather mini skirt. He shook his head.

"No, I'm leaving. Want to come with me?"

He stared at her, using his will to remove reason from her mind, bending her will to comply with his own. He felt her give, felt her lose her grip on who, and where, she was. He smiled.

That's more like it. Up yours Marinescu.

Godlike status restored, he put his arm around her, barely listening as she told him that her name was Jasmine, and he smiled when he picked up fragments of her thoughts and desires. She would give him a good time all right and at the same time satisfy another hunger.

She was docile now, but he was looking forward to releasing her mind just long enough for her to put up a struggle and make the play more interesting.

"What's your name?" she asked.

"It doesn't matter," Nik replied as he steered her into the depths of a dark alley adjacent to the club.

Blood filled his mouth and throat, and the power surged through him, sparking and arcing like liberated electricity. His chin was covered in gore and he allowed his head to fall back towards his shoulders. The whites of his eyes burned crimson and he saw everything through a scarlet veil. He laughed aloud and his teeth glistened with blood.

The girl lay inert in his arms and he let her drop to the floor. The blood had long since stopped flowing from the wound at her throat. Her heart, too weak to pump it any more, had fluttered like an injured butterfly and then slowly and finally succumbed to death. He turned to walk away.

Luke came from out of the shadows to stand in front of Nik, preventing him from leaving the alley.

Raw energy still powered through the boy, denying him focus.

"Get the hell out of my way."

He tried to push past the hulking man and then recognised him; the club heavy he'd seen arguing with his recent meal.

"I said get out of my way. I'm warning you." Nik felt the power seeking the darkness inside him. Amplifying it, charging him further.

Luke stood firm, one eyebrow arched in challenge. The guy was huge and looked exactly what he was; a hired thug in a suit.

Nik heaved himself at the man, snarling with rage at the intrusion. His breathing was erratic and rage fired through him like molten lava. He felt the now familiar tingle in his mouth as his vampire musculature began pushing his canines down, ready for more action.

It was the last thing he felt before passing out at Luke's feet from the blow that landed on his neck.

A velvet voice floated somewhere between comprehension and oblivion. It warmed him and he felt his energy returning.

The alley was in darkness but Nik's vampire eyes saw the masked man as though by daylight.

"Oh Nik, why must you do everything the hard way? Eh?"

He nodded to Luke. "Help him up."

Nik shrugged off the help, pushing Luke away. "I can manage." He snarled as he brushed himself down.

The smile beneath the mask danced around a cruel, sensual mouth and there was a strange light in the icy eyes. "Oh Nik, it doesn't have to be like this you know. You waste so much of your power and potential; you climb the hill backwards. I know how you are feeling. You are angry and quite rightly so. Tossed away at birth like last week's garbage, adopted and orphaned, bounced around the system until you could take no more. You deserve better.

You are so much bigger than all of them. They are nothing before you. Dust under your feet."

Nik tried to see behind the mask, but the sensual mouth and cold smile were all he could focus on.

"Who are you? How do you know me?" he demanded.

"I'm your future, Nik. I am the one who will take you out of the gutter and into a world where you belong. My name is Santorini, in honour of my maker's origins. You have great potential, but no discipline, and your anger is erratic and wild. You are raw and undeveloped, crude and impulsive. So much wasted energy. I can help you."

Nik's anger rose again, sticking in his throat like bile. "I don't know who the hell you think you are but I don't need your help. I'll be leaving now." It was a challenge rather than a statement.

Santorini laughed softly behind the mask and shook his head.

"What? You want me to stop you? Now why would I do that? It's a prime example of what I've been saying. A waste of energy." His voice altered, becoming harsh and devoid of any hint of feeling. "I can snuff you out with a thought. Remember that. It's not a good idea to irritate me, boy."

The word 'boy' enraged Nik further, as it was intended to, but from somewhere he found the sense to back down.

The mask nodded towards the dead girl.

"Oh dear, Nik. Rule number three. Still, we won't tell Andrei. We don't want to cause unnecessary trouble do we? And what about the Council? It wouldn't go down well with them."

The mention of Andrei Marinescu and the man's obvious superiority rankled and Nik began to feel helpless and lost in a world that he didn't really understand. It was so unfair, he'd been feeling great, invincible, a god, and now he was nothing again in the company of this silken voiced powerhouse.

"No, Nik. It isn't fair. But I can change that. You can

take your revenge on them all, and they will tremble at your feet. Yes, even Andrei will bow to you. I guarantee it. Your potential is astonishing."

He was right up close to Nik now, his face only inches away. He stood for a moment locking the boy's eyes with his own, probing, feeling his way around the anger inside. He sensuous lips curved into a lazy smile displaying sharp white teeth. He raised his hand and ran his sharp fingernail slowly down Nik's face, tracing the outline of his cheekbones and around his chin. Nik closed his eyes and leaned his head away, losing himself in the seduction of the presence.

The silken voice caressed his mind further. "You are truly beautiful. Such fine bone structure and such dormant power. I will teach you, Nik. I will teach you everything I know and you will become as I am."

He moved so quickly that it almost seemed a trick of the light as he kissed Nik softly on the cheek, leaving the impression of a butterfly's wing and sending a shiver through Nik that left him confused and afraid.

Nik said nothing, but a spark lit his eyes as something fired inside him. Hope. And something else, something that he was ashamed of.

"Good. Come with me then." He looked down at the dead girl again. "Get rid of that, Luke. I'll take care of Nik."

"Where are we going?"

"Home, Nik. Home."

CHAPTER EIGHT

Pounding on the door of Kat's cottage announced Beckett's arrival and Kat hurled herself towards it, snatching it open. She grabbed Beckett's arm and dragged him into the cottage.

She turned on Lane, "Go on then. Tell him. Tell him what you told me," she challenged.

Lane shrugged, sending a significant glance at Beckett.

"Lane?"

"Hi, Handsome. I've been trying to explain to Kat what's happening to her. She had a visit from her son last night. And guess what?"

Beckett's face was grim.

Lane continued. "He's a classic, no doubt about it. Already turned and feeding."

"Jesus. You're sure?" Her expression was enough. "Yeah, stupid question." He ran his fingers through his silver hair and then, in one stride, was at Kat's side. "Are you okay? I'm sorry Kat, I wasn't sure, though God knows the signs were plain enough. Maybe I just didn't want to believe it."

Kat recoiled. "Beckett? Don't tell me you are even considering this? Did you know she thinks she's a vampire too? That she's the niece of the grand duke something or other and that she's over four hundred years old? *Jesus!*" Her voice was getting shrill. "*What?* Am I the only sane one here?"

Beckett put his hand on her arm and she shrugged him off.

"It's true Kat," he said. "All of it. I wasn't sure if you were a latent or not. It's one of the reasons I asked you to see Lane. And because I have become ... fond of you. "

"*Fond of me?*" Kat yelled, "How can you have feelings for me when you can't even tell me the truth? And how, in God's name, can you subscribe to this insanity? Vampires, for God's sake! And you? What about you, Beckett? Do you believe you're a vampire too?" She shook her head. "Just listen to me, I sound as crazy as you two."

Beckett shook his head. "No," he said. "No, I'm not a vampire, although I've met a few. Listen to Lane, Kat, she can help you. She can help all of us."

Kat's voice rose to near hysteria and she began raving.

"Okay, so if I'm a vampire how come I haven't turned to the contents of an egg timer because, hello, it's daylight? And look, hey that's me, right there in the mirror. How do you explain that then? And do you know, I think I've got a crucifix somewhere. Bet I can hold it without burning up! I'll go and find it and prove it to you." She opened her mouth in a mock snarl. "Surprise, surprise, no fangs."

Lane caught hold of her arm and pulled her, none too gently, into the chair. "Kat, listen, all those things, that's the movies. None of that is true except for the Undead. And, as I already told you, they are something else." She pointed towards the mirror over the fireplace. "Look, that's me in the mirror, I can cast a reflection, I can cross running water, I am quite religious and go to church to pray when I feel the need, I can hold a crucifix, I don't sleep in a coffin, and I can eat and drink, although I am allergic to garlic. Most of us are. Like me, you won't age because all of your systems will change, whilst not exactly a selling point it's fair to say that is one of the plusses. Sometimes. And you will have the ability to lie dormant - asleep if you like to think of it that way - for greatly extended periods, if you turn completely. Your skin will become more sensitive to sunlight and as time goes on you will need to use sun block or you will suffer nasty ultra-violet burns. Your energy levels will be depleted during daylight hours and you'll be energised after dark. Silver drains our life force and will kill us if it gets inside us, and as for the fangs, they won't appear until you feed for the first time. A stake through the heart will kill you, but then I think that would do for most anyone don't you? Now come on, calm down. There's still a whole load of stuff we need to talk about."

"Like what?" Kat was calm but sullen.

"Like who is the father of your son? And before you tell me that it's none of my damn business, I promise you I need to know for your sake."

"Why?"

"Because you told me that until you got pregnant you weren't sick, is that true?"

"Yes. From the minute I was pregnant I felt something was wrong."

Lane was silent for a moment, then, "Your body became host to the vampire's blood or DNA for you to turn; impregnation by a vampire is the only other way you can be turned as your DNA and the vampire DNA combine in the unborn baby. Sometimes the change is completed in a very short time; sometimes it can take longer - even years - as appears to be the case with you. But the first time you feed, the process will speed up and the turning will be completed. I'm guessing you haven't so far drunk blood?"

The look of horror on Kat's face gave her the answer. "No, okay. Then I was right, you must have been feeding like a Psi. Feeding on energy - other people's life force, and sometimes even through your dreams."

Kat's eyes began to fill with unshed tears. "Suppose, just suppose you're telling me the truth, what has that to do with Nik's father?"

"I have no reason to lie to you Kat. It has everything to do with him because he had to have been a vampire to have triggered this response in your DNA and bring out the Latent in you."

Kat laughed. "Oh you're so wrong. Greg Randall is Nik's father, and no, he doesn't know and you know what, anyone less like a vampire I have yet to meet. Greg Randall is a bastard but, I assure you, he is not a vampire."

"Would you say I look like one?" Lane asked.

"Oh, we're back to that again are we? Hell, I might as well play your stupid game."

Lane became deadly serious, a steely edge creeping into her normally silky voice.

"I can assure you, Kat, that one thing this is *not*, is a game. It's not Dungeons and Dragons and there is no one to break the curse but you. The one thing you can be sure of is that if you feed, you will finally complete the transformation that has been taking place in you since you were born. You *will* become a vampire and feed on fresh blood from living people. Now it's time you stopped this and started to pay attention to me. I *can* make you, but I really would rather you do this of your own free will. Kat, there are some big bad blood suckers out there, and they'll wipe their asses with you and throw what's left of you to the rats. So, do you want me to help you or not?"

Beckett had been quiet whilst Lane had been talking. Kat looked on his solemn face and Lane's expression reflected the cold hit of truth somewhere deep in the pit of her stomach. Latent or otherwise, she was a vampire and so was her son.

"Oh God," she whispered. "Please help me."

CHAPTER NINE

Kat's voice was a whisper. "How can you be so sure?"

"There is an easy way of telling, and a blood test will confirm it, but it's a catch twenty two situation. A normal human being cannot physically drink blood in any quantity without vomiting. Blood is a very powerful emetic; as soon as it goes down, it'll come right back up again. If your DNA has changed to the vampire DNA then your digestive system will have changed too; the blood won't make you sick. But if you haven't turned and you drink the blood, well then …" she shrugged in order to emphasise the predicament.

Kat flinched. "Why the dreams? Why am I so afraid in the dark? I thought vampires loved the night."

"Because your body is craving blood. Your subconscious knows this and you are afraid of what you may do during the hours of the night."

Kat dropped her head. She didn't want Beckett to see the shame in her eyes. Hhe'd remained ominously quiet throughout and if she had dared to look into his dark grey eyes she would have seen the pain that engulfed him. If it were possible, he was hurting almost as much as she was.

Visions rose in Kat's head of the last time she'd slept with a man. She could still see the terror on his face when, near to climax, she lost control of the beast that lived deep in her soul and had bitten him savagely until the blood flowed in a crimson river from the ragged wound on his neck. She saw herself spitting the gouts of blood and tiny pieces of flesh from her mouth, rushing to the bathroom and washing her mouth over and over, crying and cursing. She left him in shock mopping the blood from his throat and the bed. An assault charge would surely have followed had he not lied about being married. He'd had a hard enough time explaining the blood and the wound to the Accident and Emergency staff let alone his wife, so his infidelity had proved her saviour.

Lane read her. "I can help you to control it," she said. "There is so much for you to learn but I will help you. So will Beckett."

Beckett's eyes told her the truth of her situation as he put his arm around her. She didn't push him away this time but leaned against him as her tears fell silently.

"I thought you said you weren't a vampire."

His hand hovered instinctively over the long diagonal scar on his chest. "I'm not," he said. "But let's say I've had dealings with them before. I know a lot about them."

Sharp painful memories flooded him as his thoughts turned to the night his sister, Grace, had died in his arms. The night she'd become the victim of a masked vampire. How she'd tried to tell him over the preceding months, asked him for help, and he hadn't listened.

Until it was too late.

The image of Grace dying and the horror of what happened after that had conceived the demons that plagued him nightly, keeping sleep at arms length.

That was the night, five years earlier, that he'd met Lane for the first time. It was also the night that, as Father Paul Beckett, he had lost his faith and walked away from the church, away from God and away from his life and into a quest that had become an obsession - to find the vampire that had robbed his sister of her life and repay him in kind.

Lane had been tracking the silken-masked vampire for years and had arrived too late to save Grace. She'd pulled Beckett together and done what had to be done for his sister. He hadn't believed her then either, when she told him that Grace was the victim of a vampire, and worse, a victim of an undead vampire. What followed that night was the stuff of bad B-movies.

They had hunted him together since then; Lane because of her overwhelming sense of duty, and Beckett because it was all he could do for Grace, and all he could do to save his own sanity. His soul could take care of itself.

The result was a massive gash across Beckett's chest stopping only just short of his heart, courtesy of a run-in with a particularly vicious vampire they'd crossed along the way. Now, he lived for the day when he could plunge a stake into the black heart of Grace's killer and watch him die. Then take pleasure in the decapitation of the corpse. That one would be for Grace. All these thoughts he put away, it wasn't the time to expose Kat to his own nightmares - she had enough to deal with without adding his burdens to her own.

Oh yes, he knew about vampires. He rested his hand over the livid reminder across his chest of their existence and his failure.

Kat hung her head and rubbed her temples as if to dislodge what was slowly taking a hold of her mind. The knowledge of what she was.

"This will be hard for you, but I want you to go back to the beginning," said Lane. "Back to where it started."

"I don't know where it started," she whispered.

Lane nodded. "You do know. Your conscious mind has blocked out the memories but I can get them back for you."

"You can do that?"

"Yes."

"Then, do it."

Lane captured and held Kat's eyes while she bent and probed her subconscious to reveal its hidden secret.

***

She was nineteen again, in her final year of medical training, examinations passed with credit, and she was dating the catch of a lifetime with the whole summer ahead of her.

I'm dating Greg Randall, she'd thought, *everyone wants a piece of him and out of all the others, he's chosen me. I can't believe it. His family has money, he's good looking, good in the sack, and he wants to spend the summer with me. There must be a god.*

"Hippocrates was supposed to have died in Larissa," she heard Greg saying, "and your grandparents' village isn't that far from there, it'll be fun. What do you say?"

He wanted her to go to Greece with him, backpacking their way through the central plain away from the tourists. What the hell else would she say?

She had insisted on using her savings to pay for her flight to Athens, they would stay in cheap rooms and hitchhike their way across the country. She would pay her own way and the idea of slumming it obviously held a perverse appeal to Greg.

Their journey had been uneventful except for Greg making a pass at the stewardess on the plane. Kat had forgiven him - he was very persuasive.

Two weeks into their trip Greg had suggested that they make for Larissa, after all they were medical students and Larissa was where the father of medicine had died.

"Where did you say your grandparents lived? Kastanavos? It must be small; it's not even on the map." His baby blonde head was bent over the map, and she ran her fingers through the curls at the nape of his neck. She already knew how he would respond and she wanted to take his mind away from thoughts of finding her roots. There was no logic behind it, but she just knew that it was not a good idea. Probably just inverted snobbery, she thought, Greg's from the elite, father and mother both barristers, living in what could only be described as a mansion. She didn't want anything to spoil their trip, especially if it was because of her humble origins. The thought bothered her.

Greg was nothing if not predictable. He threw the map aside and pulled her in close, his ice-blue eyes alive and shining with lust. Kissing him was like opening a door to another world, a world of excitement that always hinted at danger. She lost herself in him totally, reaching the plateaux and peaks of pleasure that he was so capable of taking her to, mindful of the fact that she was pleasing his ego as much as his body but she didn't care as her climax took her beyond all that.

When her breathing returned to near normal she wanted to tell him she loved him, but something intangible prevented her.

He reached across her and made a grab at the map. "So, we'll head for Larissa tomorrow," he said.

Her misgivings grew wings and flew as her whole being filled with apprehension.

They had visited the site where Hippocrates was reputed to have expired, tramped around numerous archaeological sites, drank copious amounts of local wine and now it was obvious that Greg was bored.

Bored with Greece, bored with slumming it and, she thought, bored with her. Not with her body maybe, but with who she was, or, more likely, who she wasn't. But then, she thought, Greg was the type of person to get bored easily. It was fashionable.

Leaving Larissa, he'd chosen to take the Sikouri road. Her heart sank. He was determined to expose her peasant roots. Damn him, she suspected that he was taking pleasure from her discomfort.

Several lifts and a local boneshaker bus brought them to Parthavos, as near as they could get to Kastanavos, which still left them with a hot and dusty walk. After about an hour Greg threw down his backpack, opened the front and took out the bottle of retsina they'd bought in Larissa. He drank deeply from the bottle and the bitter wine caught in his throat.

"Can't be far now. What's that place over there?" he rasped.

Kat followed his fingertip. She shrugged, "Don't know. A church maybe or a monastery? I think I can make out a cross on the roof."

"Want to take a look?"

Any delay would be welcome. "Yes, why not?"

Straight ahead through an olive grove was the most direct route. They kept to the edge of the trees and reached the white painted building quickly. It was a monastery as she'd suspected. Maybe, if it were an open order, they'd be invited in and made welcome, perhaps given refreshments or at the very least, fresh water.

At the front gate a sign announced that it was the monastery of Agios Georgios. Kat shivered. The cold dread she'd felt the night before returned. It wasn't logical or rational, but the feeling of a thousand spiders crawling up her spine held its own message.

"Greg, I don't think we should. Come on let's get on to Kastanavos."

"You didn't even want to go there yesterday. What's with you? You pre-menstrual or something?"

She wanted to hit him. It was a cheap and nasty remark and she didn't intend to forgive him easily.

"Greg, don't. I can't explain it. I just don't want to go in there. Okay?"

"Please your damn self. I'm going in." He pulled the bell and turned away from her, shaking his head and his expression said, *God preserve me from temperamental women.*

After what seemed like an age they heard a shuffling behind the gate. The bolt on the other side slid back with a harsh grating sound, and - without the imagined creaking and groaning that had taken form in Kat's mind - the gate opened. She shook herself. *Stupid. What the hell was the matter with her?*

A diminutive nun squinted at them through bottle-bottom spectacles; the only expression on her face was a faint air of puzzlement.

"Kalimera," she said. *Good morning.*

Greg was at his most suave. "Kalimera." Radiant smile, beautiful teeth. "Meelateh angleeka?" *Do you speak English?*

The nun shook her head, but her face came alive. The Randall charm.

She smiled at them and stood back from the gate indicating that they should go in. Once inside the gate, she closed it behind them, pushing back the heavy rusted bolt with its accompanying grating noise. Kat shuddered again. The tiny nun held up a hand motioning them to wait there in the courtyard. She shuffled away again and disappeared into the dark shadows of the monastery.

They stood in silence while they waited.

Eventually a young woman wearing simple clothing emerged from the dim interior of the monastery. She nodded at them. "I am to take you to Sister Angelique. Come, please."

Greg strode forward; his powerful tanned frame dwarfed her. The young girl backed away from him.

Never mind Greg, you can't charm them all. Most, but not all. Kat held out her hand to the girl, "I'm Kat," she said, "What's your name?"

The girl flushed, "I am Anna. Come with me please." She kept her head down and quickened her pace, obviously reluctant to engage in conversation. She was either very shy or her English was no more than basic.

After the heat of the day the cool interior was welcome although it took several minutes for their eyes to become accustomed to the gloom after the glare of the Greek summer sun. They came into a large square hallway with white walls everywhere and exquisite tiling on the floor. There were several doors leading from it, each bearing a wooden crucifix. Anna knocked at one of the doors and entered on hearing the muffled response from inside. "Come," she said to them.

They were greeted by a regal woman of middle age and wearing darker robes than the other nuns that they had seen moving silently through the corridors. She appraised them through her wire-framed spectacles before speaking in an excellent and cultured English. She did not offer her hand in greeting.

"Good morning. I am Sister Angelique. Forgive us, but we are ill prepared for visitors. Ours is a semi-closed order and we usually only open our doors on the feast of our Saint when local people come to pay him their respects. How can we help you? Are you lost? Or merely seeking refreshment?"

The Randall charm oozed again. He began speaking to her in Greek, determined to make his impression. Sister Angelique's expression didn't soften and she held up a hand to stop Greg speaking.

"Almost all of us here speak English and I was educated in Oxford, so please, continue in your native tongue."

Greg blushed at the rebuke and the veiled suggestion that his Greek was lousy. Kat allowed herself the ghost of a smile.

"Thank you, Sister. I'm Greg Randall and this is my friend Katerini. We are heading for Kastanavos and we saw your monastery. Forgive us but we simply wanted to take a closer look. Although some refreshment would be very welcome for which we will pay of course."

Sister Angelique smiled at Kat. She could feel the woman's eyes turning her soul inside out. The smile faded as she looked back at Greg. *Randall strikes two.*

"That will not be necessary, Mr Randall. We are not a wealthy order, but I believe our hospitality can withstand the strain of two extra meals. They will be, however, very basic. Some bread, cheese and fruit and some wine from our own vineyard." She paused. "Kastanavos, you say? You will find precious little there. Perhaps you would find Parditsa more to your liking. There are at least two decent hotels, both of which serve excellent food and wine. Perhaps you wish to refresh yourselves? Anna will show you the way."

They were effectively dismissed as Anna came back into the room bang on cue. The two women spoke briefly in Greek and in lowered tones. Anna made for the door, "Come, please."

They left Greg in a small room with an adjacent bathroom. Kat put a hand on Anna's arm. "Where are we going? I can manage in here, with Greg."

The girl shook her head. "No," was all she said.

Kat blushed. She hadn't spared a thought for their strict moral codes, and whilst she wasn't happy with Greg, his company was preferable to being alone in a strange room in the monastery with its foreboding atmosphere. She felt foolish.

Anna stopped outside another small wooden door bearing the inevitable wooden crucifix. She opened it and stepped aside.

"I wait for you. Out here." Anna nodded at her.

Kat entered the room, closed the door behind her and leaned against it. It felt surprisingly good to be alone after three weeks of Greg's company, even if it was in a nun's cell. There was a small iron-framed bed in one corner on top of which was a sheet, one pillow and one neatly folded blanket. A tiny window high in the wall provided the only light in the room. There was a washstand with a towel hanging on a single hook and she presumed the tiny door at its side led into a toilet. She decided against investigating.

"It's like a jail cell," she thought aloud. Instantly the image took hold of her imagination and she remembered her earlier indistinct fears. She threw herself at the door to the corridor and yanked at it, her heart banging against her ribs. It opened easily, almost sending her down onto the floor and she laughed at the thoughts that had pinched at her mind's eye.

Anna stood sentry duty, looking at her strangely.

"Go," whispered Anna. "Go quickly."

"What? I'm sorry, what did you say?"

Anna bowed her head. "I said nothing," she replied.

CHAPTER TEN

Anna had collected them in silence and returned them to the public areas of the monastery, showing them into a small room with a table laid for two. True to her promise, Sister Angelique had provided them with a modest meal that was both filling and tasty. Kat thought the wine to be the best she'd tasted since she arrived in Greece.

Greg did most of the talking as usual, while she listened yet again to his family history. It seemed there were vineyards in the South of France, owned though never visited. The wine they produced was, he said, far superior to what he described as the soured grape juice that they were drinking. Kat was becoming increasingly alienated from him. She'd see the trip through, not caring for the idea of making it back to the airport alone, and safely back home she'd end their relationship. She was sure he would be relieved and wondered if in fact she would be able to get in first. Not love after all.

She had been buried in these thoughts when she realised that Greg had fallen silent. His face was pale and he was perspiring heavily.

"Greg? What's the matter? You look awful."

"Stomach cramps. I need to lie down," he muttered.

She ran to the door and wrenched it open to find Anna stationed outside in the corridor.

It took less than half an hour for the stomach cramps to fulfil their potential into a full-blown bout of throwing up. Anna, under the direction of Sister Angelique, had whisked Greg away to their infirmary. Kat smiled inwardly. The Randall charm was somewhat diminished whilst vomiting.

It was quickly established that Greg would live, his

illness probably due to an excess of retsina in the heat, and Sister Angelique had offered them beds for the night. Greg had wanted to press on to Kastanavos, but his bravado hadn't stood the test of trying to stand upright.

Kat was relieved when he drifted into a fitful sleep. Anna, ever close by, touched her arm. "You come," she said. "I am to take you to the chapel."

She tried to explain to the girl that she wasn't Roman Catholic but her protests went unheeded. She decided it was easier to go along with it.

The chapel stood amid the small complex of corridors and rooms surrounding the courtyard, its huge Gothic door slightly ajar. Kat could smell the incense from outside. She turned to Anna seeking reassurance that she should enter. Anna had gone.

She pushed the heavy door open and sunlight streamed inside, immediately reflected back at her as bright beams of light thrown off the interior of the chapel. Once inside she could see the reason for this. Everywhere was the cool gleam of silver. Huge candelabra, incense burners, wall panels, even the altar, everything silver. There was something nagging at the back of her mind, something wasn't quite right, not as she expected. It had something to do with the silver but she couldn't think what.

As her eyes accustomed to the interior, she was drawn to what appeared to be a massive shrine or tomb. That too was made of silver, ornately crafted, solid silver. It must have weighed tons. One of the side panels appeared to be hinged along its length. Her eyes followed the line of the panel to the opposite edge. All along the top of the panel was a line of silver padlocks. Whatever was inside must be extremely valuable, some ancient icon possibly, the Catholic Church was famously wealthy and had massive stores of gold and silver. This was probably such a store.

And there it was - the nebulous something that had bothered her about the silver. Every church that she had seen previously had been decorated in gold or brass. Not silver.

She shivered involuntarily and turned to leave, when she heard her name whispered from inside the chapel.

"Katerini… Katerini… Katerini." No more than a breath in the air.

Kat stood still and looked around her. "Hello? Anna? Is that you?"

A movement at the rear of the chapel made her start.

Two nuns stepped out of the shadows. One was very young, a novice; a girl of no more than about sixteen, she thought. The other looked so old that she was ageless. The stark contrast in the two was stunning.

The young nun was beautiful, with wide eyes the colour of cornflowers, her face, austerely framed in her wimple, held peace in its every pore. Her wide eyes proclaimed innocence and she exuded calmness and serenity.

Like the Madonna, Kat thought.

The elderly nun had her own grace; her face was like ancient leather and her dark eyes held the wisdom of centuries.

The old one spoke to her. "I am Sister Agnes. You have come to see our Saint?" she asked Kat. "It is not the feast day, but Sister Angelique has told me that you may see him if you wish it."

"Your saint? How do you mean, see him?" An uncomfortable wriggling made itself known deep in the pit of her stomach.

The young nun had bowed her head and did not lift her gaze from the chapel floor.

Sister Agnes moved towards the silver shrine. "Our Saint, Agios Georgios, he is resting here. He was such a pure man, a holy man, that death has not contaminated his remains. He has lain in death for centuries and his body has not decayed. It is a miracle. His goodness was such that his body has survived death and decomposition. The people of the local villages come here on his feast day to pay respect to him. I have been given permission to allow

71

you to see him. You are truly honoured as Sister Angelique has never before allowed this." Her words were clipped and her voice reflected the stern expression on her ancient face.

Kat noticed then that the old nun held a huge bunch of silver keys. They hung from a belt around her habit, alongside a silver cross. She had no inclination to view a five-hundred-year-old corpse, saintly or not, but she was afraid that to decline would cause offence. *Good one Greg. Got out of this nicely.* She breathed in hard.

"Thank you," she replied.

"Katerini." The whispering came again. "Katerini."

Kat swung round expecting to see Greg on his feet again but there was no-one else in the chapel besides her and the two nuns. She shivered again, unnerved by the whisper.

On the wall behind the huge silver shrine was a massive tapestry depicting a deathbed scene in which the central figure was obviously dying painfully, whilst around him stood nuns and priests praying for his immortal soul. *Cheery*, she thought.

Sister Agnes was at the shrine.

No! Don't! Kat wanted to shout, but the words died on her lips.

She looked around her hoping for inspiration or distraction but the cold reflections of the silver were everywhere, giving her no comfort or escape. She looked up at the ceiling and even there the paintings were all edged in silver. She shivered.

The young nun had remained motionless, looking more like a waxwork now than a living, breathing and very beautiful young woman. Sister Agnes was unlocking the padlocks along the top edge of the shrine.

What will he look like? Probably like Sister Agnes, she looks like she's been around a few centuries. She giggled at the thought and instantly felt better. She'd look at the dead guy, how bad could it be? Then she'd make the appropriate noises and tactfully leave, putting some drachmas in the offertory plate on the way out. She hoped he wouldn't smell.

The side of the shrine fell forwards to the clattering of the loosened locks. Old she may be, thought Kat, but Sister Agnes had hidden strength to guide the silver panel down. *Must have biceps like a buffalo under that habit.*

Kat was relieved that there was no unpleasant odour escaping the confines of what was, after all, a coffin.

It wasn't so bad and, as she approached the tomb, she could see that its occupant had the appearance of someone in a deep sleep. No grinning skull gaped out at her, no mummy with leather like skin pulled taut over cadaverous cheek bones. Fascinating. Dead for hundreds of years and not decomposed. Atmospherics, maybe? A brilliant mortician born before his time? Something had preserved the body, though she doubted it was anything to do with saintliness. The old guy was probably only made a saint when someone found out he wasn't doing the graveyard rot, although why they would dig him up in the first place to discover that, didn't bear too much thinking about.

Sister Agnes had moved away to stand at the side of the young nun who still had her head bowed to the floor.

Kat stepped up closer to the shrine.

Agios Georgios was Greek for Saint George. *Saint George and the Dragon*, she glanced at Sister Agnes. She giggled again then bit her lip; she was determined not to offend.

His silky hair was long and grey, and beautifully arranged over his shoulders. His face appeared peaceful in death, almost restful. She expected him to yawn and stretch and sit up and only just stifled the rising scream in her throat.

Don't start thinking things like that. You'll be seeing Dracula next.

She was very close to him now, could reach out and touch him. Touch the silky grey hair that shone like the silver that encased him, touch the soft preserved flesh of his face. Stroke it. Kiss it. There was an uninvited fluttering in the depth of her pelvis.

He'd been laid to rest in a black brocade frock coat and black leather boots. *He'd have turned heads in his time. In anyone's time,* she thought.

His hands were bony and sinewy in death and the ring on his right third finger hung loose. It was the only gold object in the chapel. Old gold, with a crest, a phoenix, she thought. But those hands would have been different in life. Long elegant fingers that would stroke her face tenderly, yet could be strong with desire. She could feel them on her body, stroking, exploring, searching, and demanding.

A shiver ran through her that owed nothing to fear, it was the thrill she felt when Greg …

With a start, she realised that her face was almost resting on his and she could feel the soft tingle on her lips from where she knew she had kissed him. She recoiled as though scalded and as she did so she realised that her shirt had come unbuttoned and her breast was exposed. Her pulse was racing and her mouth was dry. Her throat constricted over the scream that threatened to choke her. She had to get out of there before she fainted. The horror of what she'd just felt overpowered her.

My God, I just got turned on by a dead guy. How sick is that?

She clutched the edges of her shirt closed and hurried to the door. Suddenly, there was a hand on her arm and she couldn't prevent the tiny scream that strangled itself at its birth. *He couldn't have …*

The scream lodged somewhere between her heart and her throat. She turned to find the young nun at her side. Of Sister Agnes there was no sign.

She tried to calm her jagged nerves long enough to speak to the girl. God, she hoped she hadn't seen what had happened back there.

"I'm sorry, I … just felt a little faint. I need some air, that's all, Sister …"

"Sister Maria," she whispered. "Please take this." She

covered Kat's hands with her own and pressed something between their palms.

Kat looked down at an exquisitely crafted silver cross with a single ruby where the arms met. She shook her head and pushed it back at her. "No," she said, "No, really. Thank you but no. I can't."

She pushed the cross back at Kat. "Please," she insisted. "You must take it. Please," she begged.

"I can't, it must be very valuable - it looks very old. I can't take it." Kat pulled her hand away and made for the door. She was altogether too freaked out to stay and argue with her.

Sister Maria was beside her as she pulled the huge old door open to the sun outside. The young nun had her gaze fixed firmly on the floor once more, but she pressed the crucifix into Kat's hand and walked quickly back into the dark of the chapel, her habit swishing around her ankles, before Kat could refuse again.

As the air hit her face she exhaled, feeling as though she'd been holding her breath for an eternity. The air was cooler than she'd expected and the sun was low in the sky. *How long had she been in there?*

She shook herself trying to lose the weird sensations that clung to her like old cobwebs.

She made a decision. Foolish or not she was leaving for the airport alone. *So long, Greg.* She doubted he would be sorry.

She refused Sister Angelique's offer of a bed, figuring that she had enough daylight left to make it back to Parthavos. She'd been given bread, cheese and fruit again, and a container of water.

As she left the monastery she sensed that someone was watching her. The sun was behind the white walled building and her eyes were drawn to a figure in one of the high windows. She raised a hand to shield her eyes against the glare unable to make out who it was that stood there, but knowing instinctively that it was Sister Maria. Her

hand had been raised in a gesture of farewell.
   Or was it a blessing?

CHAPTER ELEVEN

The only hotel in Parthavos was clean and well cared for although she would have been grateful for anywhere other than the monastery. Kat was shown to a small room on the third floor, which was basic to the extent of containing only a bed and a chair, not unlike the nun's cell back there, she thought. She wondered about Greg, momentarily feeling a little guilty at leaving him, and then dismissed the worries. He would be well cared for and probably more than a little relieved that she had gone. She was emotionally exhausted and decided to go straight to bed. As she undressed she noticed what looked like a tiny cut on her left breast, just above the nipple.

What the hell? Must've been when I legged it out of that chapel, caught it on my ring in my hurry to cover up. Oh, well, no serious damage. She lay on top of the bed, and let her thoughts wander.

Sleep came quickly as darkness fell over the village. In Parthavos, darkness always fell. In more picturesque villages, darkness may have draped itself over the tiny houses, but in Parthavos it fell like a black pall.

Around two thirty she was woken from the heavy folds of sleep by a rattling sound followed by a knocking. It took her several minutes to realise that the noise came from the wooden shutters at her windows. Someone was standing at her window rattling the shutters, trying to get in.

Icy fear washed over her as she realised that her room was on the third floor. Whoever was outside her window had somehow climbed up to her window.

But I'm on the third floor, she kept reasoning and there are no balconies. It must be Greg; he'd followed her from the monastery and was looking for a bed. Hadn't he been on the Ben Nevis expedition last year? He was an excellent climber. The rough walls and bougainvillea growing up to the roof would have provided him with a moderately easy climb. It was Greg. Well, she'd make him wait.

The rattling and knocking continued.

Damn him, she'd have to let him in before he woke the whole hotel.

"Shh," she hissed at the window. "Cool it, Greg, I'm coming."

The knocking stopped.

She opened the curtains and the window and then stopped just before unlocking the shutters.

"Greg?"

He didn't answer her.

She felt warm and mellow, almost removed from herself, like the one and only time she'd smoked marijuana. Tired, she thought, very tired.

The shutters opened easily although she had no memory of unlocking and opening them.

The man stood right in front of her in the room before she had seen him move. He was so close she could feel him on her skin. He had long dark hair the colour of anthracite and eyes like lodestones, whose magnetism pulled her into him mentally and physically, and when he smiled at her she couldn't pull her eyes away from his sensuous mouth. He had a lean, hungry look that excited her. Had she seen him before? No, not like this, and yet there was something akin to a memory seeping through her drowsiness.

"Who are you?"

"Fire," he answered.

He wore a black roll-neck sweater and a black designer suit, incongruous in this tiny peasant village. His voice sent ripples of pleasure through her as it soothed and stroked her mind.

She was in his arms and he smelled of summer, and something else. Earth, she thought, freshly turned earth.

His mouth found hers with a strange familiarity, kissing her with a depth that sent a heat through her that frightened her with its intensity, awaking flames of desire in her that had never surfaced before, that settled deep in her groin. Fire, she thought, as his words echoed in her head.

"I don't know you. I can't do this," she whispered.

"You know me. You know me as surely as you know yourself. You and I are one and the same. I can sense it in you, smell it, feel it. You know it, but you don't understand it. Not yet. But you will, Katerini."

His voice made her tingle and his hands were gentle in their art, guiding her towards the rumpled bed, slipping her nightdress from her shoulders.

"How do you know my name?" she asked.

Time slid and he was next to her on the bed, his nakedness natural and somehow once again familiar. He had a strong physique, tanned and healthy, and she wanted him, this stranger who had come to her in the night. She felt a longing like never before and she ached for him to take her. No, she didn't understand it, but neither did she care.

He was inside her and she was lost in him. He whispered to her of ancient places, past glories, and long dead cultures. Pleasing her and teasing her with accomplished finesse. She no longer felt the bed beneath her back as they floated upwards towards the ceiling, weightless, timeless, in harmony with each other's movements. She looked down to see for herself. He had defied gravity and was lifting her high above the bed but even that seemed natural and familiar and held no fear.

Waves of pleasure washed her, rising in a tide of sensation until she felt she would explode with the intensity of his lovemaking. They rocked back and forth, towards and away from the climax that she longed for yet dreaded.

Because she knew that then he would be gone.

She felt the softness of the bed beneath her again and the moist warmth of his mouth on her breast, then her stomach, as he kissed and licked her, tasting her. His lips travelled downwards to her inner thigh, sucking her deeply. When she could hold back no longer she felt her head would burst in a scarlet explosion and then there was a tiny sharp pain as his teeth sought and found her femoral artery where it passed through her groin. A red river filled her head and her consciousness left her. While he sucked at her vein and fed, she dreamed of floating on a thick, warm red sea.

His hunger had dulled but he fed some more, sucking and drinking and licking her wound, unwilling to waste a single drop of her life force that was his nourishment.

He laid beside her, propped on his elbow, his tongue travelling slowly over his teeth, savouring the last drop, relishing the taste of her blood. He looked down at her as she slept, moaning softly at the erotic dreams that he had left her with, and would be all that she would remember. Except for the haunting whisper of her name, "Katerini."

He lifted his own wrist to his teeth and pierced his skin and the wall of the vein that stood proud, and as the blood welled from it, he held it over the wound on her thigh and allowed it to drip and mingle with her own. His wrist was over her mouth and a single drop of blood formed over her parted lips ready to swell and fall into her waiting mouth. He frowned and quickly pulled his arm away from her allowing the single rosy droplet to fall onto the bed cover. He would allow her to evolve slowly. Something in her had touched him and he refused to sacrifice her on the altar of his ego. If she turned, she turned. Her destiny would be of her own choosing.

The curtains flapped in an unnatural breeze, the door banged and the shutters clattered together.

He was gone.

Kat slept, unaware of the changes already taking place inside her as the long awaited catalyst began to work on her DNA, mutating, changing, and altering.

Turning.

And soon she would discover that she was pregnant.

CHAPTER TWELVE

As the memories and images flooded into Kat's consciousness, tears ran like a river down her cheeks.

Beckett's arm was firm around her as he waited for her sobbing to subside. With a sudden movement she was on her feet, hands in her short, dark hair.

"*No*," she screamed. "God help me, no. I'm going mad."

He was at her side in an instant, wanting to hold her, knowing better but doing it anyway.

Lane stood up and walked to the window.

"So, now we know," she said.

"Know what?" Kat shouted, "That eighteen years ago I slept with a total stranger. That Greg, who for all these years I believed was the father of my son, in fact isn't. Nik was right; I don't know who his father is. He called me a whore and it seems he's right about that too."

Beckett's arm tightened around her shoulder, his face pale.

"It isn't like that, Kat. There is nothing you could have done; you weren't in control of anything that happened to you."

"Oh, please, Beckett. Not in control? I didn't see me screaming rape in any of these memories. *If* that's what they are."

Lane returned to her seat opposite Kat and took her hand. "You need to listen very carefully to me, Kat. What I'm going to tell you is going to freak you out."

Kat was shouting now, "Oh really? You think I'm *not* freaked out? You talk to me about vampires like we're discussing the goddamn weather, you try to convince me I'm a bloodsucking monster and I'm actually

83

contemplating the possibility of all this. What the hell else is there to freak me out?"

Lane's expression didn't change. "Okay, listen. This is what I believe happened back then. You have always carried the recessive gene of vampirism. Whilst it lay dormant, normal people wouldn't be able to tell but another vampire would, especially an ancient one. This saint, this Agios Georgios, is such a vampire. It is the only reasonable explanation for the state of non-corruption of his body. The Roman Catholic Church has always identified such phenomenon as Sainthood, whereas the Greek Orthodox Church knows better. When you visited his tomb he sensed you. He would have been able to follow you and find you. I believe he is one of the Undead."

"So, you're saying I allowed that corpse into my bedroom, let him make love to me, and then leave? Is that what you're saying? Because I'm here to tell you that this man was no corpse, he was drop dead gorgeous, if you pardon the pun."

"One of the vampire's capabilities is to be able to cloak the minds of their prey. He would have been able to make you 'see' whatever he wanted you to see. Have you heard the term 'incubus'?"

Kat thought for a moment, "Yes. Some kind of spirit, isn't it?"

"Incubus is the name given to a spirit or vampire who visits a woman in the night for the sole purpose of having sex with her," Lane replied. "It was him, I'm certain."

"How can you be so sure?"

Lane looked very serious. "You forget, Kat. I am a vampire too. You will learn of these things."

"Of course. How stupid of me to forget!" She appeared on the verge of hysteria, and then quite suddenly, she composed herself. "I think I'd like you both to leave now," she said quietly, "I need to be by myself."

Beckett frowned. "I don't think you should be alone,"

he said.

"Aren't you afraid I'll bite you? Drain your blood and turn you into some blood-sucking freak?"

"I'll risk it." He grinned at her, hoping to lighten her oppressive mood.

She lost it then, beating on his chest and screaming obscenities. He caught her wrists and held them firmly but gently against his chest. "It's all right. Go ahead, let it out." He stroked her hair as she sobbed against him, leaving a wet patch on his denim shirt.

When the sobs subsided, she asked him, "Do you understand any of this? "

He nodded at her, his eyes were sad and he would have given anything for this not to be true. She looked vulnerable, which was ironic given the fact that she had the potential to be stronger than him, faster than him and capable of his ultimate destruction.

Like the one before.

Still, he wanted to protect her.

Lane walked over to them. She put her hand on Kat's arm. "I want you to know that I'm here for you. There is so much for you to learn, so much for you to understand. I can help you, but I can't make you, or at least I won't make you. I'll come back later when you've calmed down a bit. Beckett will stay with you for a while."

Kat nodded.

"There's something else."

Kat looked at her questioningly.

"I want you to promise me that you won't go out. Stay here while you try and get your head around this. Promise?"

"I promise."

She closed her front door behind Lane, and leaned against it.

"Beckett, I don't want company. I appreciate your help, I really do, and it's sweet of you to care but I really need some time. I mean it's not everyday a girl gets to know she's a vampire. I'll call you tomorrow. I won't leave, you have my word."

Beckett looked helplessly at her. He couldn't insist she let him stay, but he was fearful of her being alone.

"Kat, before I go, I want you to know something. What I said before, about being fond of you, I meant it. I have … a need, to take care of you. If anything should happen to you …"

"Beckett, I'm in my own home and I'm going to bed. Nothing is going to happen to me. Remember, who's the first one I call when I need someone?" She paused, "And Beckett, about the other thing, well I want you to know that if things had been different, if I wasn't what I am, what I'm trying to say is that I could care for you too, but if what you say is true then I can't be with you. I don't know what I may do. I was already having trouble controlling these needs in me, now I don't know where it will lead. I don't know what I'll become. And I don't want you tainted or hurt in the process."

He didn't speak, he couldn't. He didn't trust his voice not to betray him. He simply nodded then bent forwards and kissed the top of her head.

He cleared his throat, "You know where I am if you need me, I'll ring you in the morning. Call Lane, she really can help you. Don't forget."

"I won't"

She closed her door and leaned against it. Beckett was still standing at her gate; she knew it. She waited for over an hour until she heard the engine of his car firing into life. Another five minutes in case he changed his mind and she would see if her car was still in one piece.

She had to find Nik.

CHAPTER THIRTEEN

She changed her mind about her car, calling a cab instead, asking him to come to the lane at the back of her cottage. The driver knew Danse Macabre and showed no surprise at this pale, thin woman that didn't dress like the usual type of punter at the club. He noted the ever-darkening rings around her eyes and the gaunt, troubled looks. Drugs, he thought. Shame, she was a beautiful woman.

She paid off the cab and sent the driver away, despite his offer to wait in case she changed her mind.

Luke strode forwards, his face expressionless. He put his hand out to stop her passing through the doorway.

"Members and their guests only Ma'am."

"I'm looking for someone. I think he's here."

"Sorry." The hand didn't move.

"I don't want to stay, please just let me look inside. I'll leave straight away if he's not here."

Luke was coldly adamant. "Sorry."

Andrei Marinescu appeared in the doorway behind him. "It's all right, Luke. The lady is with me."

He held out a hand to Kat and ushered her through the doorway.

"Thanks," she said when she was inside. "I'm not staying, I'm looking for someone."

"We're all looking for someone. Come. Let's see if your friend is here. If not, then perhaps you will allow me to buy you a drink."

"No, really, I just need to find him."

"I hope he realises how lucky he is, this friend of yours."

Kat flushed scarlet against her otherwise pale cheeks. "He's my son," she said quietly.

"Ah. Then perhaps it is I that am lucky. Come with me, I'll take you to the viewing balcony and we can have that drink while you look for your errant offspring."

He seemed to glide ahead of her and she found herself following him up the plush carpeted stairs to the yearning strains of a Goth band mourning one who was forsaken.

She perched nervously on the edge of an extremely comfortable couch with this striking, sophisticated man. His hair was like the wing of a raven, casting blue-black lights as he moved his head. It draped itself neatly into his neck and her fingers could almost feel the silkiness as she imagined herself running them through it. He was gorgeous.

What was this? What the hell was the matter with her? This man, this charismatic stranger, had touched her mind somehow. Instinctively she closed her consciousness against him, not even knowing how she had done it.

So, he thought, *she has the powers, they're weak, but she has them. Interesting.* It had been a long time since he'd had such a worthy partner. He was going to enjoy her.

"Do you see your son?" he asked.

She shook her head. "No, he's not here."

Another sign. She could see through the gloom. Yes, he was going to enjoy this rare treat. He reached past her conscious mind, bypassing her naïve attempt at blocking him. *Oh yes.*

He was excited by her, sensing in her the intensity that would match his own and something else in the Latent before him, something that always had the power to give him the ultimate pleasure. She hadn't yet turned completely.

And he was going to turn her.

He put a glass down in front of her. It contained a clear liquid that threw off rainbows as the firelight reflected in it.

"Thank you. What is it?"

"A fruit liqueur from my homeland. Plum Brandy. A drink fit for a beautiful lady with jewels for eyes."

She flushed again. This was ridiculous. She was no longer a young girl ready to be bowled over by strong drink and nauseating flattery. Nevertheless she felt herself warming inside. Something she'd not allowed herself to feel for a long time. Not even with Beckett.

The thought of him twisted inside her like a knife. Beckett was a real man, she told herself. Nothing flamboyant or overdressed about him. What you saw is what you got with Beckett and there was no getting away from the fact that what she saw, she liked. She could love him if she allowed herself to. And that was the problem.

She didn't dare allow herself to fall in love with him. There was something wrong with her, something deep inside, something rotten. Something that slumbered, but was ready to be roused to frenzy when the right button was pushed, something that could so easily rage out of control. There was no way she would taint Beckett's goodness with it. She would *not* allow herself to get any closer to him. He'd get over her.

"You seem distracted. I have sent for Luke, he will be able to tell us if your son has been here tonight. Here he comes." He beckoned. "Luke. Over here."

Andrei's henchman strode over to them.

"Luke, this beautiful lady is looking for her son. Can you help?"

Kat described Nik to the men. Andrei's expression remained unchanged.

"He was here earlier, Ma'am. He left again. With a young lady."

"Are you sure?"

"Yes, Ma'am. I'm very sure."

Kat looked despondent.

"Well, there you are. Luke is seldom mistaken about who is and is not in the club. It's why he's paid so well. Eh, Luke?"

Luke nodded deferentially to his employer.

Andrei waved him away. "So, your son is not here.

89

Perhaps you will allow me the honour of your company and I will try to take your mind off whatever terrible deed he is guilty of." He smiled at her. "He's young. Allow him some indiscretions."

Kat laughed. Suddenly she was relaxed and at ease. She felt good. It was easy to be in his company, there was something magnetic about him, compulsive. His charisma was obvious and she couldn't deny him her eyes, her customary reticence melted in his compelling aura.

She had no memory of the invitation or her acceptance but she found herself heading for his penthouse above the club.

He had his arm around her painfully thin waist in the lift and she could feel his energy transferring itself to her. She'd been feeling low and depleted and now she felt as though she could conquer the unknown world, she couldn't remember when she'd felt this good. And somewhere deep in the dark recesses of her mind she knew that it was because of him.

The lift doors opened onto what looked like the entrance to a Gothic mansion. The walls were faced with stone and the entrance to Andrei's flat was an ornate arch. The door itself was of heavy iron-studded timber but its iron ring handle was for effect only - the door opened electronically.

The inner hallway entranced her; she'd been transported back in time to the Gothic era. The entire place had been constructed as a replica of the magnificence of those days.

He led her through into the main room where a huge log fire blazed in a fireplace that would have accommodated her bathroom. The couches were antiques that had been brought over from Eastern Europe and were priceless, as were the rest of the furnishings and decorations. Her surroundings were breathtaking.

Andrei pulled her to him from behind as she stood in silence trying to take it all in. She leaned her head back against his chest as he pushed her long hair to one side and nuzzled her neck, stroking her throat and whispering into her ear. He spoke to her in a Slavic tongue but she understood his every word and gave no thought to how that might be.

"Close your eyes, Katerini. Close them and see the world with different sight. The world out there is ours; yours and mine and the rest of our kind. It is the way of nature that the strong will survive and the weak will eventually perish. Don't waste tears weeping for what is inevitable; save them for the beauty that I can share with you. I can show you Angel Falls from the inside, the mysteries of the Amazon rainforest, the ice caps and the deserts, the sunset over Montego Bay and the sunrise above the Great Pyramid. I can teach you how to watch a flower open to the morning sun and close again to the moonlight, how to be the past, the present, and the future."

His hands were on her shoulders and she could feel the overpowering rise of uncontrollable energy that she always felt when aroused - but with Andrei she had no fears. She had no doubt that her animalistic frenzy would be contained by his undeniable power.

He felt her release the barrier between them and smiled into her hair. He kissed her neck softly, alternately kissing and caressing her throat, licking and tasting her with obvious relish. Her heart was pounding and she could feel the pressure of blood in her veins; she was aware of her pulse and gradually, she came alive to another beat. Slowly but surely she became aware of the blood flowing through Andrei. She could feel the beat of his heart, slow, so very slow.

She stepped out of her dress and just for a moment she was conscious of her skeletal appearance.

He appeared to read her instantly and turned her to him. He placed his finger at her throat and slowly ran it down to her navel.

"This too will change," he said. "You are beautiful Katerini. A beautiful and powerful vampire, you simply need to cast off this human form and wear the body you were born for. You have denied yourself for too long, going without the nourishment you need so badly, going without a man in your bed because no human could stand up to the power in you."

Fleeting memories of a man mopping his throat and bloody sheets flashed into her mind. He read her again.

"He was not worthy of you, do not give him another thought. The answer to all of your problems is simple. You must turn, Katerini. Turn and become the beautiful and powerful creature that lays dormant inside you. Deny it no longer. Release it and be whole."

Kat could hear only truth in his words. She had to turn to survive. If not she would waste away and die never tasting the fruits of her potential. She would give herself up to him completely and trust in his inherent power to take her where she belonged. Into a world where there was no fear, no guilt and no pain.

"Yes," she whispered. Then silently, *I'm so sorry, Beckett.*

Her thought was reflected in his consciousness and he frowned imperceptibly.

He led her to a low couch in front of the blazing fireplace and gently guided her onto it. She watched as he opened an ancient cabinet and took out two crystal goblets that were once drunk from in the court of Louis the Fourteenth. Her anticipation was hard to contain but instinctively she knew that soon time would have no meaning.

A bell rang, and Andrei opened an antique casket camouflaging the telephone that would have been so wrong in this ancient setting.

"Yes," he snapped, then after a few moments, "Deal with it. And don't disturb me again." He put the telephone back carefully.

"I'm sorry," he said. "There has been a minor

disturbance downstairs, a drunk trying to cause trouble. It's of no consequence."

He moved over to a beautiful low marble table on which stood a crystal decanter that matched the goblets and poured a vibrant green liquid that threw off reflections like priceless emeralds. He placed a slotted silver spoon over one of the goblets, on top of which rested a cube of sugar, then poured over it some more of the bright green liquid that shimmered and danced with emerald lights. In a small deft movement, he set light to the sugar cube which burned with a blue flame and dissolved as caramel into the drink. She was enchanted by the ritual with which he was so obviously familiar.

He raised the goblet to her lips. "Absinthe", he said. "Drink, Katerini, drink to your soul that is imprisoned inside this body. Drink to your release."

The bitter liquid rested on her parted lips momentarily before she closed her eyes and swallowed. She could feel the fire, feel her potency, she felt truly alive for the first time ever.

Andrei lifted the goblet away from her lips and took her hand. He led her through into a huge bedchamber filled with elegantly carved wood and gold, lots of gold. The massive, ancient oak bed draped with exquisite medieval tapestry dominated the room and he effortlessly picked her up and took her to it.

She unbuttoned his black satin brocade tunic and pushed him backwards onto the opulent bedcovers. He let her remove his clothing, allowing her this much before he took control. The pleasure for him would be in the turning, but he'd allow her to believe in the fairy tale for a while longer.

He had his hands in her hair and he pulled her head back by it until her eyes were locked in his.

"Katerini, say goodbye to the illness and the longing, say goodbye to the wasting away."

His mouth was hot on hers and she could taste the

absinthe on his lips. His teeth were hard and sharp against her tongue and she could feel the movement as his canines were pushed downwards to become two shining white points of pleasure and pain.

The dam burst in her then as the pent up emotions and energies of the past years fell away and she became almost feral in his arms. Unlike the last time she could feel his power containing the destructive potential inside her, twisting it, turning it inwards, amplifying the force that was already birthing there.

Somewhere in the distance an animal cried out into the night and she was only vaguely aware that the scream was from her own tortured spirit, finding its way out into the world.

And she knew there was no going back.

CHAPTER FOURTEEN

Beckett had sat in his jeep outside Kat's front door for an hour before starting the clapped-out engine. He drove around the corner and followed the road to the back of her house. He saw the cab drive away and followed it at a discreet distance. Wherever she was going he'd be there to keep her safe.

He'd come to know her well over the past eighteen months and he knew she would go looking for Nik. He parked the Suzuki on the block next to the club and waited as he watched her talk to Luke, then after a few moments they were joined by Andrei. He watched as they went inside. He wanted to follow her into the club but knew also that she would be angry at him for following her at all, and she was driven to find Nik, he had to allow her that.

There would be no reason for her to stay there if she hadn't found him, and if she had, Beckett guessed they would have much to talk about, but from what Kat had said, he'd been an angry young man when they'd parted.

He made the decision to give her fifteen minutes and then go in after her. He had to know she was safe.

Luke's solid frame barred the doorway.

"I'm sorry, sir, it's members only I'm afraid."

"I've just come to collect a friend," Beckett replied, advancing on Luke.

"Are you a member, sir?"

"No. Perhaps I could join? Let me in and I'll gladly become a member."

"I'm sorry, Sir. Membership is by invitation only. You'll need the sponsorship of an existing member, or the management."

"Look, this is stupid; I only want to collect my friend."

95

Luke's face was impassive. He'd heard that line more times than he could count. He didn't move.

Beckett put his hand on the sturdy arm and tried to pass him but Luke grabbed his wrist and twisted it painfully. Beckett's knee made contact with Luke's groin and he regained his hand. Without looking backwards he was inside the club and standing at the door searching the gloom, searching the sea of faces, bombarded with the Goth anthems of the Sisters of Mercy.

The staircase at the opposite corner drew his eyes and he watched as the lift doors at the top closed behind Kat and Andrei, but not before he'd seen the arm around Kat's tiny waist.

"Kat! No! Wait!" yelled Beckett.

His voice was drowned by the music. She hadn't seen him.

He pushed his way through the crowd that moved in what looked like an ancient tribal ritual. He was pushed back.

"Hey, Bud. Cool it, yeah?"

Beckett took stock of the young man with a slender, paste white face, black eyeliner, ruby lips and black nail polish on his long tapered finger tips and decided to ignore him. He pushed forwards again.

The crowd seemed to part and he was face to face with a bear of man dressed biker-style. He had a leather band studded with spikes around his neck and similar ones around his wrists. The tattoo on his arm proclaimed him the 'Devil's Son'.

Beckett swallowed hard, he was dog meat.

Luke appeared behind him, perspiring from the insult to the delicate part of his anatomy, and his expression told of a painful vengeance.

From other directions large men were approaching purposefully. It was no longer a question of making it to the staircase, more of a matter of keeping his skin. He was nothing if not realistic and while he'd caught Luke off guard at the door, there was no way he would survive a scuffle with Satan's Army. Retreat was out of the question as Luke was closing in behind him with a serious score to settle.

The first punch was aimed low. One for one.

The Devil's Son had him in an arm lock that would tear his shoulder out of its socket with the slightest movement. The only way was back to the door. He was going to get thrown out in style.

Luke didn't move from his side, matching him step for step. He was breathing heavily and there was pure hatred in his eyes. Beckett could imagine what was coming next.

He landed face down onto the pavement, feeling the skin part over his cheekbone and his lip split. Luke's hands were on him like lightening, hauling him to his feet, one fist landed square in his left eye then pounded home under his chin. Beckett went down hard and Luke was on top of him pounding and pummelling his body.

The streetlight above him faded in and out as consciousness came and went.

Luke's breathing was still coming hard and heavy in direct relation to the pain in his groin. He gave Beckett a final savage kick and left him curled up in the gutter and out for the count.

Searing pain brought him back to consciousness.

"Hey. You still alive?" The pointed toe of an elegant black boot prodded him.

Beckett opened his right eye. There would be no seeing out of his left for some while. Through the haze of pain he could just make out the face bending over him. It was the white faced, eye-linered Goth from inside the club.

Beckett groaned.

"Man, you must have pissed them off big time. Come on, you can't lay there."

Beckett couldn't think of any reason why not, it seemed infinitely preferable to the crescendo of pain that would be involved in any form of movement. He scanned the twenty-something Goth in front of him, clad a la Blade, in an ankle-length black leather coat covering the elegant frock coat he'd seen earlier, leather pants and knee-length boots. Shoulder- length blue -black hair that owed much to a bottle, framed high cheekbones delicately painted white. His eyes were outlined with black kohl and they danced with what seemed to be amusement.

He tried to speak and realised for the first time that intelligible speech was almost impossible through his brutally beaten lips.

An arm was around him and pulling him into the vertical position before he could make any protest.

"C'mon man, give me a hand here. You've got to get your ass moving. If Luke comes back, he'll finish you off for sure. He's a mean mother."

Beckett tended to concur with this character assessment and made an effort to stand under his own power. Pain rocketed through him, finally finding a home somewhere inside his head. Breathing was painful and he could feel movement in the rib that had last been in contact with Luke's boot.

His thoughts went past the pain as he remembered Kat. She was still in there and they were mighty keen to keep it that way. He had no option but to leave, but in true terminator fashion, he'd be back.

CHAPTER FIFTEEN

Andrei made love to her in the same languid fashion that he did everything else, his coolness dampening her aggression. There was no heat or passion as he toyed with her, teasing her to the point of no return then pulling away from her. He was driving her mad, as the bestial side of her nature soared and dived. Her mouth was on his neck before she could stop herself and she bit hard into the flesh around his jugular vein.

He gave a deep throaty laugh as the blood flowed towards her eager lips.

She pulled away then, some far distant part of her mind horrified at what was taking place in the realms of deja vue. Andrei made a slow movement with his hand across his throat that somehow stopped the blood flow.

"Not yet, Katerini."

He was inflamed now, brought to it by the anticipation of the blood play. He held her with his deep eyes and calmed the rising panic in her, stroking the dark recesses of her mind into quiet submission by only the power of his thoughts.

Her agitation ebbed away and the raw sexual energy returned. His smile displayed the shining white points of the fangs that had not long ago been normal canine teeth. He was ready to enjoy her now. Now that he sensed the approach of the turning.

Their different needs were met in the same way, with a violent thrusting union that crossed the boundaries between man and beast.

She fought to regain her breath and all of the time her eyes remained fixed on his dilated pupils. The whites of his eyes were glazed with red, which darkened through crimson until they were black. Black holes in the exquisite frame of his face.

There was a subtle change in the atmosphere, a tangible change that defied description. He had a leaner, hungry look, and the sensual mouth now appeared predatory.

Kat lay back on the pillows as he moved silently across the floor to retrieve the crystal goblet that still contained the bright emerald absinthe. He brought it to the bed and lay beside her.

Her mind was trying hard to tell her something but his hypnotic hold on her was too strong. And she wanted this. She wanted it more than anything in her life before.

Andrei dipped his finger into the liquid and put it to her lips, tracing the outline of her mouth with his elongated fingernail until she closed her eyes at the sheer bliss of the sensation. He drank from the priceless goblet and put it back to her moistened lips. She emptied the glass and reached out for him, kissing him hard on the mouth, searching for the sharpness of the fangs that she knew were the key to her freedom. Her tongue touched the tip of one of them and she pressed against it, tasting at once the coppery tang of her own blood as it flowed into her waiting mouth. She pressed harder and deeper until the warm blood flowed freely, blending with his saliva and her own until she had no choice but to swallow the warm red fluid.

Andrei's eyes were completely black now, and he leaned into her, finding her jugular vein with the deftness and experience of race memory. His teeth pierced it easily and he drank deeply.

She felt as though she were floating and drowning simultaneously, knowing nothing but the ecstasy of his mouth sucking and drinking and sucking at her throat.

Drink more, she wanted to say, drink it all, drink until there is nothing left.

Andrei heard her thoughts and drank all the deeper. He drank until he felt her pulse weakening as her failing heart fought valiantly to pump the precious red fluid around her body. He heard the heartbeat slow and finally become the fluttering of an injured bird. He sucked harder to draw the blood that now had no pressure behind it.

He watched her approaching death, all the while stroking her hair and talking to her with the fascination that would never leave him.

"Katerini, I know you can hear me. I have taken the life force from you and now you must feed. You must drink from me or you will die. That is the way of it. You can feel the hunger above all else, above the pain and loneliness of death. Feel the need in you to complete what was begun years ago and turn, Katerini. Turn and live."

He bit into his wrist and covered his finger with the rising gore. Once again he traced the outline of her lips, this time with his own blood. It stayed on her lips for some seconds and finally there was a minute movement of her tongue as it tasted the tiny red pool.

He laughed seductively, enjoying this moment as always. The moment when he could decide whether she would die or live as a vampire, reborn to darkness.

His blood was welling up fast now and he held his wrist high above her mouth, letting it fall between her parted lips and splash around her mouth and chin. She would make a truly magnificent vampire. And he had turned her.

She was swallowing harder now, hungry for the life force that flowed into her mouth. She drank deep with the instinct of a child at the breast.

He took his hand away then and held it over the goblet allowing it to fill to the brim with blood: the forbidden wine of life. The midnight wine.

Again he staunched the blood flow with the tiniest of movements.

Kat sat up, her vision clouded in a sea of crimson. He held the goblet up to her lips, a priest to his communicant.

And she drank.

CHAPTER SIXTEEN

Lane finished mopping up the cuts and grazes on Beckett's face, frowning at the impressive bruising around his eye.

"Holy Mother you're a mess. What the hell were you thinking, Beckett?"

He mumbled through his cracked and swollen lips.

"I knew she'd do something like this. The creep she was with gave me the shivers."

Lane held up a hand, "Okay, I get the idea. I can't be certain but from what you've managed to tell me, it sounds like Andrei Marinescu." Her face was serious.

"Should I be worried?"

"I think maybe so."

Beckett was on his feet again. "I'm going back there."

Lane pushed him back into the chair. "No, you're not; I think you've done enough damage to yourself for one day. I'll go, I'm kind of known there."

Beckett frowned at her.

"Oh don't fret yourself, Handsome. I haven't changed the colour of my coat. I've been there a few times to help a couple of 'infants' that were out of their depth. They know I'm on the Council and they won't want to call the Elders down on their heads."

Lane's function within the vampire community was as a member of the Vampire Council who made and policed the code of conduct of the vampires, her role being to ensure the safety of all newly turned, the 'infants', and to hear charges against those that transgressed. She was a Tribune within the Curia, the higher ranks of the Council Members acting directly under, and with the authority of, the Patriarch, the supreme head of the Council. Their edict was to ensure that no vampire would harm a human in

103

obtaining their food and that all donors were volunteers. Also, no vampires should be created by turning. It was almost impossible to police the policy, as more and more of the young vampires paid little heed to the Council or their authority, and so Lane was there as a safety net for those not yet able to defend themselves against the inevitable predators. Theirs was not a pretty world.

Danse Macabre was known to be a harbour for those that flouted the rules. Beckett shook his head. "This is my fault. I should have brought her to you earlier."

"Yes, well, too late now. Let's just hope we can salvage the situation. Honestly Beckett, I could murder you sometimes."

"Bite me."

"Gladly, Handsome, I've always thought that you'd make a delicious vampire but rules are rules," she teased.

"So what do you think you can do?"

"Well, I can't kidnap her; if she doesn't want to come with me, there's not a lot I can do to get her away from there. It is still a free country you know, and if I go about causing trouble it won't be long before there's mass hysteria. I'll need to be careful."

Beckett suddenly felt very weary and put his head in his hands then thought better of it - it hurt too much.

"Stay here tonight, Handsome. Oh, don't look so alarmed, it's not a proposition. You're just too beat to go home. The guest room's made up; all you have to do is crawl between the sheets and sleep. You're in no condition to do anything for Kat tonight. Leave it to me ... and don't argue."

Beckett tried to smile but it was too painful.

"Okay," he mumbled.

Lane already had her car keys in her hand, she looked enlivened and her eyes glinted darkly. "Don't wait up. I could be a long time."

"I won't sleep," he mumbled.

"Oh, I think you will. I put some Lorazepam in your

whisky. I'll be surprised if you make it up the stairs."

He tried to protest but could already feel the drug beginning its work.

Lane didn't need to tell Beckett that she was more frightened for Kat. He was in a bad enough state without knowing what she suspected to be true - the fact that Andrei Marinescu was no ordinary vampire, not an Inheritor or a Born but one of the Undead - dead once, but reanimated by something dark and sinister, something that would take more than a string of garlic to finish it. If Kat was with Andrei in her condition then she was in a whole heap of trouble.

Time wasn't her friend. It had taken Beckett almost an hour to get the strength to drive to her place and another thirty minutes for her to patch him up. If Andrei was intent on feeding off Kat and leaving her for dead then she would already be too late. If he had a different agenda, then she feared what she would find.

Luke was back at his post, looking pale but otherwise none the worse for wear. *Should've kneed him harder, Handsome*, she thought.

He approached her respectfully. "Doc," he acknowledged. "There are no problems here tonight. Did someone call you?"

"Yes," she lied, "a short time ago. A woman called and asked me to come and get her. Do you know anything about it?"

"No. Probably someone jerking your chain, Doc. I'll just check."

He turned to pick up the intercom and Lane was past him before he even saw her move. The intercom buzzed in answer to his call. "The Doc's here. She's looking for trouble, I reckon. Where's that new broad? Still upstairs with the boss?"

"The boss is here," said Andrei from behind him.

Luke spun around, flustered. "I'm sorry Mr Marinescu. I didn't hear you."

"Obviously. What is the problem? I presume there *is* a problem. Or should I say *another* problem."

Luke went pale at the expression on Andrei's face. He would pay dearly for his incompetence that night. He swallowed hard.

"Uh, I … the Doc's here. She says someone, a woman, called her to come and get her. I wondered if it was the um …woman that was here earlier. I mean …"

"I know what you mean, Luke. We need to speak later regarding your performance. I'm very disappointed with you."

Luke felt the bile rising in his throat and prayed he wouldn't vomit.

"Yes, sir. I'm very sorry."

"I expect you are, Luke. Sorry doesn't alter the fact that we've got the Council on our backs, does it? Where is she? Already inside, I take it?"

Luke nodded. He looked as wretched as he felt.

Andrei's eyes darkened and narrowed, fixed on the unfortunate security guard until he passed out right there on the pavement. He turned and looked into the dark interior. If she was there for Katerini there was nothing he could do to prevent her finding her, but she was too late; she was already turned and by now she'd be approaching the agonies and excruciating pain of the awakening. Dr Lane Dearing was welcome to whatever she could salvage. He was in the mood for hunting now and he knew that Lane wouldn't make a fuss there and then but take matters directly to the Council. He'd soothe their complaints when that happened. It helped to have a close friend within their hierarchy that was grateful to him for keeping information to himself that would otherwise damage his standing in the Council, and for his allegiance in what was to come. According to his calculation the particular member of the Curia owed him. It wouldn't be the first time he would call in a favour.

He stepped over the inert Luke and melted into the

night.

Inside the club the music was still deafening and the mournful lyrics told of the Undead rising. Lane made her way easily through the crowd to the staircase and was at the top before another of Andrei's men intercepted her.

No, he hadn't seen anyone that looked as if they were in trouble. No, there hadn't been any new guests in the club that night. And no, Mr Marinescu wasn't in the club either.

Lane appraised the man carefully. She was reluctant to use her vampiric abilities but sometimes she just plain had to. She reached his subconscious mind in seconds and planted the idea that Andrei himself had called her to Kat.

"I'll call the lift for you, Doc. She's in the penthouse, we thought it best to keep her there, make sure she stayed safe, so to speak."

"Thank you," said Lane. A few more implanted suggestions and he was down the staircase and already he had forgotten her presence.

The lift doors opened into Andrei's hallway. Everything looked normal and there was no sound from inside the penthouse. She centred herself and could sense Kat inside. And she could sense the pain and desolation of the turning.

She was too late.

The blaze in the fireplace was already dying to embers when Lane pushed open the door to the bedchamber. Kat was sitting on the bed, still naked, and bent over double. She was weeping quietly and Lane knew that this was the calm before the storm and that it would soon change to screams of agony.

She made a quick calculation about the time it would take to get her away from Danse Macabre and back to the safety of her home. Beckett would be in the drugged arms of sleep, but she didn't doubt that the terrible anguish that Kat was about to experience would be enough to wake an entire cemetery.

She was at Kat's side almost by the power of her thoughts. She dropped her bag and keys onto the fur rug and crawled onto the immense bed to her side.

"Kat."

Kat looked up at her; bemused, uncertain of whom it was that had laid a gentle hand on her face that was still smeared with Andrei's blood.

"Kat, look at me. Focus, Kat." She pulled Kat's head gently towards her, finding no resistance. Lane closed her eyes, probing her mind to see whether sanity remained or not. It wouldn't be the first, or the last time, that a victim of turning had ended up in a padded room for a very, very long time.

She breathed a sigh of relief as she encountered confusion and terror but unimpaired reason. She reached for her bag and took out a loaded syringe. There was no stopping what was going to happen to Kat but a hefty whack of sedative would buy her the time to get her out of there.

Kat tried to push her away. "No," she wailed. "No."

"It's all right, Kat. It's me, Lane. Look at me sweetheart. Kat, look at me. It's Lane. I've come to take you home."

Kat began sobbing aloud, "I'm so sorry, Beckett. Oh no, oh no. Oh Beckett. Beckett."

Lane took her by the shoulders and shook her none too gently, time for sympathy later. "Kat. Listen to me. I'm going to take you out of here and we'll go and find Beckett."

At the mention of his name Kat looked horrified. "Oh no. I can't, I can't. I've done something terrible, I can't face him."

"You've only done what was inevitable and no doubt under the control of a powerful influence you could not possibly resist. Beckett will know that, when he's had time to think about it. Now, I'm going to give you an injection, it will make you sleepy."

Kat saw the syringe in Lane's hand and tried to push her away again.

"Kat! Stop it!" Her words were nothing against the terror that was invading Kat's mind.

This wasn't the time for misplaced subtlety and before the first scream had left Kat's lips, Lane had punched her neatly under the jaw and laid her out cold.

"Sorry, sweetie. But I had to do it. You'll forgive me later, I hope."

Lane found a vein with practiced art and emptied the syringe into it. It may have been taking a sledgehammer to crack a nut, but she couldn't risk her coming to and having a meltdown while she was driving. She pulled the discarded dress on the unconscious Kat, who was soon in her arms. She carried her like a child would carry a kitten and with just as much ease. Once again she used her natural abilities to cloak herself from the prying eyes of the throng downstairs.

When she reached the front door, Luke was still out for the count.

She hadn't previously told Kat the truth about the Undead, not wanting to panic her. She was way past that now.

The Undead were few and far betweenm thanks to the Council. They had been systematically despatched by burning, staking or decapitation and Lane had been a grisly part of that.

In the essence of folklore lay the grim truth. A vampire that had been turned by the Undead would inevitably die and be fed by the other vampire's blood at the moment of death. They would then rise again, animated by a part of the sire's soul. Lane knew all about the Undead, for she had been turned by one of their rank all those centuries ago.

She dumped Kat into the passenger seat of her MG like a sack of barley and was driving away from Newport in minutes. Kat slept the whole way to Lane's town house in

Abergavenny, moaning in troubled dreams occasionally, but moving very little.

The smart three-storey house close to the town centre was in darkness, a good sign that Beckett had succumbed to the tranquiliser and whisky. *It was the night for drugging people*, thought Lane wryly.

She carried Kat effortlessly up the stairs and laid her onto her own bed with more care than she'd thrown her into the car. She took off her crumpled dress and gently covered her with the luxurious down quilt. She stroked her hair away from her face and laid her hand on her forehead. She was perspiring and burning up in the grip of a fever, tossing her head back and forthe. Her breathing was laboured and she gasped every now then as she searched for air.

The sedative was losing its battle with Kat's transformation which was advancing rapidly. Lane closed the window and the drapes; this was likely to get noisy and she didn't want the neighbours alarmed. She turned off the main light and switched on the mellow glow of her bedside lamp. She quietly slipped out of the room to check on Beckett. His room was in total darkness and he was snoring like a pig, although Lane knew that once the torture took hold of Kat there would be no doubt that he would wake.

She stepped over to the bed and looked down at his battered face which was framed by his tousled silver hair, a permanent reminder of the grisly night that he'd been dragged into it all. "You're still a handsome bastard," she whispered. "How in the name of all that's holy did you deserve all this again? Sleep peacefully, Beckett, it may be a long time before you have the luxury again."

She closed the door silently and returned to Kat. The sheet and quilt were kicked away and she lay in a contorted huddle in the middle of the bed, whimpering softly like a child in the grip of a bad dream.

Lane went into the en-suite bathroom and unlocked a

small cabinet on the wall. She took out another syringe and a phial. There was no drug strong enough to kill the pain that Kat was about to feel, but the morphine may deaden the worst of it.

A piercing scream jolted her into swift movement. She was at Kat's side in less than a second.

Kat arched her back and her face contorted into a hideous expression of torment. The perspiration ran freely from her brow now, and her hair was slicked with sweat. Lane put her hands on her shoulders in an effort to control the tortuous thrashing that had overtaken her, but even with her vampiric strength she struggled to keep a hold on her.

Kat was snarling and spitting like a demented animal, and every now and then a stream of foul language issued forth from her lips, sometimes in English but more often in some long dead tongue.

Lane paled. This was the confirmation she dreaded. Kat had been turned all right, but it was obvious to Lane now that she'd been turned by one of the dark Undead. Andrei Marinescu. Not only was Kat in the throes of a tortuous transformation in her body at a cellular level, changing her physiology into that of a vampire, but she was also in danger of joining the species of vampire most feared and hated by the Council and the hunters.

Kat screamed again, a high-pitched keening that chilled the marrow and Lane took the opportunity to jab the syringe home and pump the morphine into her.

She was on her knees then, bent double clutching her abdomen and wailing.

"Help me. Someone help me. *Beckett!*"

Lane gripped her forearms tightly. "Kat, it's me, Lane. You'll be all right. I know it hurts like hell. It will, like nothing ever before, but it will pass. Do you hear me? It will pass."

Kat looked at Lane but there was no recognition.

She straightened up and threw her head back, arching

her spine again in agony. Her cries were pitiful, and varied from deafening shrieks to pathetic whimpering. This cycle continued for twenty minutes. It didn't matter how many times Lane witnessed this; it never failed to tear at her heart.

This time there was a deep anger boiling inside her alongside her compassion. Andrei Marinescu had his coming and she would relish bringing about his destruction.

The bedroom door crashed open and smashed against the wall. Beckett stood framed in the doorway. He was pale under the bruising that had spread to cover the entire left side of his face. The cuts and grazes were livid red marks in a sea of purple.

He stood like a marble statue, staring at the frail and tortured Kat. He had failed again, letting her down in the same way he'd abandoned Grace to her horrifying fate.

He strode to the bed and pushed Lane out of the way, grabbing hold of Kat and pulling her to him. His arms were around her in a death lock and he rocked her back and forth as she wept and screamed alternately, his tears mingling with hers.

"Shh. Shh," he soothed. "Shh. Kat, angel. Shh."

He stared at Lane, his eyes narrow channels of pent-up fury, his rage needing to find a target. He didn't trust himself to speak straight away, his cheek muscles twitching as he clamped his teeth together in an effort to control his rising rage.

When he could eventually trust himself, he asked, "Isn't there anything you can give her? Jesus Christ, Lane, do something."

Lane shook her head and put her hand on his arm, "Easy Handsome. I already did. It may work but there's no easy way. She'll either make it or not."

Beckett snapped his head around to face her again. "What in the name of God does that mean? She'll either make it or not? *What?*" He was white from his beating and his anger.

"Just that. She's strong, Beckett, and the fact that she was a Latent for so long will go in her favour. Her systems have been making ready for this for a long time. She was halfway there. We just have to wait."

"Who did this, Lane? Tell me."

Lane didn't answer him

"So, what's this? All the vampires sticking together, is that it? Protecting your own? You'd better tell me who did this, because I'm going to kill the bastard and I'm going to kill him tonight."

Lane closed her eyes against the hurt and onslaught of Beckett's rage. She sighed, "I suspect that he's long gone, at least for a while. His arrogance will bring him back eventually, but for now you may as well try to find a speck of dust in the Sahara. Trust me Beckett."

"I did trust you. I trusted you to help her, to look after her. This is the result."

He knew it was unfair but he didn't care. He wanted to lash out and hurt someone, anyone, and it was simply unfortunate that Lane stood in the line of fire. His anguish was unbearable and Lane wanted to reach out to him but she resisted. There would be no reasoning with him in this state and any way she did feel guilty about how she'd handled it. She should have realised that Kat was strong-willed enough to ignore advice and give into her instincts and go out into the night. Nothing could be done now except to watch and wait.

Fury, grief and desperation cancelled out the effects of the Lorazepam and whisky in Beckett and he was stone cold sober and wide awake.

Lane turned away from him; she didn't want him to see her tears.

"Thirsty," whispered Kat. "So thirsty."

Beckett kissed her cheek and laid her back against the soft pillow.

"Hey you, how're you doing?" His voice was thick with

emotion.

"Beckett? I'm so thirsty."

Beckett stood up and made for the bathroom to get her water. Lane was beside him before he was aware of her movement. She restrained him gently.

"Where are you going, Handsome?"

She held him with her eyes and shook her head. He read the message in her steady gaze and dropped his head.

"She needs to feed," Lane said gently. "Leave her to me, Beckett. I'll take care of her. There's a donor from the Sanctuary on the way."

He walked slowly back to the bed, not wanting to leave her but knowing Lane was right, and he couldn't bear to witness it. He sat on the bed and stroked her face.

"Lane is here for you. I'll be just in the next room. You're going to be fine. I'll be back soon. Hear me?"

Kat frowned as she focussed on his face for the first time, "Beckett? What happened to you? Your face, your poor face."

She tried to lift her hand to his face but didn't have the energy and let it fall to the bed again.

"Don't you fret about it. Hey, you should see the other guy."

Kat managed a wan smile and closed her eyes as he closed the door softly behind him.

CHAPTER SEVENTEEN

Nik stood in the shadows, admiring the young girl through her open window.

"Take her," crooned the voice behind the mask. "Use your inner nature to reach her. Remember you are no ordinary vampire."

Nik was quiet and withdrawn as he centred himself on his will. At first nothing happened, then almost imperceptibly, he felt his body rise. Slowly at first, then inch by inch, defying gravity as he willed his body to become less and less dense, giving his body up to the vampire in him, he rose from the ground until he was level with the window.

He was inside and on her before she could comprehend what was happening to her.

She didn't scream. There was no time.

The silence of the night was broken only by the wet sucking sounds as Nik feasted.

He drained her blood vessels easily of their precious cargo and as she fell limp in his arms he sensed Santorini behind him.

"Careful Nik, no more. Why take a risk of a dead body to dispose of? Make her your own in every sense of the word. Make her, Nik."

He lifted the girl from the boy's arms and laid her down onto the bed.

"I don't know how. Show me. Show me now," he said.

Santorini put a hand on his shoulder. "You do know. Close your mind to everything and just listen to what your true self tells you. What does it tell you, Nik?"

"Drain her to the point of death, then make her drink from me."

"Good. I knew I was right about you. Do it, Nik."

Nik bent his head into the girl's throat once more and sucked the blood, becoming aware of the fading heartbeat. He stopped drinking and lifted his wrist to his mouth.

Santorini reached out to him and shook his head. "So crude, Nik. Here, take this. It's yours, a gift."

Nik looked down at the beautiful solid gold lancet in his hand, tiny and exquisitely crafted. Santorini smiled at him.

"I have been waiting for one worthy to give it to. It's yours Nik, use it well."

The boy drew the tiny blade neatly across the vein in his wrist and watched, fascinated as his own blood, nourished by the rich claret of the dying girl's, welled to the surface, a tiny scarlet pool against the deathly white of his flesh. He felt the powerful presence behind him and turned towards Santorini and offered his wrist to his mentor.

"My gift to you in return," he said.

The ice-cold eyes behind the mask glinted with pleasure. He lifted Nik's wrist to his mouth and licked the wound then kissed the palm of his hand. He returned to the fount of nourishment and drank more deeply, sending waves of sensual pleasure through Nik.

"Thank you Nik. I'm touched."

Nik smiled at him, amazed at the feelings that would previously have brought shame, now they seemed natural and somehow a part of what it was that he had become. He put his wrist over the girl's mouth and squeezed hard, watching his lifeblood coat her lips then drip onto her tongue, pooling there until she swallowed. She opened her eyes to him.

'No," she said. "Never."

Nik felt the anger rise inside him like a flood tide. He slapped her and she began to fight back against him as Santorini watched from behind the silk mask, laughing quietly.

'Finish her, Nik. Take it all."

Images came into Nik's head, images of the pale thin woman who had tried to care for him even though he had attacked her. She smiled at him in his mind and shook her head.

"No," he said.

Santorini frowned, and his ice-flow eyes hardened to cold diamonds. He read Nik easily.

"Don't forget, Nik. She abandoned you, gave you away to a life of misery, to fend for yourself and find out for yourself what you are. Don't listen to her now. You are powerful, Nik. You have the potential to be one of the greatest amongst us, but you mustn't give into weakness. They are our nourishment, Nik, nothing more. Like beasts in the field. Listen to me."

The dark velvet voice caressed his mind, soothing his doubts, filling him with power. He'd done it before, carelessly and not in control, he could do it again, consciously this time, coldly, in full knowledge of his actions. He opened his mind to the flow of crimson that filled his being and drank from her again. Not gorging in his usual feeding frenzy, but slowly, savouring every drop. He drank until there was no more. Until she was dead.

"I'm proud of you, Nik. You truly are incredible. Stay with me, I'll take you where you belong, I'll take you to where your destiny will become so clear that you'll wonder how you ever existed before."

"Where?"

"I'm going to take you to your father."

Nik's face was flushed from the feeding and he was high on the energy taken from the lifeless girl stretched out on the bed before him, but he felt himself pale at the words.

"My father? Even my mother doesn't know who he is. I'm the result of nothing more than a whore who slept around until she couldn't tell who fathered the child in her belly. How can you know my father?"

117

"I know many things, Nik. More than you can imagine. Yes, I know your father. He is in Greece, Nik. We shall go there and you will be together and I will be the one who made it possible. Remember that. You will be reunited with a father that will love you and teach you things that only he is capable of. He is the greatest vampire alive on the earth at this moment. He is the fountainhead. And he is waiting for you."

CHAPTER EIGHTEEN

At Lane's house, the donor, a young medical student named Jill, arrived.

Kat lay quietly, unsure of what was about to happen but trusting in Lane. Jill was a fresh-faced blonde with green eyes and freckles, attired student fashion in threadbare and frayed jeans and obligatory faded T-shirt. She carried two hefty books under her arm.

"Hi," she said disarmingly as though there was nothing out of the ordinary in the proceedings.

Lane nodded at the books, "I see you've brought some studying with you."

Jill pulled a face, "Yeah. Mid-term papers are due in next week. I thought that while I was just sitting here, I might as well bone up on my bacteriology. "

Lane laughed, "As I recall, bacteriology is why I specialised in psychology."

The girl made herself comfortable in a reclining chair in the corner of Lane's room with a familiarity that came from regular practice.

"Thanks for coming so quickly, Jill. You're a gem," said Lane. "This is Kat, and as you can see she is in need of your help in rather a hurry."

Jill smiled at Kat, "It's a bummer, isn't it? Don't worry; you're in good hands with Doc Dearing. And no need to worry about the red stuff, I'm certified free of HIV and anything else undesirable, right Doc?"

"Right." Lane was connecting the transfusion kit to Jill's arm as she spoke. She was worried about Kat; she wasn't out of the woods yet. This was the beginning of a long and lonely road for her.

The blood ran from Jill's arm into a standard collecting

119

bag laced with an anticoagulation agent to stop it clotting before Kat could drink it.

Jill stuck her head into the mysteries of bacteriology making no more comments or conversation, appearing to be unaware of Kat's profuse sweating and growing agitation and lust for her life blood.

Lane took the usual pint, removed the needle from the girl's arm, swabbed the puncture wound and taped some cotton wool over it.

"Don't forget, go lie down on the couch downstairs for a little while, there's a drink and some cookies on the table. Get plenty of rest for the next few hours and drink lots of fluids. The money is in an envelope next to the cookies. I won't come down, Kat needs me here. Good luck with the bug exam."

"So long, Kat. Glad to help."

"Thanks," Kat mumbled.

Lane was busy at the dressing table, transferring the precious blood into a small cup. Although there were other ways for Kat to feed, as she herself fed or gained the necessary blood, the first time was different; she was in a weakened state and would soon be driven mad with the hunger. She had to drink.

Lane helped her sit up against the soft pillows. She looked like a frightened child, a far cry from the powerful vampire that she had the potential to be.

Kat's pallor was frightening, she was almost transparent and her emaciated frame looked dangerously close to skeletal. She made a sudden lunge towards the cup and Lane only just managed to keep it from spilling on the bed.

Kat's eyes took on a blaze of crimson and she opened her mouth wide as the vampire muscles under her canine teeth pushed the sharp white fangs downwards in anticipation of the bite that would normally bring sustenance. She grabbed the cup with bony fingers and drank greedily, instantly feeling the energy coursing through her body. Cell by cell she could feel new life pervading her being.

She drained the cup and handed it back to Lane who watched her anxiously for any signs of adverse reaction.

As the minutes turned to an hour her pallor became less prominent and the crimson veil over her eyes faded until her amethyst eyes shone like brilliant jewels. Her hair lost its lankness and sprang back to its former ebony beauty. She listened as she heard sounds like never before, with an intensity and clarity that was almost deafening. She heard the ticking of the clock in Lane's sitting room downstairs and the refrigerator humming in the kitchen. More sounds came flooding in now; the sound of quiet lovemaking coming from the bedroom in the house next door, and the snoring of the elderly man two houses away. Her nostrils flared as scents and aromas came to tantalise her. She could sense the blood in Lane's veins; smell the richness of the precious red fluid. She smiled, somewhere between saint and lost soul.

Something was wrong though. Something was missing. She concentrated hard and Lane picked up her thoughts instantly. They could both only sense each other in the house. Beckett had left.

"He left as soon as he was through that door," Lane said. "The damn fool, I felt him leave but I had to stay with you. I know where he's gone and if I'm not very much mistaken he's in for another rough ride. I need to go to him, Kat. Are you alright?"

She nodded at Lane and jumped out of bed with unfamiliar energy. She made for the mirror, and then hesitated. What if she cast no reflection? Lane did, but what if she, Kat, didn't?

She brushed aside the fear and went to the dressing table.

Her reflection looked back at her, healthy, invigorated, alive. She lifted her hair that had somehow reached her shoulders and felt the luxurious softness, her skin was like down and her lips had a rosy hue that she hadn't seen for eighteen years.

If vampires were the creation of the devil, then she thanked God for it. Whatever she was or had become, she was glad of it.

"Where is he? I'm coming with you. Wait for me to get dressed. Where did he go, Lane?"

Lane sighed,"I'm rather afraid he went swimming out of his depth in shark infested water."

She saw Kat's puzzled expression and put her arm around her shoulders. "There is so much to tell you, so much for you to learn, I hardly know where to begin."

Kat's eyes glinted, the vampire in her already assertive and confident. "Begin with Beckett," she said.

CHAPTER NINETEEN

Lane's cell phone rang and made her hesitate, although she was tempted to ignore it. She turned sharply on her heels, it could be Beckett.

"Lane Dearing," she said abruptly into the receiver.

"Lane, my dear, you seem somewhat agitated. Perhaps this is not a convenient time?" The silky, arrogant voice of Michael Rabb took her by surprise.

"Michael, to what do I owe this pleasure? Or am in some kind of trouble?"

"Now why would you say that? Can a fellow member of the Council not telephone his colleague for no particular reason?"

'Fellow member of the Council' was hardly how Lane would describe Michael Rabb, and to her knowledge he would always have a reason for everything that he did. Her immediate superior and Proconsul of the Curia to the Vampire Council, Michael Rabb was as ruthless as he was successful, and it was not a secret that he had aspirations to the Secretariat. He was suspected of having radical, if not downright dangerous, ideas of revising the Vampire Code, and to get on his wrong side was not a good idea. She had always been wary of him, not least right then.

"I'm sorry Michael; I was expecting a call from someone else. How may I help you?"

"Simply, that I realised that I have not spoken with you since the last Council meeting some time ago, and rather than you being of help to me, I wondered if there was anything that I may assist you with? You are after all, our leading Tribune. So, is all well with you?"

She felt his mind searching hers across the ether, and wondered why he had chosen the clumsy medium of the telephone to contact her. She was now deeply suspicious of him and his motives. The call was unprecedented. She closed her mind to his probing.

"Yes, thank you. Everything is fine. In fact I was just about to go out." *Actually, everything is not fine and you are the very last one I would tell about it.*

She had placed him in an awkward position. Politeness would ensure that he terminated the call if his real reason had been purely social. If there was something else on his mind he would need to show his hand and he was skilled enough to sense her mind being shielded from him.

He hesitated. "Then I will leave you to your evening plans. I trust you will be present at the next meeting of the Council, set for two weeks time I believe. I understand that there is to be an interesting addition to the agenda."

So you do want something. OK, let's have it. "Oh, really? I hadn't heard. Perhaps you would bring me up to speed. I may have overlooked the notification, although I don't think so. It seems that I haven't received the information." *Or more likely haven't been included in what's really going on.*

"Of course, my dear. It wouldn't do for you to be unprepared. It seems that our Patriarch has ideas of ... how shall I put it? Retiring. Yes, retiring is perhaps the best way. There is to be an election, and our Patriarch arrived in the country today. The Council is to convene in London this time."

Holy Mother of God, not now. Not with the whiff of corruption at the very core of the Council. Two weeks! Not enough time. She managed to keep her voice level and her inner thoughts shielded.

"I see. I am surprised, naturally. I expect he will give us his reasons. I take it that you will be applying to fill the vacancy that will be left on the Secretariat?" she asked quietly.

"Actually, no. That is not my intention. But you might want to begin thinking about where your allegiances may lay, my dear. There will obviously be big changes and it wouldn't do to stand behind the wrong banner, now would it? It would be regrettable if any of our leading Council members were to make a mistake at this time. There is unrest, which I am sure you know, but I fear that it may be escalating. I have heard murmurings of another War. In fact, I have been assured, quite off the record, that there are to be investigations into any behaviour by Council members that may be construed as 'unusual' or unauthorised. It may be prudent for you to ensure that I am kept informed of all of your activities from now on. It would be beneficial for you to have a friend in the Curia. So, you are now, as you say, 'up to speed' and I will leave you to enjoy your evening. Take care of yourself, Lane."

The line went dead abruptly, as he gave her no time to continue the conversation. Her mind was in turmoil. What was the Patriarch thinking? Surely he was aware of the undercurrents and suspicions within the Curia. She wasn't sure who she could trust within her own kind anymore and she was all too aware of the veiled threats from Michael Rabb. And another Vampire War? Dear God, no. There had always been tension between the Born and the Made or Turned Vampires. Talk of unclean bloodlines and pure blood had always been a problem, but that was why the Council existed. Born out of the last Vampire War which had left hundreds of thousands dead, both human and vampire, the Vampire Council was there to ensure that vampire and human could co-exist in balance with harm to neither species. Another war would be unthinkable, the consequences unimaginable.

A horn blared on the street outside, bringing her back to the present with a jolt. Kat had been listening intently to her conversation.

"I don't suppose there's any point in asking you to stay here?" said Lane.

"None," replied Kat.

Lane shook her head. "Thought not. Okay, then. We'll talk on the way."

"So, tell me," Kat persisted as Lane drove.

"I first met Beckett ten years ago, almost to the day. He was a Catholic priest then: Father Paul Beckett. His first love was God and his church. His sister, Grace, was the victim of a particularly evil vampire, one of the Undead. I've been after him for some time but he always proves elusive. His name is Santorini and he wears a black silk mask, very seductive and very deadly. He has no conscience and kills or turns indiscriminately. He's also spectacularly gifted in his ability to cloak himself and conceal his thoughts from other vampires. He could be in the same room and if he was concealing himself, even I wouldn't see him. He is an adept of the Dark Arts and that is the reason he has eluded me for so long.

"Anyway, Beckett's mother had suffered badly from depression and she killed herself. His father became a chronic alcoholic and walked away from their children leaving Beckett to look after Grace, and he did a damn good job of it too, considering. Grace got in with a bad crowd and gave him plenty of grief, experimenting with alcohol and drugs, a wild child. Anyway, Beckett pulled her out of all that and for a few years she seemed to have calmed down, enabling him to concentrate on his own life. After a while, Grace took to staying out all night again and lying to him about where she'd been and who with. Beckett's a good man, Kat, and he tried everything he could to get her back on the rails. He thought he'd done it for a second time when Grace started seeing someone, she wouldn't tell him who. She became secretive and sullen and he was at the end of his tether, frantic that Grace was rapidly going down the road to self-destruction. "

"How old was Grace?"

"Eighteen by then. A woman, not a child anymore and Beckett knew if he pushed her too hard, she'd be gone. Just after that, she told him that she felt unwell. She began to lose weight, had no appetite and couldn't sleep. When she did sleep the blood dreams almost sent her mad.

Sound familiar? Beckett thought she was depressed and begged her to get treatment. Things got worse until she went to him one night and told him that she'd been 'feeding' her boyfriend who was a vampire. Well, you can imagine Beckett's reaction, not unlike your own initial reaction, or any normal person who didn't know or believe in vampirism. He thought she was delusional and dismissed what she was saying as part of her condition. Only thing was, Grace's condition was vampirism and not depression. She persisted in trying to get him to believe her but gradually stopped when Beckett just couldn't get his head around it.

"Two weeks later she came home very late and collapsed from loss of blood. The boyfriend, Santorini as it turned out, had dumped her literally back on her own doorstep to die, but only after he'd made her drink his own blood. She died in Beckett's arms, or at least the human in Grace died."

"Oh Jesus."

"That's not the worst part. Santorini, as I told you, is one of the Undead. Dead already and reanimated by an evil spirit that is the basis of the vampire of popular fiction. Dracula lives, big time. His victims become the Undead as well, although not all are evil; some of us retain the humanity that enables us to fight them. I thought I had found him that night, but I arrived too late to put an end to the bastard and I found Beckett nursing Grace on the floor where she fell. He was in shock and out for blood. He lost his faith that night and took off his clerical collar right there in front of me, and he has never put it back on since that night. He walked away from the God that hadn't saved his sister, despite the hours of praying. He made a vow that night that he would search and find the one who did this to Grace and kill him."

"Sounds like Beckett," said Kat quietly.

"He didn't believe me at first, but something about Grace in death made him listen. I stayed with him watching over her to see if she rose. She did."

"So what are you saying? She got up out of her coffin and you did a Van Helsing on her?"

"Not quite. She wasn't in a coffin. I stopped Beckett from involving anyone else until I was sure. We laid her on her bed and watched and waited. She got up when it got dark the next night. You know the rest, or at least you know how the stories go. True, I'm afraid. The thing that had infested Grace was staked and decapitated."

Kat's face was a mask of horror. "And Beckett did that?" she whispered.

"No. I did. There was no way that Beckett could do that, but he watched it all."

Kat was silent. Lane's face was grim as she drove, sensing all the time the fear in Kat. Would this happen to her? And if so, would it be Beckett?

"How can that have happened and there be no enquiries? What did you do with the body?"

"We have, shall we say, a support system. There are those amongst us that are doctors who will sign death certificates and there are always undertakers that will ask no questions except for how much are we prepared to pay?"

"And all this goes on without anyone knowing anything? Surely somebody has become suspicious in the past?"

"Of course. You will learn to be able to control people's thoughts, implant suggestions and even alter their memories. It will become as easy as breathing after a while. The hard part is knowing when to use that ability and when not to. Believe it or not there is a strict code amongst the vampire community. The trouble is that too many ignore it. Ah, there he is."

"Who?"

"Beckett. Seeing in the normal sense isn't the word, but I can see him, telepathically. As I thought, he's at the club."

Kat leaned back in her seat and closed her eyes. "You know if I hadn't been through this, if I hadn't ... well, I wouldn't believe any of it. It's too fantastic."

"That's what makes it possible for us to live among normal humans. They don't believe, or they don't want to believe."

"What will happen to me now? I mean will I change into something like Andrei? I'd kill myself now if I thought that."

Lane was quiet for a moment. "Anything is possible but I believe that there has to be the seed of evil deep inside for anything like that to take a hold. The ancient ones say that evil can't live where love abides. I think it's true. And don't go trying to kill yourself, it's not that easy. Believe me, I know."

Kat heard the bitterness that lay beneath those two simple words. Obviously somewhere in Lane's long past there had been a time when she had been desperate enough to try and end her existence. Hard to believe now, looking at the beautifully elegant and confident woman who spoke calmly of staking and decapitating one of the Undead as though it was a normal everyday occurrence. The memory was apparently still very vivid. Lane reached into the pocket on the driver's door and pulled out a packet of Marlborough. She saw Kat's automatic look of disapproval

"Don't lecture me. It's hardly going to kill me now, is it?"

CHAPTER TWENTY

Beckett hurled the door of the jeep shut so hard it bounced open again and he left it that way.

The door to Danse Macabre was locked and bolted and there was no light showing at any of the windows. He slammed his fist against the heavy wood, again and again until his knuckles bled.

He looked up at the small windows high on the smooth elevation of the building. None had a sill and there were no footholds anywhere on the almost polished wall. He kicked the door, nursing his battered hand. He kicked it again, swearing forcefully, unaware of the police patrol car that had pulled up behind his jeep.

"I think that's enough, sir. There's no damage done by the looks, best stop before you do some, eh?"

The policeman was young and Beckett detected a hint of uncertainty in his voice. New to the job he suspected. He smiled. Maybe he'd be the lad's first nick.

He turned round fully and was surprised to see the look on the young copper's face change to one of concern. In the heat of his anger he'd forgotten how he must look after the earlier beating.

"Would you mind telling me how your face got into that state?"

Yes, I do mind. It's like this; I came to save the woman I love from being turned into a vampire. The doorman of the club is nothing more than a henchman for a whole nest of vampires based here at the club. He kicked shit out of me and I didn't get to save the damsel in distress. Instead I watched her change into a vampire and now she's at my friend's house drinking blood. He gave a short harsh laugh.

"Not really, officer. I'm afraid I got into a bit of a

barney here earlier. Came back to finish it."

The policeman looked at the darkened windows and locked door.

"I think you're a bit late for that. Have you been drinking?" He cast a long look at the jeep parked at a crazy angle from the curb.

Beckett thought of the whisky and tranquiliser cocktail Lane had dispensed. "Just one." He grinned. "A big one, though."

"Is this your car, sir?"

The lad was more confident now, on more familiar ground, he'd obviously practiced this one.

Beckett nodded. "Guess I'll call a cab, right Constable?"

"Just as well, sir. Do I have to ask you for the keys?"

"No. I think I've had enough trouble for one night." He pulled his phone from his pocket and dialled Lane's number. It rang unanswered so he tried her cell phone.

Lane answered straight away. "Wait there Beckett, I'm about three minutes from you, and don't antagonise the nice policeman."

"Yeah, yeah. Thanks, Legs."

He turned off the phone. "A friend is coming to pick me up. I won't drive, honest."

The young policeman looked dubious. His car radio crackled and a muffled voice talked to the empty patrol car. He hesitated then leaned inside and answered it. A couple of minutes later he re-emerged.

"I have to answer a call. I don't advise you to drive, sir. You'd do well to wait for your friend." His face told Beckett that he didn't trust him not to get back behind the wheel anyway, but something more serious was claiming his attention. "Goodnight, sir. Oh, and I've made a note of your registration number so if there's any report of damage to this property I'll know where to come." He got back into the car, spoke into his radio again and drove away.

Lane and Kat arrived minutes later.

Beckett yanked open the driver's door. "There's no-one home. Help me get inside; I'm going to find the bastard, if it's the last thing I do tonight."

He stopped abruptly, suddenly aware of Kat's presence.

He was speechless at her transformation, her eyes dazzled amethyst lights even in the gloom of the car and the ever-darkening circles beneath them had vanished. The reason didn't bear thinking about but she was alive and obviously no longer in pain.

He didn't know what to say to her that wouldn't sound trite and pathetic.

"It's okay, Beckett. I'm sorry. I'm sorry I let you down but this was inevitable you know. If I was going to live that is. Can you forgive me?" The lights in her eyes dimmed with sorrow at the pain she knew that she'd caused him.

"Forgive you? It's me that let you down. I should have sent you to Lane much earlier. I just didn't want to believe what I could see with my own eyes. I was a jerk."

Lane yawned. "So that's the sticky sentiment over with and we're all friends again, so let's go home shall we?"

Beckett shook his head. "No chance. I'm going in. With or without you. It would be easier with you but either way …"

"What the hell for? Don't be a bloody fool, Beckett. Isn't a close call with law enough for one night? Not to mention the beauty treatment. Besides, it may look empty but we don't know who's at home and neither of us is flavour of the month in there." She nodded at Kat, "And I don't think it's a good idea for Kat to go back in there."

Beckett glared at her. "I'll tell you what for, I'm going to settle with this creep and I'm going to try and find something that will lead us to the bastard in the mask. This is just the sort of breeding and feeding ground that he'd haunt. Take Kat home if you like, but I am going in."

Lane sighed. She knew Beckett when he was in this mood. "You think I haven't tried to find a link to him in there? I need to be careful if I don't want to lose my entrée into the place."

Beckett's face was intractable. "All right," she said, "but you stay here with Kat. On no account is she to go back in there and I'm more likely to be able to hold my own in there if anyone is home. Is that clear?"

He didn't answer.

"Beckett?"

He nodded.

Lane got out of the car and indicated to Becket that he should get inside.

"If I can get in the place, I'll try and open the door for you from inside. Stay here. And I mean it. *Both* of you." Her eyes glinted dangerously and Beckett knew better than to argue with her; a friend she may be but a powerful vampire she was first of all.

She tied back her hair into the nape of her neck with a band from inside her pocket and stood looking up at the smooth exterior to the club, hands on her slim but shapely hips. Whilst for Beckett there were no footholds, for her the wall presented no challenge.

She was at the wall so quickly that even Kat, with her new vampire vision, didn't see her move. In seconds Lane was scaling the straight wall, though crawling would be a more appropriate description.

Thoughts flashed like forked lightening through Kat's consciousness. Her life had changed so dramatically in such a short space of time. Knowledge and awareness of such strange concepts that previously she would have denied without hesitation she now accepted as cold fact. Vampires had been the stuff of legend, myth and fiction, the product of fevered imaginations and now in the cold light of day not only did they exist but also she now numbered one of them. Now she was watching Lane climb the outside of a building like some crazy incarnation of Spiderman.

Kat closed her eyes. "Holy Mother of God," she said under her breath.

Beckett reached out to her and took her hand. "Get used to it," he said.

CHAPTER TWENTY-ONE

Santorini and Nik stood at the dead girl's window.

"Go ahead, Nik. Jump. It will be fine."

Nik looked into the ice-blue eyes and knew he spoke the truth. He trusted this man, this vampire who had become his self-appointed friend and mentor. And he knew that he wanted to be more, he wanted Nik to be his lover.

Nik had never before questioned his sexuality, but along with the other changes in him that had developed since he had acknowledged his vampirism and drunk the blood of his first victim, had come this unnerving acceptance of Santorini's subtle but erotic kisses.

He stood momentarily on the sill then threw his hands high above his head and leaped into the night air.

Instantly his vampire senses took over and he slowed his descent down by the same method that he had risen in the air and in through the girl's window, until he landed on his feet directly on the firm ground beneath the window.

Santorini smiled at him. *Well done*, the smile said. He stepped out onto the sill and turned back to face the room. Nik saw a subtle movement and a tiny flare of light. As Santo stepped off the sill into nothing, the room behind him began flickering with light. Flames soon engulfed the room and the dead girl. There would be no drained body to find; no evidence of their visit.

Nik sensed disquiet in his friend. There was an uncertainty. Hidden somewhere amongst Santorini's pride in Nik's new achievements there was a maggot of doubt. Santo was unsure of him for some reason.

He read the boy and put his hand on his shoulder.

"Very good, Nik, you learn quickly. Yes, I was

wondering if you would be so bold on your own. Would you remember to leave no trace? Would you be disciplined enough to remove yourself, in every sense, from the scene? I said once before that the weakness of compassion would be your downfall. Beware, Nik. None of us is invincible. Almost, but not quite."

"What about my father? You said he was the greatest vampire on the earth. Is he not invincible?"

"Of all of us, he is the one who is closest to it. But even he has his own vulnerability. Enough of this now, we're going home."

Nik's face fell.

"Come Nik, you think I don't know where you have been living? You think that I don't know that besides the clothes you stand up in you have precious little else. That's in the past now. You are coming home with me."

"I don't know," he said doubtfully.

Again Santorini read the boy. He laughed. "Oh, I see. You think I intend to seduce you and keep you against your will. Is that it?"

Nik's face, flushed from the feeding, deepened in colour.

"Relax Nik. There are no strings. Just a comfortable room, a full wardrobe, keys of your own to come and go as you please. Yes, I find you desirable, but not exclusively so. I have taken a liking for you in every sense, Nik, and I want to see you fulfil your potential. Besides, there is much to do if we are to go to Greece. You do want me to take you to your father?"

"Yes. I'm sorry. It's just ..."

"I know. A lot has happened in the past few nights. On top of which you find the mother who abandoned you, a new friend in me, I hope, and the knowledge that your father will welcome you. You see, Nik. I do have some slight selfishness in my motives. I want you to tell your father that it was I that taught you to be all that you can be, and I that looked after you and brought you to him."

"Why?"

"You'll see, Nik. You'll see. Now, home?"

Nik nodded. "Home," he replied.

***

Lane reached the topmost window easily and to her surprise found that it was not locked from the inside as she had feared but she was able to lever it open far enough to get her hand inside and open it fully. Nik and Kat watched as she disappeared into the dark void.

Andrei's penthouse apartment was in total darkness but to Lane it may as well have been floodlit. This was the second time in as many days that she had been there and a quick visual examination of the bedroom and en-suite marble bathroom confirmed that the flat was empty and her vampire senses told her that there was no other vampire presence.

She closed the window behind her but knew that if Andrei were to return soon he would detect her scent. It was a gamble she had to take, Beckett was not going to be satisfied until she had searched everywhere and then let him in to do the same. She didn't know what she was going to do about Beckett. He was dangerously obsessed with what he saw as revenge for Kat's turning, though she realised it was still as much about Grace. She couldn't blame him. Grace had been no innocent, but the violent degradation of her eventual 'death' made her despair of her own kind. This crusade wasn't going to end quickly and she knew that before its close there would likely be more tragedy.

Kat was another matter, vampire in essence already; her turning had been inevitable if she were to survive the anaemia and approaching insanity. Beckett was obviously falling for her but Lane wondered how much of his feeling had been transferred from Grace, and he'd found Kat a convenient hook on which to hang his lust for revenge.

She knew him well enough to realise that he wasn't going to stop until the vampire responsible for Grace and Kat's condition was dead, and that, she knew, was going to be almost impossible.

In the sitting room Lane saw and smelled the remains of the absinthe. Traditionally and historically the vampire drink, distilled from powerful hallucinogenic herbs, this would have ensured Kat's compliance, in her already confused and emotional state, to the advances and undoubted attractions of Andrei. She was reluctant to allow Beckett to see the evidence of the seduction here and in the bedroom but she knew that she didn't dare to move anything. The less Andrei knew about her incursion into his apartment the better.

Designed to keep people out, the electronic locking system was easy to bypass for her to leave the apartment. She pressed the call button on the lift and heard not only the whirring of the mechanism as it brought it up to the penthouse, but also the buzz of electricity through wire and cable. She dismissed the awareness and transferred her thoughts once more to Beckett.

As the doors began to slide open she sensed the presence of someone inside less than a second too late to avoid the garlic oil that was hurled directly into her face, blinding her for just long enough for the occupant of the lift to take advantage of her temporary confusion and drive home a wooden stake hard into Lane's chest.

CHAPTER TWENTY-TWO

"Something's wrong. She should have been down by now."

Beckett voiced Kat's thoughts.

"She's been inside for over fifteen minutes, I'm going to try again, there may be a way in from next door. You'd better come with me; I don't want you hanging around here on your own."

"What if Lane comes back? She'll be mad as hell with you. She may be trying to talk her way out of there right now if Andrei is home."

Beckett scowled. "Andrei is it? I don't have to remind you what he did to you, do I? Or maybe you enjoyed it? You have no idea what these monsters are capable of."

"God help me, I did enjoy it. Does that shock you, Beckett? And I have a very good idea of what they are capable of, or have you forgotten? Perhaps you'd like to rethink your feelings for me; I'm a monster after all." Her face was pale and for a moment the old vulnerability reappeared.

Beckett's jaw tightened as he fought to gain control of his emotions. He got out of the car suddenly and slammed the door. He'd lost Grace to these foul creatures and it looked increasingly as if Kat was lost to him too. His rage simmered dangerously close to explosion, and he wanted to get his hands on any one of the bloodsuckers no matter what it cost him, although he knew the price was likely to be high.

Kat was out of the car and beside him, her movements imperceptible. Beckett shrugged.

"I'm sorry. That was unfair. I just feel so bloody helpless; not your typical hero. Maybe if I were a vampire too, then I could get even."

"Don't even think that Beckett." She knew he wasn't in the mood to listen, but without Beckett she'd have taken her own life long ago. One day she'd tell him, but not now. It would sound like a platitude.

Beckett moved as though to walk away, intent on finding a way into the building. Kat didn't try and prevent him, it would have been a waste of time and her senses were alerted to something else. Someone was approaching the inside of the door and they were breathing heavily. She sensed something akin to panic. She reached out and held onto Beckett's arm.

"Wait," she said.

Beckett looked at her questioningly then followed her eyes to the door. He could hear nothing but was aware of Kat's heightened senses that were still in their infancy. He knew he was holding his breath and continued to do so.

He took a step forward and Kat made no effort to prevent him, whoever was hurling themselves towards the front door of the club was frightened. Badly frightened.

The door flew open with a crash and the building seemed to forcibly eject the white faced, eye-liner-ed Goth that had helped Beckett earlier. He appeared not to see either Beckett or Kat as he flew towards them in blind panic.

Beckett put out an arm and grabbed him as he tried to run past them. Recognition dawned slowly, his wildly dilated pupils returning to near normal size as his panic began to subside.

"Oh, it's you," he gasped. "Well, I'd vanish if I were you. This is no place to be pushing your luck, mate. This place is bad. Real bad. A beating's not all you'll get round here. And I'd 'preciate my arm back. I want some space between me and it. Pronto."

He tried to pull away from Beckett, who increased his grip on the boy's arm.

"Not so fast. What do you mean 'it'?

"Got me a Sucker, that's what. Not the one I was after, but still a Sucker. Staked her good and proper."

His eyes were still displaying panic and he was perspiring as the adrenaline and fear pumping round him kept him on a high of fight or flight. Beckett kept a firm grip on his arm as he tried once again to pull away.

"Let go. I mean it, you owe me, mate. Remember?"

Kat was already through the door sensing for Lane while Beckett dragged the boy back towards the club so fast his feet were dragging on the floor in Beckett's haste to get to Lane.

He snarled through gritted teeth. "Don't worry, my friend, you'll get what's coming to you. You'd better be praying that the Sucker you staked isn't who I think it is. *Mate.*"

"Fuck you. Let go of me. What are you? Some kind of Sucker lover?"

Beckett's free hand made hard contact with the back of the boy's skull and his grip tightened as he twisted the arm behind the boy causing him to yell out in pain.

"Move it," snarled Beckett, "You praying yet?"

The club was in darkness and without the advantage of Kat's developing vampire sight he stumbled on the stairs but held on to the boy's arm, sending him tumbling over his own feet.

"*Beckett. Get up here. Quick!*" Kat's voice made his chest tighten. He dragged the boy along on his knees not giving him time to stand. He could just make out a darker rectangle in the gloom. The lift.

Kat was on her knees bending over Lane. *Jesus, if this little creep had....* Beckett pushed him forwards sending him reeling against an armchair. His head cracked against the hard floor as he went down, and stayed down.

Beckett pulled Kat back roughly as his eyes fought to focus in the gloom. "*Lane?* Get me some light, Kat. *Now.*" His hand was wet and sticky and he knew it had come from Lane's chest. He could hear the wheezing, bubbling sound as she fought to breathe. She coughed and choked on the blood that was welling up into her throat. "Hang on, Legs. *Kat, where's the Goddamn light?*"

A soft glow answered him and he took stock of Lane's situation for the first time. A wooden stake protruded from her chest where it had mercifully missed her heart by several inches and her eyes were swollen and streaming. Kat leaned over him, horrified at what she saw. She couldn't tear her eyes away from the stake. She reached out towards it.

"Leave it," Beckett snapped. "It's the worst thing you can do. Get me something to wrap her in, she's freezing."

Kat ignored him and reached out for the stake again. "Trust me on this, Beckett. I can hear her. She's telling me to pull it, she hasn't the strength to pull it herself and she can't heal herself whilst the stake stays in her." She took hold of the jagged wood and tugged at it, pulling it from Lane with a wet, sucking sound. Blood bubbled and frothed out of the wound in a crimson foam.

Lane gasped as the stake left a gaping hole in her chest. Beckett tore open her shirt.

"Sorry, Legs but I need to get to it." Beckett's face was grim.

Lane opened her reddened eyes and held up a hand to stop him from touching the bubbling crimson wound. She closed her eyes again as if to sleep. Kat could sense the rushing sound in her veins and her vampire eyes saw the healing begin seconds before Beckett did. Slowly the wound pulled together, muscle and sinew beneath the hole closed first, then finally the skin drew together. There was no scar.

"Holy shit." The white face of the Goth paled naturally as he regained consciousness in time to witness the healing.

Beckett lunged towards him, grabbing him by the shoulder of his jacket. He dragged him towards Lane and pushed his face close to her.

"Look! Look at her, you ignorant bastard. Look at what you almost destroyed." Beckett's anger was raw as he pulled the boy to his feet and yanked him around to face him. His jaws were clamped tight together, his fist balled at his side.

Lane coughed as she sat upright. "Leave him, Beckett. I'll be fine. Thankfully his knowledge of anatomy is lousy, though my eyes hurt like hell, you little thug!"

Beckett hit him again anyway. It had been a bad night.

He hauled the lad to his feet again. "Be glad she's okay. Be very glad."

"She's a goddamn Sucker man. You her 'boy' or what?"

Beckett's fist slammed home into his solar plexus and he held him upright ready to receive another.

"*Beckett!*" yelled Lane. "Quit it, Handsome. He may know where Andrei is." She turned to the boy. "What's your name? And I can tell if you're lying. You need to choose your words carefully, you really do."

She stood up and brushed herself down, seemingly oblivious to her half naked state. Her eyes were still stinging and full, the garlic oil having done its job. She'd been able to avoid the full extent of the attack, instinctively covering her face seconds before the garlic essence was thrown but it was the action that had exposed her chest to receive the jagged wooden stake.

The boy was clearly terrified and Lane used the fact to her advantage as she narrowed her eyes and pushed down her canine teeth. She snarled at him and moved right up to him with vampire speed. It was at that point that he lost control of his bladder.

Beckett let him go and stepped back quickly. "Very nice. Not so brave now, are we? Maybe I'll just leave you to her. Mate."

"No," he snapped. "No ... please."

Lane's eyes twinkled at Kat. *Watch me,* she said silently. *Watch how you can use your abilities to your advantage. Watch him squirm. He deserves it. That bloody stake hurt.*

145

Lane's elegant fingernail hooked under the boy's chin. "I asked you your name Pee Wee."

He drew himself up. "Darius. Darius Luca, I'm a hunter."

"Tut tut. Now's not the time to try and be clever."

He lost height suddenly under Lane's glare.

"Well, Hunter to what did I owe the pleasure of your attention? Hmm?"

"I wanted Andrei Marinescu, he's a Sucker... like you."

"No," she said icily, "No, he's not at all like me. Because if he had you here now, I rather doubt that he would resist draining you of all your blood then taking your goddamn head off. I *may* not do that. Besides," she looked down at the puddle by his feet, "I think you're in the wrong job."

"A hunter, eh?" Beckett mocked him. "What shall we do with him?"

Lane eyed him coldly. "Let the little creep go. He's not worth the effort."

"You heard the lady. Go." Beckett pushed him roughly towards the stairs. "Go. And take my advice, Hunter, quit whilst you're ahead."

"Just like that. You expect me to leave, just like that? After what I've seen? I mean, man that stuff is way past weird. If you can all do that, how the hell do I ... you know?"

Beckett's harsh laugh made the boy pale. "You know how to push your luck, I'll give you that. It occurs to me, Hunter, that you need a few lessons. Vampirism 101, how's that sound? And you know what; I think I may enjoy being the teacher."

"My name is Darius," the Goth said quietly but with belligerence.

Lane sighed, "Okay Handsome, let's get out of here." She turned back to Darius, "I'll just tell you this once, you're way out of your league here, and for your future information we do know how to police our own bad guys.

Leave it to us, all right?"

Kat had been quiet during this exchange, looking around her thoughtfully. She put a hand on Beckett's arm and nodded towards Darius. "He may have seen Nik," she said quietly.

Beckett grabbed the boy firmly by the shoulder again. "This lady wants to know if you've seen her son. Think very carefully before you answer."

Kat described Nik and what he had been wearing the last time she had seen him.

Darius adopted a foppish pose and looked thoughtful. Beckett tightened his grip on his shoulder and Lane moved menacingly closer.

"Okay! Okay! Yeah, he was here earlier. He left though, I saw him talking to Andrei just before he left. Don't know what was said but your son looked more than pissed off."

"They said he hadn't been here," said Kat,

Darius shrugged. "The one in the mask followed him, in case you're interested."

Lane stopped abruptly and Beckett's face was paler than death itself.

"The one in the mask?" Lane asked. Her eyes were gimlets in her intense features.

Darius nodded. "Yeah, he's been here several times recently. I noticed him take an interest in this guy Nik. Left straight after he did. I got the impression he was following him."

"Oh God," whispered Kat. "Nik."

CHAPTER TWENTY-THREE

Santorini had taken great delight in Nik's awed expression at his home. Set back in dense pine forest at the foot of the Brecon Beacons and separated from the road by a quarter of a mile drive, the vast new house had surprised Nik. From within the luxury of an exquisite drawing room, Santorini had laughed at his assumptions.

"What? You expected a crumbling old mansion? An ancient stately home, perhaps? That would be far too draughty and uncomfortable for my taste, Nik. You have been watching too many tasteless films. I see I will need to educate you. Come, I will show you to the guest suite. You need to rest and refresh yourself."

"I ... err ... I didn't know what to expect really." He felt foolish and that angered him as he was reminded yet again of his low status on the ladder of vampire hierarchy.

"There are many things that you need to understand, Nik, however tonight is not the time to begin your education."

Nik resented Santorini's attitude and arrogance; the way he assumed Nik's ignorance and lack of intelligence. Circumstances had robbed him of many things but intellect had not been among them, and one thing that was apparent was that his self appointed mentor needed him as some kind of passport to the presence of a vampire much higher in the pecking order than he was. His father. The thought emboldened him. His father would welcome him and he would no longer need for anything. He would play along with Santorini for the time being, using him for his vampire education and well being, until he knew who and where his father was. Then he wouldn't need him - he wouldn't need anybody.

"Do you ever take off that mask?"

Santorini laughed again, a musical sound that flirted on the edge of seduction. "Of course. Perhaps you believe me to be somehow disfigured? I assure you that is not so. I wear the mask for amusement only. I like to be amused Nik."

"Show me, then. Show me your face."

"You challenge me? How utterly charming. Very well."

With a deft movement of his hand the mask fell away from his face. His features were classically exquisite; finely defined eyebrows framing ice-blue eyes that sat above an aquiline nose. His cruel mouth seemed harsher now that it was in context with the rest of his face. HIs haughty demeanour irritated Nik, making him feel inferior and clumsy. Well, that would change.

"You see. I do not hide an ugly scar, or putrid skin. It is as I said. For amusement only."

"And me? Do I amuse you? What will you do with me when you tire of me?"

Santorini's eyes narrowed momentarily. His voice was cold when he said, "I don't believe that will happen, Nik. I told you, I intend to educate you and present you to your father as an accomplished vampire, a son of whom he can be proud, and a son worthy of him. And for that I expect to be rewarded. In the meantime, yes, you amuse me." He paused, appraising Nik's expression. "And I believe that I have awakened something in you that you do not understand."

Nik's eyes darkened. "I'm tired," he said.

"But of course. Where are my manners? Come with me."

Nik followed him. Whilst he was of value to Santorini, he felt safe.

The house would not have been out of place in Beverly Hills, with it's marble floored hallway and sweeping staircase that led to another two floors. His host strode ahead of him on the first floor to a set of double doors of heavily carved oak. He flung them open with a dramatic gesture.

"Please make yourself comfortable."

Nik stepped into the room. An enormous four poster bed with silk drapes took centre stage. The furniture was elegant and extravagant and even to an unaccustomed eye must have cost a fortune. A door stood ajar and beyond it he could see a bathroom and what was obviously a dressing room. He looked down at his ragged jeans.

"You will find all you need in the wardrobes, Nik. I think you'll find everything will fit. Help yourself."

Something that had been nagging at Nik gelled within his mind. He turned to Santorini.

"How do you know of my father? I mean, how do you know that the man you speak of *is* my father?"

"Because, Nik. I have been looking for you for a very long time. He sent me to find you."

"That doesn't make any sense. How does he know of me? That slut, who is my mother can mean nothing to him."

Santorini smiled. "Too many questions for tonight. Get some rest and we will talk further when you wake up." He read Nik's thoughts and laughed aloud. "Yes, you will sleep through the day, and not in a grimy coffin. You will sleep during the day and wake and feed at night. Not because you'll turn to ashes in the sunlight, but simply because you will be tired. You will be nocturnal because that is your nature and when you are most comfortable. That is when you will play and stalk your prey. We live by night because the darkness triggers our hunger."

"You didn't answer my question. How does he know of me?"

"Because he senses you."

"He *senses* me? "

"I told you Nik, you owe your great potential to being the son of one of the most powerful vampires of all time. You were conceived of the Born, albeit a Latent and an

151

Undead, one of the most awesome combinations of vampire genetics. Enough for now, Nik. Good night."

It was nothing short of a dismissal and Santorini was gone before Nik could utter another word, but there was no sleep in him - he was wired, high on the events of the night and the flattery of his mentor. He had gorged himself on the blood of his prey and discovered new abilities that he had only previously wondered at. Now, instead of being homeless, living on the floor of a filthy warehouse, he found himself befriended by one of his own kind who was refined and sophisticated, obviously wealthy beyond his imagination, and proficient in all the vampire arts. His mind explored the possibilities and above all else, he thought about his father.

He had always known he was different, special somehow. Now he knew why - he was the son of someone great. He wondered how much of his father he had inherited. A glance in the mirror reflected his mother's dazzling amethyst eyes at him. He scowled. He wanted no part of her and there was nothing he could do about this, her gift to him. His mouth had hardened into a cruel line, a copy of which he had yet to see for himself.

In Greece.

CHAPTER TWENTY-FOUR

Outside Danse Macabre, Beckett swore colourfully and kicked out at the door.

"Frustration has never been easy for you to handle, Handsome. There's nothing we can do here now", Lane soothed. She turned to Darius, "And as for you, I suggest you think about making yourself scarce. You've had your share of excitement for tonight and I should also think about walking away from all this. If you want to stay alive for some considerable time that is. You've seen what our kind is capable of and believe me they won't hesitate in using you as a light snack. Understand?"

"No way. I'm not leaving."

Beckett moved towards him. "Perhaps I can persuade you?"

"What? You're going to beat me up? Is that it? Go ahead. I'll just be back another night. I told you, I'm not quitting."

Lane put a restraining hand on Beckett's arm. "Down boy. He's not worth the effort and I think you've had enough agro for one night. If he wants to be Andrei's breakfast, that's up to him. Let him go."

Beckett scowled again - he wasn't going to let it go. "Did you forget what he just did to you? Or is that okay all of a sudden? Because from where I was standing you were a delicate part of a gnat's anatomy away from checking out."

Lane sighed and looked suddenly weary. "All right Beckett. You win. Beat the crap out of him if that's what is going to make you feel better. Then what?"

Beckett looked sheepish. He took a step back and raked his fingers through his hair. "I'm sorry. It's just that

I feel so damned helpless. Darius, I'm sorry, and I owe you for earlier. But she's right you know. You need to get the hell out of here, and do yourself a favour and stay out. You don't have any idea what you're dealing with. Trust me."

Darius paled visibly, even under the white make-up. His entire demeanour changed as if a mask had dropped. "You think so? I'm sorry to disappoint you, because in fact, I know more than you can imagine and I believe that you can imagine a great deal. My name isn't Darius Luca, it's Darius Marinescu." He gave a short harsh laugh at the surprise in Beckett's expression. "Yes, that's right. Andrei is my brother. And I am going to kill him."

They stood in stunned silence for a moment until he spoke again. His voice had lost the affected foppishness and had acquired a cultured European accent.

"I should attend to her if I were you. She looks unwell." He pointed an elegantly manicured and black nailed finger at Kat, who in the previous minutes had begun to feel woozy. She leaned against the wall of the club and as Beckett moved towards her, she slid quietly to the floor.

Lane was at her side instantly, her fingers at her neck feeling for her pulse. "She's okay," she said quickly. "It's just a faint, she'll be all right. She's had a rough night." She pulled Kat up into a sitting position as she had begun to stir and mumble.

"Tell me about it," Beckett muttered. He turned his attention to Kat. "Hey, sweetheart, wake up. C'mon Kat, wake up honey. We need to get you out of here."

Kat appeared confused momentarily, and then the confusion gave way to a look of horror, as the events of the night replayed in fast forward on her memory screen. She tried to get to her feet, she needed to run. Run away, as far as she could, from the madness that was centred on the three figures that swam before her unfocussed eyes.

Lane read her, and pre-empted the flight. She gripped

her arm as Kat tried to shake her off. "Let go of me. Leave me alone, all of you."

Lane's grip tightened. "Get my car, Beckett. I'm going to take her to the Sanctuary. She's having a bad reaction to the turning. Her old immune system is putting up a fight. It happens sometimes but it will pass, I just need to get her somewhere safe until it does. The keys are in the ignition"

Her words were not lost on Darius. "Jeez! She's a Sucker too?" Fortunately, it was out of Beckett's hearing.

Kat was trembling and weeping when Beckett pulled up in Lane's MG. "What the hell's happening to her?" he demanded.

"It's an allergic reaction. It's temporary, but while it goes on it could get nasty. Her new immune system is rejecting her normal tissue as her vampire DNA takes hold on her body. I have what I need for her at the Sanctuary. I'll call you later."

She bundled Kat into the passenger seat of the car and locked it from the outside, before driving away with the screech that left half of the rubber of her tyres on the road.

Darius had remained still and silent whilst they attended to Kat. Beckett turned his attention back to the boy.

"So what's the story? Andrei's your brother? I have to tell you, that doesn't endear you to me. Tell me about it, and I'd better be impressed."

"Oh, I think you'll be impressed. I'll tell you what you want to know, but not because your scare me, but because I think we can help each other. And if he stays true to form, Andrei won't be back here tonight."

"That's your first mistake. I should scare you. You seem confident about Andrei not returning. Where will he go?"

"Anywhere he wants. You forget what he is."

"I assure you, I forget nothing. But you're right about one thing, it's a waste of time staying round here. I'm going to ask you nicely to come back with me and tell me a story."

Darius smiled. "You have no need to threaten me Beckett, however you dress it up. I'll go with you, but only on the understanding that you tell me your story in return. It's only fair."

"Maybe. My jeep is around the corner. Do you drink, Darius Marinescu? I hope so, because I'm going to get stinking drunk and I would rather do it with company.

CHAPTER TWENTY-FIVE

Kat had continued to shake and weep quietly as Lane drove too fast through the empty streets of Newport towards the Sanctuary. Behind, above, and below the façade of an Indian restaurant, the Sanctuary was a warren of rooms and corridors where vampires who obeyed the code could go to feed from donors in safety, and those who were in any kind of trouble could find help. The Council had set up such establishments in most major cities, concealed behind innocent eating or drinking establishments where the comings and goings at late hours of the night would not attract too much attention from locals or the police; their facades were always respectable businesses which operated legitimately. The Sanctuary was a lifeline to many.

Lane stopped the car outside the Taj Restaurant, ignoring the double yellow lines at the kerbside. There was no time for the niceties of legal parking, she'd send someone out to move the car as soon as she had Kat safe inside.

She was prepared for Kat to try and run but as she opened the car door she could see that Kat was in no state to be running anywhere. She gently put her arm around Kat's back and helped her out of the car. "It's okay, Kat. You're going to be fine. You're safe and you're going to stay safe. This will pass. I promise you. You have to trust me again. Can you do that?"

Kat nodded feebly. Lane's voice held a quality that made it hard to resist her. Besides, she really had no choice - she couldn't even stand unaided, let alone run.

Inside the front door there was an entrance to the left into the restaurant and another directly ahead which led through to the rear and upstairs, into the Sanctuary. Lane pushed the door open with her shoulder as she held on to Kat and guided her into a lobby that would have not been out of place in any elite hotel. A reception desk at the rear of the lobby was manned by a pretty young girl. She stood up immediately as Lane and Kat entered.

"Hi Doc. You'll need a room I guess. Your usual one next to the clinic is free. I'll come with you, it looks like you have your hands full." She lifted a key from a large board behind the desk.

Lane smiled warmly at her. "Hello Jane. Thanks, you're a sweetie. This is Kat and we'll need the room for the rest of the night and maybe part of tomorrow. OK?"

"Always glad to help. Do you know the blood group?"

"Not yet, but it's all right, she's fed. It's a reaction to the turning, she needs some Anti-HVV and a long sleep and she'll be fine. If Paul Beckett calls, put him straight through will you, and I'll need to make a call to the Council later. We have a problem. Anyone else check in tonight?"

"No. It's been quiet. Thank God. There's just me and a couple of donors."

Lane frowned. She knew the vampire community in Wales had grown and a quiet night at the Sanctuary meant only one thing – people had died. Either a vampire or some innocent victims were no more.

Jane opened the door for them and flicked the lights into life. They were subdued in deference to vampires' photophobia and their painful reaction to bright light. She walked ahead and pulled the long drapes closed, even the lights of the city could hurt the delicate retinas of a newly turned vampire. She tossed the key onto a small table on her way out.

"Just ring down if you need anything. I'm on duty all night; I'll get your call to the Council when you're ready."

"Can you be an angel and get my car moved around the back? I'm not in the mood for the clampers."

"Sure. I'll keep your keys behind the desk. G'night."

Lane sat Kat down onto the comfortable bed and knelt down in front of her, taking her hands in her own.

"I'm sorry, Kat. It's been tough and I'm afraid it's going to get a hell of a lot worse at some point. I'm going to give you a shot. It's an Anti-HVV serum that will help your immune system to accept your new DNA.

Kat seemed bewildered but offered no resistance as Lane bared her arm yet again. She didn't flinch at the sting of the needle and allowed Lane to lay her down and cover her with the warm quilt. In minutes the shaking subsided and she gave herself up to the sleep that she needed so badly.

Lane didn't relax though, she knew that Kat's dreams would be lurid and frightening as her mind tried to assimilate the horrors of her new life. She paced the room and smoked continuously, clicking her thumb and fingernail together as she prowled, panther-like, around the room, trying to put some order to her erratic thoughts. It was obvious that the situation locally was escalating and that there were some hard core vicious vampires operating in her territory.

It also meant that she was close to her quarry and the thought made her quicken with anticipation. Her hunt over the past centuries, constantly changing her identity and location, losing loved ones in a steady stream of grief and death, could soon be over. She knew that she should notify the Council, but there was a dark nugget of doubt somewhere deep within.

Recently she had begun to fear that there was corruption at the very heart of the Council, and she didn't know yet who she could trust. She knew though that she would be bound by any decision they made and that wasn't acceptable. She had waited too long to let go of the satisfaction of seeing her maker perish and now thanks to sharing Kat's long buried memories, she knew where to find him. With the instinct of ages she knew that she would find Nik with him, so maybe she would be able to help Kat in the process by bringing back her son. She would ignore her allegiances to the Council and see this through on her own.

She looked at Kat sleeping soundly and pulled the drapes aside to see the sky streaked with the mauves and lilacs of the coming day. Kat would sleep for the next few hours at least.

Lane made a sudden decision and snatched up the telephone. Jane answered quickly.

"Jane, I need a babysitter."

"No problem, Doc. I'll get one of the donors to take the desk and come up myself. Be right there."

Lane put down the phone and slipped on her shoes. "Sleep tight honey," she said to Kat.

Not waiting for Jane to arrive, Lane left the door ajar and met her in the corridor. "She should sleep for hours," she said. "When she wakes, tell her to call Paul Beckett. She knows the number."

"What about your call to the Council, Doc?"

"I've changed my mind. I'll be in touch. Thanks, Jane."

"No worries, Doc. Um ... you sure everything is okay? I've never seen you like this."

Lane gave the girl a reassuring smile. "Never more sure. Goodnight."

She swept out of the Sanctuary grabbing her keys from the desk as she passed. Her obsession had won the day and she gave it free rein to cloud her judgement, now only intent on one thing. Finding the vampire that had eluded her for so long.

CHAPTER TWENTY-SIX

Beckett pushed the pile of books and magazines on the coffee table aside, flicked away a layer of dust, and set down two glasses with a new bottle of Jack Daniels as he flopped down onto the battered old sofa beside Darius. For a few minutes he didn't speak.

Darius remained quiet and still, sensing the anger and pain that had the potential to erupt in a lava stream of rage from Beckett if he poked a hole in the tight containment. Eventually Beckett sighed and leaned forwards and poured two glasses of the Tennessee whisky.

"Don't know if this is your poison or not, but tonight, I really don't care. Here. Drink."

Darius took the glass from him. "What shall we drink to?"

"Oh ... I don't know," Beckett said in a slow quiet voice. "Let's see. How about old ghosts? And new tragedies. Yep, that about does it, old ghosts and new tragedies."

Darius raised his glass. "To old ghosts and new tragedies." He took a sip of the harsh spirit and waited. Beckett was calling it, and he knew if he was patient he may gain an insight into where to look for Andrei next. The bruising on his head from Beckett's handling of him earlier still throbbed like a son-of-a-bitch and he had no wish to repeat the scenario.

Beckett downed the whisky in one and said nothing, just poured himself another large glass of his favourite 'JD', which followed the first in swift succession. He poured the third.

"So, Hunter, sorry, Darius, tell me about the blood sucking bastard that you call brother. And I want the truth.

All of it."

If Darius had doubted Beckett's purpose should he hold anything back, the hard glint in the storm grey eyes told him the reality of his situation. They might be playing at drinking buddies, but the truth was a gazillion miles away.

"There isn't a whole lot that I can tell you that you don't already know." He held up a hand as Beckett shifted his weight on the sofa and inhaled deep and loud, his expression beyond warning.

Darius took another swallow of the fiery spirit. "Whoa, calm down. I'm going to tell you everything, it's just that apart from the beginning, when it all happened, you probably know as much as I do about the thing that used to be my older brother."

He felt Beckett relax a little. "Andrei is fifteen years older than me, I was a late surprise to my parents, you may say. My family are from Romania, Bucharest to be exact, although Andrei and I were born in London. My father and mother came to this country on old money and we were educated at the best schools. Andrei always had the knack of getting into trouble, he never seemed content with anything, always searching, always looking for something better. Then when I was ten, I found my mother crying one night. I hid and listened as she told my father about Andrei's latest obsession. It seemed that he had become involved with a satanic cult that included the drinking of blood in its nasty little rituals. Apparently it was mixed with wine and herbs, and I use the word 'herbs' loosely, to enable the sick acolytes to stomach it whilst getting high on the atmosphere and the drugs. At first she thought he would get bored and move on to the next thing, as he usually did. But that didn't happen. He just got more and more obsessed by it all, and especially by the leader of the group. Then one night he came home covered in blood. It was ugly. There was dried blood on his face, around his mouth and chin, and his hands and chest were plastered with gore. My mother had gone to bed early, thankfully, and my father tried to get some sense out of him and get him cleaned up. Oh, yes, I know what you are going to say. Why didn't my father call the police? It wasn't that simple. Andrei insisted that he didn't know what he had done, just that he was covered in blood that wasn't his and that he was obviously under the effect of drugs. Father honestly believed he would sleep it off and we could try and put things right. And then there was the issue of our being here. I said we came here on old money. Well, that is true. But we were also here illegally. That is why he didn't involve the police or a doctor."

Darius paused, then, disturbingly devoid of emotion, continued with Andrei's history. "As it turned out, it wouldn't have made any difference. Everything that was my brother died that night. We didn't know what was happening to him then, not that we would have understood or known what to do for him. It seems that during one of the bloody rituals Andrei gave himself over to evil and allowed their leader to feed from him, and then Andrei drank his blood. That much he told us before he fell into a fever and a coma. It was all over in less than two hours - the screaming and obscenities, the thrashing and the vomiting of blood, and then the death. He'd fallen quiet and we thought that was it, that he would sleep and recover but he simply slipped away. He never even opened his eyes.

"Not until later."

Beckett leaned forward and poured another Jack Daniels; the story was getting uncomfortably familiar. He moved the bottle over the other glass but Darius covered the rim with his hand.

"I think I know what happened next," said Beckett, thickly.

Darius appeared not to have heard him, he carried on, talking to his own soul then and not just to Beckett, as if by doing so he could purge the horror of what had followed.

"My father and I cleaned him up then, washing him, getting rid of the blood, putting him into clean clothes. We didn't want my mother to see him dead and in that state. Her health was delicate and the shock may have killed her too. So, when we had finished, my father broke the news to her gently. He told her that Andrei had taken a drug overdose. It was all we could think of to explain it."

Darius went quiet again, the memory too vivid to carry on.

"It's okay," said Beckett. "I think I've been there."

This seemed to anger Darius. "*How can you know?* That wasn't the end. We laid him out and as is the custom in my homeland we sat vigil with him, saying the prayers that were to keep his soul safe while it travelled back to God. Though we may as well have saved our breath for the good it did. We sat there until the next evening, taking it in turns, while we waited for friends from the old country to come and help with his burial. When the darkness came, Andrei sat up. He just sat up as if nothing had happened. Then . . ."

"Then," prompted Beckett.

"Then he killed both my mother and father. Just ripped them apart with his bare hands."

"Jesus, that was rough at ten years old." He couldn't help but note the calm coldness as Darius had recounted the story without emotion.

"I grew up quickly."

"Why do you think he spared you? Compassion?"

Darius let out a harsh laugh. "Compassion? No. He left me alone because I ran away. Yes, I ran like hell. And I ran until I couldn't run any further. I was found exhausted and in shock. They took me into care because I pretended I couldn't speak. Kept it up for years, then when I was old enough I just ran away. It seems to be what I'm good at," he said bitterly. "I've been searching for Andrei ever since, always one step behind him. I thought I'd found him tonight, thought I was at last going to be able to put an end to it all. And what did I do? I ran. I ran away again. So I'm in the market for some help after all. I have recently come to understand that there is more to hunting and killing vampires than the movies would have you believe."

"Well, I don' know 'bout that." Beckett had begun slurring. "Seems t'me that you almost did the job on Lane. You got the right ideas. Balls is what you're short on. S'understandable."

Darius glanced at the now empty bottle on the table. "If it wasn't that you're drunk I would take offence at that."

Beckett shrugged. "Take away, sunshine. Take away."

"So, I told you about Andrei. Now it's your turn. What's your story, Beckett?"

"You told me nothing. A sad story is all you told me. I already know Andrei is a bastard. I already know he's a vampire of the worst kind - one of the Undead. I know he'll kill without mercy or feeling of any kind. All this I already know. And my story, well, that's kinda private. This ain't no support group, kid, I just wanted to keep an eye on you while I got myself anaesthetised - which incidentally, takes more than a bottle of my friend, Jack, these days. Now, that's got to be a worry, eh?"

Despite the bravado, Beckett eyes were almost closed and he leaned heavily against the young man. Darius stood up.

"I'm not gonna keep you against your will. There's no need to run," he said pointedly to the boy.

Before Darius could reply, Beckett was slumped into the corner of the sofa. The young man stood for a few moments watching him as he slipped deeper into an alcoholic stupor. "What happened to you? Whatever it was, it haunts you. Haunts your dreams and your waking hours. I know how that is. Maybe we have more in common that you admit to. Sleep while you can, Beckett."

A cocktail of Tennessee whisky and the events of the

previous twenty four hours made a perfect catalyst for the action replay of the night it had all begun for Beckett. His subconscious released the lock he'd placed on it and his darkest memories played out like a movie on the screen of his nightmare.

***

It had been raining and he was waiting for Grace to come home, determined to stay awake and talk to her, no matter how late it got. He wanted her to see a specialist, a friend of his from the seminary who had traded the pulpit for the shrink's couch. Her constant ramblings of vampires and blood drinking were out of control now. He had no choice; he would get her psychiatric help.

His hundredth glance at the clock told him it was just past three o'clock. Late, even for Grace. He went to the door to look out for her and almost fell over her inert body lying soaked to the skin and in a pool of blood on his doorstep.

"Grace! Dear God, help me."

Beckett picked her up into his arms - no great effort needed; Grace had lost at least three stones in weight and was no heavier than a small child. She stirred in his arms.

"Paul? Paul, I'm so sorry."

"Shh. Don't talk. Let me get you dry. Dear Jesus, what happened to you? Where did all this blood come from?" A quick inspection told him that it wasn't hers, but the smears around her mouth sickened him and he didn't dare think about how it had come to be there.

He strode up the stairs and laid her on her bed, took her soaking clothes off her shivering body, leaving her underclothes. He flinched at the emaciated frame in front of him, the protruding ribs, and paper thin skin covering bones and precious little flesh. He'd had no idea.

In that moment, shame and guilt swamped him. He should have listened to her, taken her seriously. But if he had then that meant he would have to accept that she was telling the truth. That vampires did exist. That his God had allowed such creatures of hell to walk the earth. That all he believed in had no meaning. All lies. His life was based on a lie.

Grace stirred on the bed and Beckett covered her with a blanket. He sat down beside her and took her hand in his.

"Grace? Gracey? It's me, Paul. Listen to me. It's going to be all right. I'm going to get you help. I'll look after you. It's all going to be all right."

It was then that Beckett's world descended into an even deeper pit of madness.

Grace sat up and stared into his eyes, her pitiful screams tore into his soul, held him transfixed and unable to move to telephone for help. He reached into his pocket for his prayer stole, and put it around his neck with shaking hands. And he prayed. He prayed until the screams subsided and Grace lay still and calm again. Her breathing was shallow and barely perceptible. And then it stopped. Grace was dead.

Beckett didn't know how long he sat in disbelief, unaware of the tears that slid down his face and off his chin onto his shirt, unaware of the presence of a tall beautiful woman standing behind him, unaware that he had left his front door open in his haste to get Grace inside and safe, unaware that the woman was speaking softly to him, until she put her hand on his heaving shoulder. Somewhere someone was sobbing, he looked up expecting it to be whoever stood there in the room with him, but gradually realised that the sobs were his own.

"Father? I'm, afraid it isn't over. There are things to be done. She needs to be given peace. Do you know what I'm saying?"

Beckett shook his head. "Um, I need to call our doctor. He . . . um . . . needs to come and . . . certificate . . . something. I don't know."

"No, Father. That isn't what I mean. She has died, but there is something inside her, something unclean. Do you understand?"

"Possession?" he whispered, vague memories of distant lectures in the seminary, filed away for future reference, a future which thankfully had never arrived. Until now.

"Not in the way you understand it, Father. Your sister is dead. There is no bringing her back. But what lives in her will animate her unless we do what is necessary."

Beckett nodded and stood slowly and opened the drawer of Grace's beside cabinet. It was still there: the Bible he had given to her on the day of his ordination. He lifted it reverently, still not questioning the woman's presence doing everything automatically, his mind far removed from that place.

Impatience flickered momentarily around her sensuous mouth. "No, Father. That won't help. Not now, maybe not ever. Your sister is the victim of a vampire and her body has become host to something unholy. Unless her heart is cut out and her head removed she will rise and become a filthy creature of the darkness, living only on the blood of the innocent, killing and corrupting as she herself was killed and corrupted."

"*Get out!*" Beckett yelled. "Whoever you are, get out of my house and take your filthy lies with you. I'm calling the doctor and then I'm calling the police."

She moved so quickly his human eyes did not see it. She was in front of him, holding on to his arms, pinning them to his side and staring into his eyes. He couldn't move. It was as if he was paralysed. But he heard her. She didn't speak, yet he heard her, and he became quiet under her gaze.

"I hate doing that, but it's the only way to get you to listen to me and let me do what has to be done. It would be better if you could do it, loving her like you do, but you can't, I can see that. But you have to be there. Someone who loves her should be with her."

She sighed, compassion for the broken priest outweighing her instincts.

"All right Father, have it your way. We'll wait. We'll wait and watch and when the last rays of the sun disappear from that window, if she rises as one of the Undead then you must allow me to do what is necessary. If not, then I will stand aside and you can do it your way. Is that a deal?"

Beckett somehow knew at the deepest level of his soul that he was hearing the truth, and now he was being given the opportunity to see for himself. He looked down at Grace's lifeless face, she was still beautiful, and it was hard to believe that she was dead. Hard to think that only minutes earlier her screams would have chilled the coldest soul, her torment undeniable.

"Father? Do we have a deal?"

Deal with the Devil, he thought. He gave the smallest of nods. He had no reason to trust her, but he did.

In the long hours that followed they sat beside Grace, watching and waiting. For what? She may rise, the woman had said, but what did that mean? Surely if she rose again it didn't have to mean that she was a vampire. It could be a miracle. After all he had been praying hard enough for one. Jesus had risen and promised eternal life to all who believed in him. And that was the problem. Grace had vehemently denied Christ; she had shunned religion in all its forms, especially the Church, which in her eyes was responsible for the fact her brother was allowing his life to drain away. She didn't see the joy or the love, just the burden of others' suffering. In fact, that's what it all seemed about: suffering. Well, not for her, she was going to live her life to the fullest because there was nothing else after it. No angels, no heaven or celestial choirs, no long tunnels into light, and no ancestors in blessed reunion, it was all crap. This was all there was: finito.

Father Beckett prayed silently. *Oh Grace, I pray it's not too late. Dear Lord, she is so young, give her another chance, give* **me** *another chance to show her, to bring her to you. I can do it, I know I*

169

can. Please, God, I have tried to be your servant and I have failed with Grace, if anything her waywardness is my fault, I have not seen what was before my eyes. I promise Lord, if you spare her I will bring her to you. Amen.

The woman's voice brought him back to the present. Her name was Lane, she said, Lane Dearing. She was a psychiatrist with an exclusive private practice. For hours she talked to him although he remembered nothing of it later. All he would remember was what took place after the first infinitesimal movement of the sheet which covered Grace up to her shoulders.

At first he wasn't sure if he had seen it at all, he was tired and his eyes stung. He held his breath, trying to hold time in a frame that would remain unchanged, becoming unaware of anything outside the arena of Grace's bed.

The atmosphere changed subtly. The temperature dropped and the air seemed rarefied, his chest was tight and his lungs struggled for essential oxygen, making him feel dizzy and disorientated. He felt Lane tense, on the alert after hours of waiting. Whatever it was that she waited for was about to happen.

There was a heavy silence and then Grace's lips parted and her left arm began to move under the sheet. In what was a fraction of a second but in what seemed like an eternity to Beckett, Grace brought her arm from beneath the sheet and turned her face to look at Beckett.

And he knew.

Lane brought the wooden stake from out of nowhere it seemed, and without warning she plunged it deep into Grace's chest. Beckett was stunned, unprepared for the brutality of it but knowing from the depths of his soul that somehow, unbelievably, this was right. The howl that came from Grace bore no semblance to any humanity and the fetid smell that issued forth from her could have come only from hell's bowels.

Lane moved swiftly and deftly with a surgical scalpel. In seconds she had cut through her chest, broken her ribs and cut out her still heart. Beckett stood fixed to the spot in horror at the defilement of his precious sister, unmoving because of his instinctive knowledge that this was what Grace needed, however evil it seemed. He didn't know how or why, just that it was so.

With practiced skill and alarming dexterity, the woman surgically removed Grace's head and placed it on her ragged chest.

She turned to him.

"*Now* you pray."

Beckett felt the first hysterical laugh rising in his throat, and let it out. He laughed, and then he screamed. And he was awake, shaking and sitting up on his sofa with perspiration soaking through his shirt and there was a young man looking at him oddly.

"So, Beckett, you do know. You poor bastard."

Beckett didn't reply, he'd passed out again.

CHAPTER TWENTY-SEVEN

The Sanctuary had been quiet all night, apart from Lane and Kat there had been no visitors. Jane, the young receptionist had sat beside Kat all night as her immune system battled to become compatible with her new DNA. Lane had left without explanation of where she was going and Kat had slept fitfully, tossing and turning, muttering and mumbling, perspiring and shivering. The transformation for her had not been an easy one, surprisingly, as she was born a Latent vampire with her body already carrying the blueprint of the vampire slumbering within her at genetic level.

It was close to seven a.m. when the harsh buzz of the intercom on the wall near the door brought Jane from her doze to fully awake in a millisecond.

"Hello," she whispered, not wanting Kat to wake whilst it was still dark.

"Jane, there's a guy down here asking for Doc Lane. He won't accept that she's not here; in fact he's being an asshole about it. Can you come down and sort it?" The young donor that Jane had left in charge of the reception desk sounded anxious.

Jane looked across at Kat who was now sleeping peacefully and apparently very deeply. She hesitated. She'd promised she wouldn't leave Kat. Lane had been adamant.

"I'm with someone, a client who isn't well. Can't you deal with whoever it is? Did he give a name? If it's treatment he needs, you can give him a room to wait for Doctor Dearing, or if it's a meal, then honey he's all yours."

"No, he won't tell me his name. He insists on seeing the Doc. Won't deal with anyone else. Quite stroppy he is too. Says he knows she's here."

"Well, he's wrong. Look, can't you get rid of him?"

"He's not going anywhere and he ... *excuse me, sir!* You can't go through there! Sir, come back...shit, Jane he's on his way up. Want me to call the Council Cops?"

Jane sighed heavily. Why on her watch? "No. It's okay. I'll head him off and get rid of him. Just call them and come quick if I hit my alarm. Okay?"

"Sure. You're welcome to him. Loves himself a bit, right up himself if you know what I mean."

Unfortunately Jane did know; without the assistance of the girl's colourful vocabulary.

She cast another quick glance at Kat. She hadn't stirred, so Jane opened the door quietly and tiptoed out into the hallway. It was empty and there was no sound anywhere. She frowned. There were only two flights of stairs from the reception area, and even with the heavy carpeting she would have heard someone approaching. Unless . . .

Too late, she sensed the presence behind her. The cold shiver that ran down her spine told her before she felt the press of his cold hand on her shoulder, before she heard the seductive tone of his voice commanding her to do as he bid. Before she fell into the hypnotic trance that prevented her from pressing the red button on her personal alarm.

Michael Rabb leaned into Jane's shoulder and whispered into her ear. Willing her to remember nothing of his visit, or of Lane and Kat's earlier presence. She was to dismiss the young donor, telling her all was well. She would remember nothing. Especially, she would not remember him taking Kat away from the Sanctuary.

His seductive whispering caressed Jane's sub-consciousness and she responded to him invitingly, arching her back and murmuring, as she fell deeper and deeper under his influence. He kissed her on her neck, softly, enticingly. It would keep her enthralled in an erotic dream long enough for him to take Kat.

"Go," he told her telepathically.

Jane remained motionless for several seconds, then walked towards the staircase and down into the hallway below.

The Proconsul opened the door to Kat's room with the merest of movements and stepped inside. His vampire eyes penetrated the darkness immediately and came to rest over the sleeping Kat. His mouth, moments earlier full of sensual promise, now held a hint of the brutality that he was capable of also. His eyes, once the darkest hazel, now shone a luminous yellow in the darkness, like toxic waste.

He lifted Kat roughly from her bed and she woke immediately. Her new vampire sight and senses alive with the night, she pulled away from him, snarling at the restraint. With a swift movement of his hand he dug his long, manicured fingers into her temple and subdued her, claiming her mind for his own. Then he threw her over his shoulder with ease, as if she was nothing more than a silk scarf.

He opened the window with his free hand and stepped out onto the ledge and out into the breaking dawn.

Lane had brought her MG to a silent halt outside a tall building, grey against the lilacs and yellows of dawn. It was in darkness except for the glow of light behind heavy curtains on the third floor. In it's time it had been a school, a hotel, a government office building and more recently renovated in style to become a private home. Home to one of the wealthiest and most ruthless vampires that had set foot on British soil and who now held a prominent position within the government of the nation. Lane sensed for his presence and detected it, along with several young female energies, engaged in a variety of acts of indecency. Here was another that seemed untouchable by the Council mainly because, although his actions were despicable, they had not yet crossed the threshold of the Code in its strictest sense and human laws were not within her jurisdiction. She walked around the perimeter of the house, looking for the easiest route of entry. All the windows were closed but the lock on the rear door that led into the garden gave way at her push.

She entered the house and stood still, sniffing at the air, her hearing tuned into the conversation on the third floor, though conversation was not how she would term it. She shivered. Her own kind made her sick sometimes.

The atmosphere was heavy with marijuana smoke and the coppery scent of fresh blood. She heard the distinct beating of three hearts, and smelled no essence of any death. At least the old man was still staying just inside the vampire law. She knew that he had not sensed her presence, too engrossed in his own deviance. She leapt to the first landing and listened. Then in a split second to the next and third before crashing through the door into what could have been a tasteful salon. Instead it harboured what had once been instruments of torture and an enormous bed. The three girls screamed in a chorus of fright and protest. He looked up at Lane and sneered at her.

"You need better security, Old Man. The lock on your back door is feeble."

"Councillor Tribune. How nice of you to join us. Isn't it nice, girls?"

"Enough, Minister. I'm here for information. In exchange for not reporting the death of one of these sweet young things to the Curia. Incidentally, just how young are they? Sixteen? No? Fifteen? Shame on you, Old Man. I wonder what the national press would make of it. They do seem to thrive on government sleaze these days."

He rose into the air with an indignant cry and landed before her face to face, his jaws wide open and his hands reaching for her throat, fangs down and ready for action. The girls huddled together, too terrified to move, all traces of drugs and suggestion fleeing from their brains in an instant of clarity.

Lane was too quick for him and overpowered him

immediately, throwing him onto his back and bringing down her elegant stiletto heel onto his throat, her right hand clutching the razor sharp knife that she used for beheadings. He squirmed beneath her foot that stopped short of throttling him.

"Don't ... even ...," she said icily. "After what I've seen I may just take your goddamn head off anyway. So be nice."

She released the pressure on his throat just enough for his larynx to work.

"What ..." he rasped. "What the hell do you want from me? I've broken none of our Laws and none of the girls is dead. I've enough power in the Cabinet and the Press for your threats to mean nothing." Despite his arrogance his eyes remained focussed on Lane's right hand.

"Dear me, you're right, none of them are dead. Yet."

"I don't believe you. You wouldn't dare."

"Try me," she snapped, and increased the pressure on his throat, closing his windpipe and carotid arteries.

"I want to know the whereabouts of Andrei Marinescu. And don't tell me you don't know who I mean. I've seen you in the private rooms at the club. You disgust me."

"How should I know where he is? I have no contact with him outside of the club."

She bent forward and leaned into him, placing the knife above his heart. He whimpered.

"Wrong answer," she hissed. The knife blade bit through the silk of his shirt and into his flesh, through muscle and sinew, down to the bone. She held it there.

The old vampire was writhing under her control now. "Wait! Wait. I may know something."

"Better," she snarled. "So, tell me. And if I don't believe you, the next thing my knife hits will be your rotten heart before it slices it from your body."

"There's a house, in the Brecon Beacons. Only a few of us know of it. I was there once when Marinescu showed up briefly. He seemed to know his way around the place, as though he had been there many times."

"Who owns this house?" she demanded.

"I don't know." The old vampire was clearly afraid.

Lane leaned into his chest hard and heard the crack of his ribs as the knife bit deeper.

"No!" he screamed. "I swear. I swear I don't know who he is. He throws extravagant parties, inviting only a chosen few. I suspect it's those of us that can be useful to him. But he never puts in an appearance himself. Always sends his apologies via his butler, welcoming us to his home and asking us to enjoy his hospitality. I swear it."

"You will tell me now, mind to mind, how I find this place, and if for one second, I sense you are trying to deceive me, I *will* kill you without hesitation."

As if to demonstrate, she pressed down on the knife until the tip of it rested against his heart wall.

She closed her eyes, never for an instant relinquishing her control over him, probing his mind, seeing the country roads become lanes in the foothills of the Welsh mountains. She saw the house nestling among the pines and locked it into her memory.

She withdrew the knife from his chest but kept her heel hard against his throat. He laid still, eyes closed in healing mode. She turned her attention to the huddled girls. Her eyes blazed into their minds. "Get dressed," she commanded silently. "Leave this place with no memory of what has taken place here. Never come back, but retain some fear, it may keep you safe in future. *Now.*"

There would be sub zero temperatures in Hell before she allowed them to witness what was about to happen.

She watched them do her bidding without a word spoken between them but she felt their pain and the pain and suffering of every young woman that had gone before, and her eyes welled with their tears. When they had left she bent once more to the old man. The ribs had begun to knit together again and the cut in his chest had stopped bleeding. She slipped a small case from her pocket and took out a loaded syringe, her intention to buy herself time. She wanted no warning given to Andrei or his unknown friend. She played with the idea that it may be Santorini, and shook her head. She wasn't that lucky.

She looked down on the healing vampire and remembered the frightened girls. She took out the knife and bent low over him.

"To Hell with you. I'm going to kill you anyway, you bastard," she hissed.

She gave him no mercy, cutting his heart out and decapitating him with the ease of experience and without hesitation.

And no regret.

CHAPTER TWENTY-EIGHT

The house stood in its own architectural splendour amid the backdrop of pine forests which clothed the foothills of the Brecon Beacons. Beyond it the wild mountains dominated everything, dark purple peaks against the lightening sky. A Welsh dawn cast unique magic.

Nik had been unable to sleep, his mind and vampire body alive with new promise. He was no longer just another vampire who had to hide by day and prowl the midnight streets, taking what he could find. He was special, he had always felt it and now he knew it as fact. His father was highly respected and revered among the vampire community and he had been taken under the wing of a sublimely powerful and exciting being.

Santorini had promised him the world and along the way he was going to teach him the refinements and abilities that would one day make him, Nik, one of the greatest of his kind. Little wonder that sleep eluded him, even as the first streaks of the daylight stung his retinas, he could not sleep.

As if summoned by Nik's restlessness, Santorini appeared silently at his bedside. He handed Nik a silver goblet.

"This will help you get the rest you need, and I have special blinds that will keep out the strongest rays of the sun at noon. I have to leave you for a while; I have an important meeting to attend. And when I return we will continue with your new experiences."

Nik looked into the goblet, unsure of what to find there.

"It's a simple sleeping draught, Nik. You need to rest. By the time I return you will have slept and be refreshed and ready for the night."

Nik swallowed the amber liquid. "When do we go to Greece?" he asked.

"Soon, my young friend. Soon, you begin the journey to your father and to your destiny. Before then I have a great deal to teach you, to prepare you for what the future holds for you."

"Why can't I go with you today?"

Santorini clicked his tongue impatiently. "Because I said so. And that is reason enough. I do not intend to explain myself to you, now or ever. If you wish to continue under my patronage then you will respect my wishes and obey my instructions without question. I trust we have an understanding?"

Whatever emotion raged inside Nik at being treated as an errant schoolboy yet again he kept in check; he was wise enough to gauge, quite correctly, that Santorini's arrogance was bred of a deeper power that Nik could not even begin to comprehend.

He nodded sullenly at his mentor.

"Whilst I am gone, you will sleep, with the aid of the draught you have just swallowed, and when you wake I will have returned or will be about to. If the latter is the case, please make yourself comfortable and use whatever you wish. My home is yours now, Nik."

His eyes penetrated deep into the boy's mind, burning, searching. He appeared satisfied at what he saw there, and with a sudden movement appeared at the open door. He turned and nodded once at Nik, and was gone.

***

The windows were heavily veiled against the midday sun and there was an air of cool gloom pervading its walls. The men present had arrived wearing dark glasses and their faces lightly glistened, betraying heavy sunscreen.

The Patriarch showed little sign of emotion, it was his

way. It was the trait that made him popular with some and frustrated others. It was more than a century since he was elected Patriarch of the Vampire Council and in his time he had seen change coming. Now was the time to hand over the reins to another. He had made his decision and made it known to the senior members of the Curia.

"Patriarch," one of the visitors said, "You must surely be aware of the unrest within our world, indeed within the very Council itself. We live in very different times from the days when the Code was written. How can we expect to be able to live by it, when all around us there is bloodshed and violence, and our food supply is tainted and diseased? The Code is outdated and has to be revised."

The Patriarch was slow to reply and when he did, his speech was quiet and measured. "I think you move too swiftly. The Code has enabled us to live alongside humans undetected for many hundreds of years. To change it will mean exposure and exposure will mean death. The death of thousands of humans and vampires alike. There is a great need for caution."

His opponent was on his feet then. "These humans are intent on their own destruction; they need no help from us. And what then? Where does our food source come from then? We have tolerated your 'caution' for too long. Unless we act now, our kind will be driven into oblivion along with them. If they are going to disappear anyway, we should do what we can to protect ourselves. We must. Our survival depends upon it. You should know that there has been a vote within the Curia and it was unanimous. As from this moment, you are no longer Patriarch of the Council. I am to give you notice of your dismissal and to inform you that I have been elected temporarily as Patriarch until such time as the full Council can convene for a formal election. We have need of younger blood."

The Patriarch remained seated and the tone of his voice was rigid. "*Election*? Revolt is nearer to the truth. Led and fed by whom? I have no doubt regarding your part in this. Very well, then here is my reply. I have no intention of standing down as Patriarch until formally asked to do so by the full Council. Until then, you may consider yourself as operating outside of our Vampire Laws. I shall issue orders for your apprehension to the Tribunes. Now, if that is all, I would ask you leave."

"You leave me no choice. It has been agreed that I may remove you in any way that is necessary. I deem this necessary. And it is why the Prelate is also present."

The Proconsul nodded towards his companion signalling his contribution.

"Patriarch, I too believe the Proconsul is premature in his call for revision of the Code, but with the pressure from the Born we are facing unrest that could escalate to a second war. Perhaps it would be prudent to show ourselves willing to compromise?"

The Patriarch remained adamant. "I will compromise on *nothing*. How dare you? You who have bought your way into the Curia - oh yes, I am aware of the background machinations. And why? This so called Anti-HVV serum of yours. Are you insane? You can have no idea of the consequences of such a thing. The Council members that support you are as insane as you are."

He saw the blade coming, saw murder in the other's eyes, and did nothing.

Proconsul Rabb turned to his companion. "Leave now. I will attend to what has to be done here. There is no need for us both to be a party to this. I will be in touch soon. Your support will not be forgotten, Prelate.

"I am grateful, Mihai. You will always find me loyal to you when you are officially our new Patriarch." He bent low in an almost mock bow.

"Thank you, but there is much to do before that is assured. And you should know that only my oldest friends call me Mihai. I don't believe you qualify. I would be grateful if you would recall that in future."

"I apologise, Proconsul. Some of us have had so many

identities over the centuries, protecting ourselves and those we love."

Michael Rabb seriously doubted whether the Prelate had ever loved another soul in all of his comparatively young life. "It is as you say. Now, if you would leave, I will continue here." He nodded significantly at the bloody blade still in his tightly clenched fist.

The Prelate bowed again and left without Michael Rabb seeing the resentment that played around the sensual mouth and hard eyes. If he had tried to read his companion he would have heard his thoughts. *'Take your glory now Proconsul. I am going to be rewarded by greater than you, and then we will see who will revise the Code and who will be elected Patriarch. My benefactor has the greatest of all influences with no need for titles and Councils. When I return to him his son and . . . ah yes, the mother of his son, he will deny me nothing.'*

***

Nik had indeed slept heavily and the sun had weakened and was low in the sky when he awoke but even so his retinas stung, and it was a feeling he relished. It was a reminder of who and what he was and what his potential was.

The house was silent, it appeared that Santorini had not yet returned from wherever it was that had claimed him so importantly.

Nik yawned leisurely and strolled across to the dressing room. He opened the vast wardrobe and flicked through the clothes hanging pristine inside. Versace, Armani, Dior. He glanced down at the crumpled heap of old denim jeans and T-shirt and a slow smile spread its way across his face, almost, but not quite, softening the cruel mouth and hard violet eyes. He picked the old clothes up as though they were contaminated and tossed them into the bin standing in the corner of the room. Goodbye uncertain teenager, hello sophisticated, soon to be, man of the world, well, vampire of the world.

He laughed aloud at his thoughts. What had seemed a curse was now a blessing and when he was reunited with his father, he would no longer have need of Santorini and his arrogance. In the meantime he would use his power and knowledge and obvious influence to his own advantage, that way he would not appear to his father as a troublesome burden but a youthful vampire with a world of promise.

He became aware of Santorini's presence as a wave of unwelcome uncertainty washed over him. He spun around to find him leaning against the open doorway, arms folded, with an air of amusement that only served to feed Nik's resentment.

"How long have you been standing there?"

"Long enough to enjoy your pleasure at your new life, Nik. That's all. You are quite right, you will make a beautiful, sophisticated vampire and your powers will bring you anything that you desire. I am only pleased that I will have played a part in your transformation."

Nik was uncomfortable. Santorini had read his thoughts. Had he also picked up on his resentment and plans to abandon him once his father had accepted him as his own?

The older vampire came into the room and reached inside the wardrobe, retrieving a summer weight Versace suit and accessories.

"This one, I think. The soft grey will enhance the purple in your eyes. And it will be hot when we land in Greece. You will be glad of the comfort of the silk."

"Greece? We're going today? But you said ..."

"I have changed my mind. There are things about to happen here that I would prefer not to be a party to. It will be good for me to be in another country for a while. I will expect you downstairs and ready to leave in an hour. Pack what you want, I find Greece sadly lacking in creature comforts these days. Quite frankly, it amazes me that your father chooses to remain there."

Once more, Nik was irritated by Santorini's tone, especially as he was close to criticising his father. He doubted that he would voice his amazement so freely to his father in person.

"What is about to happen? Why do you need to leave?"

"Nothing that need concern you, Nik. Although I do need to teach you some of our history, about the Vampire Wars, the Council, and the Code. Yes, the Code is about to become a part of our history, along with the Council in its present form. Get ready, Nik. I will educate you as we travel. One hour."

He was gone.

CHAPTER TWENTY-NINE.

The bright sunlight burned against Kat's delicate new retinas, and she quickly closed the blinds on the window again. Unsure of her whereabouts and totally disorientated she began pacing the room, prowling, fuming.

She had awoken as Michael Rabb took her from the bed at the Sanctuary and even though her vampire strength and senses were at a new height, she had been unable to fight against him, either physically or psychically. Whoever he was, he was indeed a powerful vampire. He had not spoken to her except to tell her that fighting him would be futile and the truth of his terse statement was immediately apparent.

Rabb took her to a room that was little more than a prison cell. There was a simple divan bed and an en-suite bathroom and nothing else. There was no clock, but by the degree of burn in her eyes she knew that the sun was high in the sky. She thought it was probably somewhere around the early afternoon. Michael Rabb had not made an appearance since he had dumped her unceremoniously on the bed and told her that he would return later in the day, that she would not be able to escape and that she would be better resting than wasting her energy in trying to do so.

Her thoughts were solely on Rabb and his motives. Why had he taken her from the Sanctuary? Who was he? A vampire of considerable power, that was obvious, but there was something else, something that she couldn't define. He had an air of authority and was obviously used to having his instructions obeyed, but beyond that she thought she sensed ruthlessness and compassion. The whole picture was confused.

She wondered where he had gone. To sleep ahead of

the night, when presumably he would be at his best and be out seeking to feed? The house had been cloaked in the pastels of the dawn when she had arrived with him after travelling, seemingly, hardly any distance at all. And throughout the house there had been no sign of any other presence. He had carried her from the moment he had picked her up from the Sanctuary bed and stepped from the window ledge out into the night. His physical strength was phenomenal and even with her own new-found abilities she had been unable to free herself from his iron grip.

Reaching out with her heightened senses she knew that she was still alone in the house, a solitary prisoner. She had tried for over an hour to open the door to the room and failed and from the pain in her eyes when she opened the blinds it was obvious that she would be unable to cope with the sunshine without darkened lenses. It was easy to see where the literary and Hollywood myth of vampires burning up in sunlight had come from, however exaggerated.

It seemed she had to be content with waiting for his return.

Kat sat on the bed and listened, searching the neighbourhood to try and identify sounds and aromas that may give away her location. She locked onto a woman, frustrated and worn out by her crying baby. Concentrating on her hearing she was suddenly surprised when she found herself 'looking in' on the scene. The woman was young, not much more than in her late teens. Her hair was unkempt and her face was lined and haggard with lack of sleep. Her one room flat was untidy and Kat could sense the despair even from her distance. Her heart went out to her and the child and she wondered if she could make her presence known and give some kind of comfort.

Before she could put this to the test, her consciousness returned to her own predicament and her surroundings. It had been a shock and one that she hadn't thought about.

Her physical senses were heightened to the ultimate degree, so why not her psychic abilities? Both Lane and Andrei had both shown this capability but she had assumed that it was a trait that came with time and experience. She tried to re-centre herself back on the young girl, but although she could still hear the infant crying she could not overlook them again.

Thoughts of Lane brought Beckett into her mind - if only she could reach out psychically to him; draw him to her, to her rescue. She became irritated at her own frustration and scorned herself for the fantasy of her ideas. Then, as suddenly as it had happened before, her consciousness travelled outwards again, and this time it found a target that responded to her immediately.

She sensed him at first and then 'saw' his burning eyes, felt the searing power of his thoughts and heard him as he whispered to her across the ether.

'Where are you, Katerini? Ah ... I see you; a beautiful prisoner and you wait for your rescuer, no? How romantic. Sadly, real life is not that way. Or perhaps, it is. Shall I be your rescuer Katerini? Will you come with me? Shall we journey together? I appear to be too late here, and have missed those I sought, but instead you have found me. I will come for you, it seems that you have transformed into a very beautiful vampire. I sensed that potential in you when I gave you the darkest of gifts and I can see that I am not to be disappointed.'

Kat surrendered her mind to the seductive depths of Andrei's consciousness. She had no idea of how she had managed to connect with him, but the warmth that arose within her, softly stroking her mind and being with its sensuous tentacles, robbing her of any resistance.

"Andrei," she whispered aloud. "Help me. I will come with you. I want you, want to be with you."

His voice was at the very centre of her being and she heard his every word within her essence, within her cells. *'Remember,'* he whispered, *'Remember how you became what you are now. Relive it, moment by moment and I will come to you, following the energy of that memory. Always there will be this*

191

connection between us, Katerini. It is I who made you.'

"I remember," was all she could say; her whole being now somewhere else. She saw again the emerald light within the absinthe, the heavy velvet drapes on the ancient four poster bed, the flicker of the seductive firelight. Then she felt his hands on her body, persuading again, searching her again, finding her again.

She writhed in pleasure at the sensation of his mouth at her throat, breast and thigh, and as he released the crimson life force from her vein she passed from pleasure through ecstasy and finally into hunger. A hunger so deep that she felt that it would never be quenched.

Until she drank from a vein that still pulsed with life.

In the time it took for the thought to lodge in her mind, she was off the bed, alert, sensing the other's presence.

He had come.

"Katerini, go to the window. The sun will burn your eyes only momentarily. Step out onto the ledge and I will be there should you fall. Trust me Katerini. I will not allow you to come to harm. I need you too."

Kat sensed truth in his words and warmed to him again; he was not as bad as Lane and Beckett had tried to paint him. They had their own agendas, and after all it was Andrei that had come to her aid, not Lane or Beckett, and it had been Lane that had left her vulnerable at the Sanctuary. To hell with them both.

She went to window and only hesitated momentarily in pulling back the heavy blind. The sun had lost some of its earlier potency but the tingle on her retinas was instant and progressed to a burning in moments so she squinted against its glare.

"Come Katerini. Trust me. I will shield you from it."

She opened the window with little more than a thought; it had been unlocked all the time, her captor relying on her daylight blindness to confine her. Her painful eyes streamed and the dazzle was almost unbearable. She put her forearm over her eyes and stepped out onto the window ledge.

"Step out, Katerini, step out and into my arms."

She took her arm away and found herself looking into Andrei's sultry face, his hungry eyes, his high cheekbones. His arms were outstretched as he once again defied gravity and hovered in front of the window ledge. His eyes blazed crimson and his sensuous lips were parted revealing the white sharpness of his elongated canines.

And she stepped out.

***

The reception area and desk at the Sanctuary was deserted and no sound came from anywhere within when Lane eventually returned. She had driven directly to Santorini's home to find the place empty. It didn't matter, she had his lair now and there would be another time.

Despite the advancing daylight, Lane felt more alive than she had for days. Although she possessed an innate dislike of violence and killing, she had no qualms in dispatching anyone of her kind who preyed on the innocent and the vulnerable. Killing the old man had been distasteful but tinged with satisfaction that there was one less perverted predator prowling her territory and preying on young girls whose mother's should be taking better care of them. She despaired of modern society and its lack of cohesion. It all stemmed from the breakdown of the family and family values; no wonder the kids were angry, they had every right to be. It was such a shame that their reaction was one of violence and disrespect. She shook her head, trying to dispel the path her thoughts were taking. She needed to be positive for Kat, she was going to travel to hell and back before she could come to terms with her new condition and she needed Lane and Beckett's protection. Already she'd been away too long, but it had been necessary, finding the whereabouts of Andrei was equally important if she was going to protect Kat properly, and it coincided with the quest for her own answers.

She was at the foot of the stairs before the stillness of the place hit her. She stopped and reached out with her vampire senses. Something was very wrong. She could only detect a single heartbeat in the building, and that was human.

In a single fluid movement she was on the landing and seconds later she threw open the door to Kat's room. Jane lay curled up asleep on the bed. Of Kat there was no sign.

Lane shook the sleeping girl forcibly, immediately aware that her sleep was unnatural.

"Jane. Jane, wake up. What the hell ....?"

The girl stirred and struggled to open her eyes. Lane crossed to the window and yanked open the curtains.

Jane sat up slowly. "Doctor Dearing?"

Lane lost no time in probing the girls mind, sensing immediately the shield on her memory placed there by one of her own kind. "Jane, release your mind to me. I need to see what happened here."

Jane nodded, all too aware of the nature of the Sanctuary and its business and its patrons. Lane's tone left her in no doubt of the urgency of the situation. She took a deep breath and closed her eyes, willingly allowing Lane entry to her deepest consciousness.

"Good girl. Thank you," said Lane softly, trying to allay the girl's fears.

She saw Kat asleep on the bed and Jane answering the intercom. The scene flashed to outside the room then and she felt the thrill of the seduction as Jane surrendered to Michael Rabb. Then she saw the empty bed and Jane falling asleep on it, totally oblivious of all that had taken place. Now though, with Lanes probing, she was all too aware.

Her hand flew to the tingle on her neck and throat where Rabb's seduction still lingered. The thrill of his touch was still fresh on her skin and she felt her response as if she still lay against his chest. Her eyes filled with tears as she realised the enormity of what had happened.

"Oh, God," she whispered in a strangled voice. "Oh, my God. I am so sorry. I ... I should have ..."

Lane put her arm around Jane's shoulders. "Shh. It's OK. It's my fault. I shouldn't have left her. At least I know where to find her, thanks to you allowing me in." She took in the girl's distress; it wasn't fair to leave her this way. The fault hadn't been hers. Lane didn't know the human that would be able to withstand Michael Rabb's intentions, fair or foul. It wasn't without reason that he held such a high post in the Curia and given her earlier misgivings, she was alarmed to the edge of panic.

She probed Jane's mind one more time, erasing once more the memories of what had taken place. '*Sleep again,*' she instructed the girl.

Jane would wake unaware of the events of the previous night and Lane had left the suggestion that she had slept for only moments.

Lane closed the door gently, a grim expression etched on her face, now for Michael Rabb. What the hell did he want with Kat, and how did he even know about her? And where in God's name was Beckett? This would be the second time she would have to tell him that she'd lost Kat and didn't look forward to it in the slightest. She felt an unreasonable resentment of him. *Damn the man.* As for Rabb, she decided that surprise would be her best tactic, although this relied on the fact that he wouldn't be scanning his surroundings for other vampire presences.

Proconsul Rabb lived in an old Celtic manor house, a stereotypical dwelling place for a vampire of his great age, as the ancients seemed to take comfort from the history in the fabric of their homes, especially when built of stone which probably stored more memories than they did, having been on the Earth longer.

Her thoughts were interrupted by the harsh sound of her cell phone. Irritably, she clicked it into life. "Lane

Dearing," she snapped.

The silky smooth voice that replied did nothing to soothe her. "It appears we are both missing something, my dear. I sense you already know of my interest and are planning to visit me. Come, dear. I look forward to receiving you." The line went dead.

Lane fumed inwardly at the arrogance of Michael Rabb and at her own transparency to him. What the hell did he want with Kat?

Lane had the distinct feeling of being summoned to the headmaster's office and it irritated her. Her problem was that she had no choice than to obey the summons as Michael Rabb was her immediate superior within the Curia. Well, she would go, but he could wait.

She turned her attention back to her phone and dialled the number by heart. It rang for longer than normal and she was about to hang up in frustration when a young voice answered.

"Hello? Paul Beckett's phone."

Recent memory cells kicked in and she recognised the voice. "Oh it's you Darius. Put Beckett on, I'm in no mood for games."

"Dr Dearing? Um ... Beckett is ... asleep right now. Can I give him a message when he wakes?"

"Asleep my arse. Passed out drunk, more like. Shake him, pour water over him, whatever it takes to get him conscious and on this phone in thirty seconds. Starting now."

Lane's foul mood communicated itself immediately to Darius and remembering her power and potential fury; he blanched and let the phone slip from his hand. He turned on Beckett who appeared unconscious on the sofa. He shook him by the shoulders vigorously. There was no response.

Darius briefly contemplated the water option but a glance at the size of Beckett's fist changed his mind. He shook him again. This time Beckett grumbled incoherently.

The third shake brought his eyes open, unfocussed initially, then processing his surroundings quickly. His gaze landed on Darius.

"What? What's up?"

Darius nodded to the phone lying on the coffee table. "It's Dr. Dearing. And, um, she sounds upset."

Becket had experience of Lane 'upset'. He snatched the phone.

"Lane, what's happened? Is it Kat?"

"I'm afraid so Beckett. I left her for a while …"

She didn't finish the sentence before Beckett was down her throat.

"You left her? *You left her?* What the hell were you thinking? *Were* you thinking? Where is she?"

Lane's silence said everything. Beckett's anger slipped into fear. "Christ, Lane. Where is she?"

"I'm sorry Beckett. I had to leave her. I'll explain when I see you, but I didn't leave her alone. Jane was watching her. I thought she'd be up to it. I was wrong."

"What to do you mean? What wasn't she up to? Lane?"

"Michael Rabb. He turned up just after I left. He must have been watching me, waiting for me to leave. He wouldn't have risked trying to take her if I'd been there. But Beckett, I had no idea he had an interest in Kat. I can't imagine why or what he wants with her. Any ideas?"

"Michael Rabb? The Proconsul of the Council? I have no idea what the hell he wants with Kat. Unless … didn't you say that the vampire that made her in Greece, was an Ancient, and a powerful one at that."

"There's more to this Beckett. I don't like it. And I'm afraid for Kat. You see there's a problem. Rabb doesn't have her anymore."

Beckett ran his hands through his silver hair. "*What?* What do you mean he doesn't have her anymore? Lane?"

"Look, this is getting us nowhere. I've been summoned to Rabb's house. I'll come over when I'm done."

"You're not going there alone. Wait for me Lane. I'll

come get you."

"Don't be ridiculous Beckett, you're still drunk. I know I can't die in the normal way of things but getting mangled in a car crash isn't my idea of fun, no matter how fast I'd heal. Stay there, just in case Kat contacts you. I'll see you later." There was a click and she was gone.

Beckett stared into the phone as if it would give him answers. He shook his head, as though to clear it. It didn't work. Darius had been silent while Beckett had been on the phone, but as he moved quietly into Beckett's kitchen his presence became apparent again. He filled the kettle and began searching the rag tag collection of cupboards for Beckett's coffee supply. Whatever was going on, it was obvious that Beckett needed to shape up and quick. He heard the shower running and opened the fridge; he'd have time to get some food into Beckett. That's if he had any. A quick glance gave him the option of left over pizza, some suspect looking sausages, eggs, or something that he couldn't identify wrapped in crumpled tinfoil. He opted for the eggs, and grabbed the milk along with it. A sniff told him that while it wasn't the freshest, it was unlikely to cause any lasting damage. He doubted that herbs were ever an item on Beckett's shopping list but found some dried chilli at the back of one of the cupboards - that would wake him up.

Beckett appeared in the doorway, his long silver hair was wet and tousled but his eyes were clearer. He looked bemused at the kitchen activity.

"Coffee and devilled eggs, no pun intended," said Darius.

"Coffee's fine, bin the eggs," Beckett replied.

"You need to eat. Something tells me it will be a while before we get the chance again.

"We? What's with the 'we'? I brought you home with me because I thought it would be better than getting drunk on my own. You didn't tell me anything I didn't already know. So, there is no 'we'. Okay?"

"No. It's not okay, actually. My brother Andrei is involved in all of this. I know it. I may not be the Hunter I wanted to be, but I'm still going to kill him when I find him. Besides which you have no idea where to start looking. From what I gathered from your phone call, Kat is missing again. Do you think she's with Andrei?"

Beckett was silent for a while then he said, "You know I think maybe she is, there's no-one else that would be able to take her from Rabb. And they have a connection now, he turned her and he won't want to let her slip away while he can still control her. Come on, you can drive. I'm still way over the limit."

"After you've eaten. Trust me, you need something inside you beside Jack Daniels."

Beckett laughed, "Who made you my mother?"

"Not likely, but the sooner you eat, the sooner I'll drive you. Where are we going?"

"We'll start at the club. I know he wasn't there earlier but maybe we can find a clue as to where he may have gone. Hey, these eggs aren't half bad," said Beckett through a mouthful of chilli and scrambled egg.

Darius was thoughtful. "She must have something he wants. Or can get him something he wants. That's the way it works with garbage like him."

Beckett mulled it over. "If he's got her, and I think he probably does, her sire would probably be very grateful to have her back, don't you think?"

"Her sire?" Darius queried.

"It's the vampire term for the one who made her. Made her, mind you, not turned her."

Beckett paused and paled as a look of horror crept over his face. "Oh, my God, he's taking her to Greece."

CHAPTER THIRTY

Andrei relied on everyone assuming he wouldn't show up at the club for some time. They knew he was arrogant and reckless, but even he wouldn't be so foolhardy. They knew him not.

Once inside his penthouse apartment again, his confidence soared and he turned his attention to Kat, prepared to enjoy her before he took her to her fate. To her sire in Greece.

His elongated fingernail hooked itself under her chin, lifting her face into the candlelight of his darkened rooms. He looked at her long and hard and her newly awakened vampire senses began a dance of their own. His arm was around her waist and he began to slowly turn in a tight circle, never once moving his eyes away from her own. He didn't speak, allowing the intensity of the moment free rein.

Suddenly she felt her consciousness leap into his and become wrapped in his memories and experiences. His earlier promises of exotic places and secret locations viewed from vampire eyes were now become reality. She felt as if she had never lived before, born right then at that moment, all her life prior to that minute erased as nothing. He held her in his power and transferred nothing of it to her, enjoying her for what she was, the most beautiful vampire he had ever seen, her own power still quiescent but hinted at, her potential as yet untapped, waiting for the moment when its release would make her one of the most powerful also, a queen among the vampires. At that moment he had no doubts, she held the power of the ancients, her sire had bequeathed to her the ultimate gift: immortality, power and a blood lust that would emerge untamed and unquenched. He was going to enjoy her in a way he had never enjoyed a woman before.

It is said that when two vampires make love, the energy released contained the power of a nuclear explosion. It was why it rarely happened. The two parties would vie for control over each other and what began as lovemaking would inevitably end in a fight that brooked no mercy. Vampires on the whole found sexual gratification in their victims and not their own kind. But Kat was different, she was a challenge he could not resist, provoking his appetites to action and prodding his arrogance into a blind search for dominance. He knew that while she was still under his influence, her potential was no threat to him, but he was excited by the fact that at any time she could become a match for him in every way.

There was no need for seduction. Kat was aware of the power building within her that had little to do with animalistic sex. That would simply be the vehicle which would carry her energy outward into the world until she stood alone in her vampire state. Her own potential, unharnessed as yet, thundered like a river in full flood through her veins needing the merest heartbeat to send it coursing through her. She tore her eyes away from Andrei's hold, in itself a demonstration of her latent power, and searched his throat for the hint of a pulse. Her disappointment exploded as she realised that he was indeed one of the Undead.

Reading her, he pulled her to him. "Katerini, you cannot drink from me again. It would be your undoing. Drinking once from my veins conferred on you eternal life and unending possibilities. To drink twice would end your life as surely as ripping out your heart."

Incandescent light flared in her eyes and in a single moment Andrei realised that he had vastly underestimated Kat's power. Her canines elongated in an instant, leaving her no time to adjust, and the bloodlust raged to the surface in a snarl. Her face contorted into a bestial mask and hissing, she turned on Andrei, pulling free of his vice-like grip. Surprise had given her the edge, but only momentarily. He threw his consciousness over her like a mantle, subduing her just enough to gain control. He grabbed her and pulled her to him, fury replacing lust. His strength when given full rein was immense and he tossed her across the room onto the four poster bed as though she were a helpless kitten, and was on top of her, pinning her to the bed by her wrists, before her crazed efforts to gouge his face bore fruit.

She lay under him breathless and tears of frustration welled into her eyes and fell onto the pillow. Sensations and emotions eddied inside her like a demented vortex. Desire, lust, rage, hatred and hunger. Most of all, there was the hunger.

"Katerini, stop. I cannot feed you, not without destroying you. Calm yourself and I will take you with me. Together we will hunt and feed and you can feast on the living blood of your prey and live as you were meant to live. Not spoon fed, half-dead blood from insipid donors, but fed on blood taken from pulsing veins, still warm, still with the scent of the life-force enhanced by the terror your prey will feel. It is truly the most sensual fragrance in this dreary world, Katerini. Let me share my world with you and then ... then I will take you home."

Kat had ceased to fight him, his overpowering physical strength way out of her league despite her newly acquired vampiric abilities. And his voice still had the power to enchant her, to take away any resistance to his demands. She lay quiet; her rage hushed rather than abated, her hunger at a peak that tormented her to the point of agony.

"I am going to release you now, Katerini. But I warn you, if you try again to attack me, I will kill you. You know that I can and will, in an instant and without remorse. Do you understand?"

She nodded. The fire in her eyes became more subtle, almost muted, but it remained, fuelled by the intense hunger. She turned her face to him.

"What did you mean, 'take me home'?"

"Your true home Katerini. I will return you to your father. In Greece."

"My father is dead. He died several years ago. They said it was tuberculosis, but I know better now. He died because he carried the vampire gene."

"I don't mean him. I mean your vampire father, your sire. The one who made you."

Understanding dawned on her as she pictured the tall, elegantly dressed man that had sparked in her the latency that was now in full bloom, and the night she had fled from the tiny monastery, leaving Greg behind her.

"What makes you think that I need you to take me there? Or if I actually want to go there?"

"Because Katerini, I know something you don't. At this very moment, your precious son, Nik, is in the hands of one of the most ruthless vampires I know. And they too are on their way to him. He calls you to him from across the oceans, from beyond the tomb that holds him. It will be quite the family reunion. Very touching. And you need me, because if Santorini gets hold of you, he will not spare you, he will not flinch at watching you die as he takes off that beautiful head of yours. Now I call that a shame, and such a waste. I can protect you. He will only see you as a distraction for the Ancient One, taking away the kudos of him retrieving the ultimate prize, his son."

"Nik? Nikolos is going to him? Why? Why would he do that? He hates the vampire in him and came to me looking for a cure. He wouldn't go there willingly."

"You think so? I should tell you that Santorini is very pleased with his progress. He has made his first calculated kill and has begun the path to refinement. I do not think he will be looking to you for any cure, my beautiful one. Not now. Not ever."

"You bastard. How long have you known this?"

"Only since last night. It was this knowledge that gave

me the idea of finding you and taking you to the Old One. He will be delighted with you. Any vampire would be. And I expect he will show his appreciation to me for bringing you safely to him."

Kat attempted to wrench herself free of his grip one again. He pinned her harder to the bed.

"Now did I not just say that I would not be happy if you kicked off again? Do I need to remind you?"

He let go of her left wrist and slapped her hard across her mouth. Blood appeared at the corner and her tongue was on it in an instant. Her eyes flamed red and the hunger surged inside her teased by the taste of her own blood.

He let go of her and she threw herself on him and began kissing him with a frenzy that came from her own tainted soul. He laughed at her from deep within his throat, sending her into the passion that he knew had only just been contained beneath the surface.

He allowed her to rip his clothing from him, and treated her in the same way but denied her full dominion over him. Her senses swam and she was aware of her body rising from the bed in union with his. He held her there in mid air, caressing her, stroking her hair and murmuring to her, implanting pictures of such beauty they took her breath away, then replacing them with scenes of carnage that only served to fuel her appetites to the extreme. He took her from the depths of despair at her hunger, to the heights of moaning ecstasy, enthralled at her own ascendancy from the pitiful woman she had once been, to the awe-inspiring creature she now was. If there had been no going back before this, there would be none now; her transformation only seeking her first raw feeding to complete the circle of her rebirth.

It may have been the Old One that had created her, but it was he, Andrei that had transformed her into this awesome vampire, and he took her so far into ecstasy that he almost became lost in her wildness as she met him as an equal, energy for energy, raw power for raw power. A volatile cocktail of destruction waiting to happen.

CHAPTER THIRTY-ONE

Beckett had grabbed a small Hessian bag as they prepared to leave his apartment.

Darius looked pointedly at it and then at Beckett.

"Want to know what's in there, do you?" Beckett growled.

Darius nodded.

Beckett threw the bag down onto the hall table and opened it roughly. Inside was a pointed wooden stake, a cook's knife and a butcher's cleaver. Darius paled.

"That's serious shit, man", he said huskily. "Or is it just the stuff of mediocre fiction?"

"It's serious shit we're dealing with, or didn't you realise by now? And I can assure you there's nothing fictitious about it, mediocre or otherwise. Get your head around it; there are limited ways to kill these bastards. They won't burn up in the sun. Not unless they get stuck out in it for extended periods, and even then it's not like the Dracula movies. Unless they are deeply religious and of the Christian faith, a cross or crucifix will do squat. They have to be separated from their head and their heart and fire won't do it. Now can we continue with your education as we go? You haven't done much homework for a slayer, have you? I still don't believe you realise how serious this shit really is."

"That's not fair. You know I do. It's just that knife and cleaver. You know, I guess it makes all this a bit more real."

"Lesson number one, Hunter. Sometimes it's not enough to ram a stake into 'em. You have to take their heads off. Otherwise, well, not to put too fine a point on it, no pun intended, they just keep coming back. Especially the Undead. They have to have their heart's cut out and their heads chopped off or they'll be back on their feet and ready to rip you apart before you can blink. So ... still want to be a slayer?"

"Not as a career, no. But I *am* going to kill Andrei. For my parents, and for me. You see, I remember the old Andrei; the one who used to play with me and read to me, the one who used to stick up for me when I was in trouble. It's for him too. That thing is not my brother. Where the hell are we going by the way?"

Beckett didn't answer him; he was busy dialling Lane's number on his cell phone. It was switched off and he cut off her voicemail message abruptly. No point in leaving a message; he'd keep trying until she answered him.

Darius drove in silence; they had not exchanged a word since they had left Beckett's apartment, and tension had developed between them that had no particular origin.

"Take me to Andrei's place, and if you can't drive any faster I might as well have driven myself. Pull over."

"I'm already driving over the speed limit. At least if we get stopped, I'm sober."

"All right, I get it. Beckett's drunk, well it won't be the last time and it sure as hell isn't the first. Now put your bloody foot down or pull over and let me drive."

"We're almost there, calm down. Have you thought about what we are going to do when we get there? I mean, assuming we can get into the place without the Spiderman act? And if we do and he's there, what then? Do you *have* some sort of plan? Because let me remind you, he's a mean son-of-a-bitch and he won't blink while he rips me apart. His own brother."

Beckett remained silent. The same thoughts were swirling in his head, accompanied by a crashing pain that was the beginnings of the Mother of all hangovers, and he was beginning to regret the eggs and chilli.

"Say we get in, say ...." Darius began.

"Say you shut up! Just for one damn minute, will you

please shut the hell up? I'm trying to think."

Beckett knew he'd acted impulsively. He knew he had little chance of gaining entry into the place without Lane, wherever the hell she was. And he was only too well aware of the enormity of taking on Andrei. The alternative, however, was too much for him to contemplate. He'd not acted in time to save Grace, not that he'd have known back then what to do anyway. But the outcome was the same. Grace had died. Turned into a feeding vampire by one of the Undead and she had risen as one of them. If Lane hadn't been there to end it, Grace would still be out there now, feeding and corrupting and tainting. His Grace, his sweet, innocent Grace, violated and destroyed while under his protection. He had failed her and now history had repeated itself but this time he wasn't going to stand by and do nothing. This time he knew how it would go and he was prepared for it.

Darius brought the car to a slow halt; they had arrived at the club whilst Beckett was deep in thought. He turned the engine off and sat motionless, staring at the Victorian edifice, focussed on the Gothic artwork around the sign 'Danse Macabre' which did not seem out of place against the stark frontage of the building.

"You know what that means don't you?' he said quietly. Beckett frowned. "What?"

"Danse Macabre. It means Dance of Death."

"Yes, I know." He looked into the young face, lined with anxiety. "Look, I think it would be better if you stayed in the car. I may need you to drive me the hell away from here a bit sharpish. Keep the engine running and if I'm not out of there in ten minutes, call Lane. Understand? No stupid heroics that won't do any good. Just get Lane."

"No way. And in any case, you're not in yet."

Beckett laughed harshly. "No?" He pointed to the front door that was obviously open. "Arrogant son of a bitch is inviting me to the party. Well, it wouldn't do for me to appear rude by refusing such hospitality. And you will do as I say, or I'll lay you out cold myself. I mean it, sunshine."

Darius was deeply resentful of the way Beckett spoke to him and wasn't about to take orders from someone that he saw as a beaten, drunken ex-priest on a quest for vengeance that he had little or no chance of gaining.

He remained silent but gave a cursory nod in Beckett's direction.

The door stood ajar onto a dark entrance hall, normally peopled with Andrei's heavies. In darkness and silence the club was bathed in a more sinister atmosphere than when the all the dark music, Goths and vampire wannabees, were present en masse. Beckett felt his heart thumping in his chest and his throat was dry.

In his haste he had left without a torch or light of any description so had to feel his way into the club's main area where he had seen Kat and Andrei take the lift to the penthouse apartment. As his eyes accustomed themselves to the darkness he could see the overhead sign proclaiming the room as 'The Lair' and the outline of the various booths and seating areas around the place as he headed towards the far side of what to him seemed like an arena. He trod lightly across the central open space where Goths and vampires alike regularly gyrated to the Danse Macabre. A quick glance around told him there was no staircase other than to the viewing balcony, no alternative route to the penthouse; he would have to use the lift. He hoped that Andrei would be sufficiently occupied with Kat to not hear the whirring of the lift mechanism as he ascended and at the same time wished her a million miles from there.

The silence was heavy and even the sound of his breathing seemed to reverberate through it. He held his breath and approached the lift doors.

He pressed the button to call the lift and the clanking that accompanied it shattered the deathly quiet.

"Shit!" he hissed. *Ah well, if he didn't hear that he's either not here or he's one dead vampire.*

The lift doors opened surprisingly quietly, and closed behind him in the same way. He pressed the only button inside and the lift juddered to a start and then ascended smoothly and silently. *Maybe he still hasn't heard anything. Maybe I'm Queen Elizabeth.*

Andrei lay on his side next to Kat, propped up on his elbow. He had never seen such awesome beauty and power in a newly turned vampire and the power their lovemaking had unleashed had left him weakened as both sought ascendancy over the other without actually shedding blood.

He stood up and leaned over the ornate antique dresser, opening the small door to a cupboard on the top. He took out sparkling crystal, two goblets and a decanter glinting with the emerald light of absinthe.

Kat moved across the bed and stroked his back, nuzzled his neck, then pulled herself away as the urge to bite overwhelmed her. She slid her tongue across her teeth, willing the canines to retreat. They didn't.

Andrei read her, penetrating deep into her psyche.

He held up the crystal glass of absinthe. "Drink this, take in the green fairy that lives in the absinthe. She will enhance your pleasure in the feeding. I sense your hunger Katerini, soon it will be over and the hunger will be satisfied. Come. Drink."

Kat took the glass from him, her eyes locked into his. She took a sip from the bitter liquid that lit a fire deep inside her belly. Since her turning she had eaten nothing and drunk nothing other than the tiny cup of donated blood in the Sanctuary. She looked at him questioningly.

"How?" he asked. "It's the magic of the absinthe. You will be able to tolerate it in small amounts. It brings your heightened senses. And speaking of which, your old boyfriend is here."

Kat looked stunned, momentarily thrown off balance. Then she closed her eyes and concentrated, reaching out with her vampire sense, listening, feeling, smelling. It was true. Beckett was in the building.

Andrei laughed from deep in his throat. "How very convenient, my love. Your dinner has come to you."

In a fraction of a second Andrei was off the bed and into his clothes, his shirt hanging loose and torn where she had ripped it from him in the height of her passion, his taut muscular chest glistening in the half light. He was at the door before a human eye could have detected his first movement. Kat was at his heels.

Beckett stared at the lift door, somehow knowing that on the other side, Andrei stood waiting for him. He needed no vampire senses; his gut told him.

Momentarily he wondered if he should pray, then dismissed the thought. Prayer had done him no good when Grace had stood on the threshold of life and death, and he had been a priest back then. Back then he'd had faith. He realised now that didn't give him any advantage at all. When you were stuffed, you were stuffed. He had turned away from his God that night and not looked back at him since. To him, there was no God. God was dead.

His throat was dry and the minutes ticked away, and with each second his chest tightened and his heart hammered harder under his ribs. He swallowed hard, unzipped the hessian bag and took out the wooden stake. Hawthorn: deadly to vampires. More effective than impotent prayer.

This one will be for Grace.

Bile rose in his throat as he lunged forward and hit the button to open the door. Stake raised above his shoulder he powered forwards as the door slid open. Andrei stood in front of him and Beckett brought his arm down towards the vampire's chest. Midway through the arc of descent his eye caught a glimpse of Kat as she was suddenly standing at Andrei's right hand. He hesitated for less than a second before striking. It was all Andrei needed to bring him to the floor.

Beckett had been up close and personal with several vampires since Grace and he had no illusions as to their power and potential. Now, flat on his back, half in the lift and half out, with Andrei's vice-like grip on his throat, he was at the mercy of one of the most heartless of their kind.

Andrei bared his fangs and sensed the warm throb of the precious liquid in Beckett's veins. He gave his characteristic throaty laugh as he read the resignation in Beckett's mind.

I'm going to die. Right here, right now. And I don't know what will happen to my soul. I have no faith. I can't pray. I'm lost.

Andrei threw his head back, his sensual mouth wide and ready for the kill.

"*No!*" Kat screamed.

Andrei spun around his eyes blazing, the ravening mouth framing a bestial snarl. He hauled Beckett to his feet with one hand and with other he struck Kat hard across the mouth and grabbed her by the hair. In a few strides he was back inside the apartment and he threw Kat, whimpering against the wall with a heavy thud. Andrei's grip on Beckett's throat had clamped off his windpipe and his face was a rapidly turning to a deepening purple. He dragged him into the elegant living room and down onto the sofa. He tightened his grip even further and Beckett felt the waves of unconsciousness washing over him for the second time that day. The last thing he heard was Kat sobbing.

"Katerini! Here!"

Kat tried valiantly to control her weeping, to find the power that she knew lay within her but the fire in Andrei's eyes held her mind and she could do nothing but obey.

She moved towards him, afraid for the first time in his company.

Andrei's face was suffused with rage and even though she closed her eyes she was unable to block the image. Beckett lay, out for the count and Andrei had grabbed her arm and wrenched it behind her, his face only centimetres from her own.

"Don't ever, *ever* do that again. Consider yourself fortunate Katerini that you have a value, or I would be feasting twice this night."

He hit her again and this time her sharp canines split her lip. Instinctively she licked at the blood and instantly felt her power returning. It was not enough. She was facing Andrei's anger for the first time and she knew who – inevitably - would win the contest. She tried to control her breathing and began to feel the thunder in her veins subside to a muffled throb with a deathly pace. The blood continued to run onto her chin.

Andrei's rage had not been spent and he hurled her on top of Beckett.

"Now, Katerini. Now, you will show me where your allegiance truly lies. You are hungry and need to feed, and here you have a meal. Feed."

Kat's voice shook, "Please Andrei, please, I beg you. Not him."

Andrei grabbed her hair again and thrust her head forwards. "If you do not, you will both die. His death will be painful and demeaning and you will watch. Then I will feed from you and force you to feed from me. I told you what will happen if you do that, but until you have witnessed it's agony you cannot begin to imagine the exquisite pain. Now, *feed!*"

Katerini leaned forward over Beckett's pulsing throat. She smelled the blood in his vein and felt the tension in her mouth as her canines elongated into deadly spears. She hesitated inches from his flesh and choked as a sob birthed somewhere deep in her soul. She swallowed hard, a mixture of her own blood and saliva. She looked into Beckett's worn and beaten face. The lines seemed deeper than when she had last seen him, and he looked tired beyond measure. His torture was etched on every crease on his face. A release? His self torture would be over, and he would find his peace in Grace. She had to believe that.

A hiss sounded from just behind her ear. "Feed. Drain him or watch him die at *my* hands."

She knew she had no choice. If she didn't obey Andrei she knew they would both be dead. If she was careful, maybe Beckett wouldn't die. Andrei tightened the grip on her hair painfully and pushed her once more towards Beckett. She closed her eyes and leaned into him, but before she allowed her mouth near to his neck, hidden from Andrei's eyes by her curtain of silky hair, she kissed him on the lips. Tenderly at first, then allowed herself the last moment to kiss him deeply, momentary flashes of regret about what might have been, quashed by the cold hit of reality.

She buried her head in Beckett's throat. Her long sharp teeth piercing his skin and vein easily, her mouth receiving the crimson flow as if it were consecrated wine. She swallowed and the red veil descended over her as she was oblivious to the man that had once been her friend and would-be lover, aware only of Andrei's distant laughter.

She was lost in the blood.

CHAPTER THIRTY-TWO

The voices were strange. Familiar somehow, like voices that had been distorted for a movie, slow and drawling and deep, like a tape being played on the wrong speed. There were two of them, a male and female. Images tried hard to gain entry in his upper consciousness but they melted away like ice in a hot bucket. He was weak and sick and incredibly thirsty.

It all came into focus then. Kat. And Andrei. And what followed. This was it then. He was dying. In all the times he had gone against a vampire he had never once thought that he would die, not even when his chest had been laid bare and bleeding, bloody broken ribs open to daylight, not even then. And Kat, poor Kat, he'd failed yet again. Maybe it was better this way. Maybe this was his payback for Grace. Maybe …

"Aaargh!" the pain ripped through him sending searing tongues of agony throughout his entire body. His back arched and went rigid before a massive seizure took hold. Foam forced its way from between the clamped jaws. His breathing stopped and he felt the pressure as his lungs fought to draw in air that would not oblige. The blinding pain again, and this time he could not scream. He had nothing left. No breath, no spark, no fight. He slipped into the nothing of the darkness.

He felt himself being pulled upwards into the nothing. There was no light, no tunnel, no Grace and no God. If he had been alive he would have laughed at that. Now he knew the truth. After death, there was only eternity in the dark void of your own consciousness. Son of a bitch.

Something was wrong. There was someone else in his

eternity and a delicate fragrance that reminded him of someone.

"Grace?" he whispered.

"Oh, my God. *Oh, my God.* Get him on the stretcher *now.*"

"Grace?"

"It's me Beckett. I'm here. Hold on."

He felt himself being lifted and set down and then movement. And the movement heralded the return of the searing agony. He felt a sharp stab in his forearm and then slow warmth that cloaked the pain and shrouded him in a mist of confusion. He surrendered to it.

"Get him to the Sanctuary. Don't stop for anything, blues and twos. Go."

He rested in the warm haze; whoever was barking the orders was obviously in control. He'd ride it out and see what happened next. Maybe there was a process, some sort of half way station between life and eternity.

Maybe he was going to be one of those souls that roamed the earth in endless unrest. Ah, shit.

There was another pain, this time centrally in his chest. A tight pain that sent its emissaries into his face and down his arm. It was then that he realised he had been breathing again. Until then, that was. Because then his heart constricted and stopped. It was in the split second before that, that he heard the alarm of the monitor. A thump on his chest and a voice high and commanding. "You get back here, Beckett. You hear me? Get back here, right now!"

And it was then that he saw her.

"Grace," he said.

Her arms were extended and she smiled at him.

Now he was hallucinating.

"It's all right Paul. It isn't your time yet. You'll be going back in a minute. I just wanted you to …" She faded out.

"No, no wait. Grace."

There was a rushing sensation as though he was riding

the tornado to Oz. His eyes jerked open.

Then Lane was leaning over him, listening to his almost imperceptible pulse. No need for a stethoscope, she heard its every feeble beat and sensed its unsteady return. She let out a deep breath.

He looked at her, confused and hurting like hell.

"You had me going there for a minute, Handsome."

He wanted to ask her if he was in Kansas. He wanted her to smile, to lose the fear in her ancient eyes, fear where he had never seen it before, but all he could do was blink. The quips could wait for later. It wasn't the time: it wasn't his time.

He slept then, a deep natural sleep untroubled by bad dreams. They would come later.

He opened his eyes three hours later to find Lane sitting by his side, her aristocratic features lined with concern.

"Hello Handsome, nice to see you back. How do you feel?"

"I feel like crap, how do you think I feel? How did I get here? How did you know?"

Beckett struggled to sit up but Lane put a restraining hand on his shoulder. "No, don't try and sit up. Not yet. I need to check you out first."

"Thought you did that years ago." He tried again unsuccessfully to get up. Lane pushed him down gently.

"You can thank Darius for the fact you're here and not dog meat in a dark cupboard at the club. He called me as soon as you went inside. I was on my way to Michael Rabb's place. "She pulled a face, "I'll still have to face the music for disobedience. Anyhow, Andrei must have thought better of an encounter with a member of the Council, especially as he seems to have plans for Kat and in any case, I had to make a choice. Go after them or get you out of there." She smiled at him in a way he'd never noticed before. "No contest, Handsome. And it's hardly surprising that you feel like hell, given the thrashing your body's taken over the last few days, to say nothing of the empty bottle of Jack. I think you have a death wish, Beckett, but I'm sorry to disappoint you, it looks as though you'll have to wait a while longer. Now lie still, I need to take some blood from your arm."

"Hungry, are we? And for the record, you need to work on your bedside manner, Doctor."

"Not funny. Though I have often wondered how you'd taste. But again, I am going to disappoint you, I'm afraid. Now don't be difficult, I need a syringe full of the good stuff to test it. I need to see if the Anti-HVV worked."

"Anti-HVV? What the hell have you pumped into me? Bloody leech. And just how long have I been here?"

"You know, you are so charming when you are in this mood, Beckett. I'll explain when I'm sure you really are okay. You've been out for hours, and you've had seven pints of blood. Now, *please* lie still."

She lifted his arm and attached a syringe to the needle already in his vein and withdrew the blood she needed. He didn't take his eyes from her face, watching as she became the professional in an instant. As she turned to leave, he caught her wrist.

"Lane, tell me what's going on. Kat ..." There was a fleeting second when he saw shadow, a hint of pain on her face.

"Rest, Beckett. We'll talk when I've done the test." She wrenched her arm from his grip.

"It wasn't her fault. She had no choice," he persisted.

"Beckett we *all* have a choice. Now rest. I won't be long." She turned to leave, "Do I have to lock you in? Or send you to sleep again?"

He knew that he wouldn't be able to stand and shook his head, a movement he instantly regretted as the room swam around him and he felt violently sick.

He heard the door shut quietly behind her and closed his eyes against the whirling walls. Kat's image came unbidden on the screen of his memory, she was leaning over him, her amethyst eyes had been clouded with pain, but not the pain of her latency. This was a deep, emotional pain. He put his finger to his lip where he remembered her kiss. It was soft and gentle and spoke of something that could have been kindled into life given the opportunity, but was now firmly in the past. He tasted her blood in his mouth and when she bit him, he had felt the salt of her tears sting the tiny puncture in his throat. He felt his own eyes fill and squeezed them tight, and the first tears slid down his face. He sniffed hard and swallowed. He didn't hold with a man crying. It wasn't what he did. What he did, was to get even.

He turned his thoughts towards the whole scene. Andrei in a rage, manhandling her and pushing her down to his throat. He would pay for that. But not that day.

Lane returned before his thoughts took him into further misery.

He looked into her eyes and saw the relief in them, which instantly transmitted itself into his own being.

"Don't tell me. I'm pregnant."

Lane laughed aloud. "God, Beckett, what will it take?"

"To do what?"

"To make you take your own life a little more seriously."

"Don't know what you mean. So, what happened? What did you give me? And I want it straight"

"A new Anti-HVV. It's still under development. I've never used it before and it was either going to bring you back safely or enhance the virus she transferred to you in the bite and kill you. I still don't know if it's only temporary or if we'll have you around for a while longer. Straight enough?"

"It'll do. So where did you get the stuff? Doctor Frankenstein?"

"I can't go into that right now. Let's just say I acquired some for the Sanctuary in not quite a legitimate way. Like I said, it's experimental. You're my first lab rat."

"Such an honour. Now, help me up. I always think that a man falling flat on his face lacks dignity, don't you?"

Her arm was around his shoulders, supporting his abortive attempt. The twitching muscle in his cheek betrayed the clenched teeth as he tried again. This time Lane lifted him with her arm. He sat on the edge of the bed, keeping his eyes firmly fixed on her, away from the carousel that was the walls of the clinic.

"So, what is this Anti-HVV then? And what the hell happened? I can't remember anything after Kat ... well, you know."

"She drained you. Or near as damn it. You, um, well it looked as though you were starting to turn. "

He started to protest and she quashed his outburst with a look. "Hear me out. Something strange is happening, Beckett. I have never seen anyone other than a Latent turn like that, and never so quickly. The Anti-HVV is supposed to arrest the process. It gives a massive boost to the immune system, attaching itself to the white cells in the blood and attacking the virus, at the same time it actively works to kill off the mutated cells. Well, that's the theory. The problem is that it causes such a shock to the system it can kill instantly if it takes the wrong way. The last time it was used the patient died immediately. I had to take that chance," she said abruptly as she sensed his outrage. "It was either that, or sit back and watch you turn. I couldn't do that Beckett. Not you. So, I took a chance."

The enormity of what she was saying weighed on him like a leaden cloak. "Thank you," he said thickly.

"It was touch and go, you had a seizure and your heart has taken a bashing. I still don't know if it was the Anti-HVV or the virus that caused it. Beckett, I had to do it. I had to try."

He caught hold of her hand, "Of course you did. So, is it working?"

"Honestly? I'm not sure. It looks hopeful. There are definitely less vampire cells in your blood. And there is an increase in your T cells."

"I hear a 'but' coming."

She nodded. "But there is a marked decrease in your red cells. The Anti-HVV seems to be having a detrimental effect on the cells carrying haemoglobin."

"So, what does that mean? I'm anaemic?"

"If it doesn't continue, yes, anaemia is the result and I can treat it easily. It's called haemolysis, the red cells are dying off rapidly and if it gets out of control, it will mean a transfusion to see if we can arrest the process. Then if that doesn't work, there's haemodialysis."

"And if that doesn't work?"

She was quiet for a moment, then, "It's not good Beckett."

He remained silent, his cheek muscle twitching.

"Like I said, it's looking positive but I need to keep testing your blood to watch the progress of the Anti-HVV. You need to get some rest, now. I'll be right here. I'm going nowhere."

"Lane, I'm worried about Kat. And before you say anything, I know she wouldn't have done this unless Andrei had forced her to. "

"It doesn't matter Beckett, she crossed the line. I don't know how long I can protect her now. She's turned and feeding and that isn't the worst part."

"What?"

"There's a difference in the virus. It's mutated from the original viral strain. It's the vampire virus but it's stronger, more resistant. That's why I risked the Anti-HVV. Beckett, you have to know that it may come to the worst for her."

"No. Lane, no. There must be something. " His memory of the event played out again, there was something that bothered him and it suddenly became clear.

"There's something you don't know," he said.

Lane looked at him intently, trying to probe him but failing. She was too damn close to him. "What?" she asked.

"Before she bit me – well, took out half my throat I should say -, before that, she kissed me."

"Goddamn it Beckett, this is no time for romance. So what? So she kissed you, I'm glad for you, I really am, now can we move on?"

"You don't understand. She was bleeding. From the mouth. It looked as though Andrei had roughed her up a bit. Anyway, when she kissed me, her blood was in my mouth. It didn't register at the time. But I remember it now. Her blood was in my mouth … and I swallowed it."

Lane shook her head, biting the inside of her lip to control her emotion. Damn Beckett. If he wasn't involved she wouldn't hesitate when she caught up with Kat. Why was everything so complicated?

She looked directly at him, "Beckett, I'll try, but I can't make you a promise I may not be able to keep."

He saw through the mask to her emotions, he knew her better than anyone else. He was the only one she'd allowed close in centuries. "Try is good enough for me. But I am coming with you and that is that, I'm feeling stronger by the minute."

She looked serious. "That's what is bothering me, Handsome. By rights you should be in intensive care on some goddamn machinery. But look at you. I've seen you look a damn sight worse."

"So, what the hell are you saying?"

"I'm saying that either the virus or the Anti-HVV is somehow making you stronger while at the same time it's killing your red cells. I'm saying that because you drank her blood and she infected you with her bite as well, unless I can reverse this process you will end up like her."

"Holy Mother of God," he whispered.

Lane nodded. Her heart ached for the man who had become her dearest friend. Over the centuries she had avoided forming unnecessary relationships where she could, but somehow Beckett had got under her skin and into her heart, albeit a vampire one.

"Let's hope it works then," he said quietly.

CHAPTER THIRTY-THREE

Beckett slept in between Lane taking blood samples. He opened his eyes to find her standing at his side looking grim.

"Oh God, it's happening isn't it?"

Lane didn't reply, she turned her head but Beckett had already seen the glisten of a tear on her cheek. Lane didn't do crying.

She turned to him quickly, "I don't know Beckett. There's still a battle going on in there. I'm afraid that if you lose any more red cells I'm going to have to set up a transfusion."

"If you're going to do it, get on with it. I told, you I can't hang around here, they've already had a night and day's start. He's taking her to Greece. I know it."

"Beckett, how can you be so sure? And as your doctor I should tell you that you aren't fit to go anywhere, but I know I may as well save my breath. I'm going to take one more blood sample before I set up the transfusion. Lay still a minute."

She took his arm and attached the vial to the needle taped into his arm. The blood flowed slowly into the glass tube in her hand.

"Lane, if it – you know – well if it does go that way. I want you to take care of it."

She took a sudden breath in and gasped at him, her eyes wide. Shocked at his meaning, her hand clenched involuntarily around the tube which immediately shattered into her fist. A mixture of Beckett's blood and her own crimson flow ran down her arm and dripped into a shiny pool on the floor.

Beckett lunged at her before she could react. His face

contorted into a mask of something wild and dark, he snarled at her and the sound that came from him was dark and tortured as he grabbed her hand, pulling her towards him, his mouth wide.

Her vampire senses and strength took over and she yanked her arm free and grabbed at the chair which she had sat vigil in. She brought it easily high above her head and crashing down towards Beckett's head.

As quickly as the insanity had arisen, it faded and she brought the chair down to the floor instead of cracking his skull. The look of horror on his face mirrored hers. He locked his terrified eyes into hers and slowly shook his head. Lane pulled a towel over her hand and wrapped the already healing wounds inside it, then moved to his side and put her other hand onto his arm.

"Beckett…"

"Don't. Don't say anything. I'm sorry, Legs. Well, that's it I guess. There's your answer. Now, what are you going to do about it?"

"I'm going to figure out a way to fix this. And you are going to have to co-operate. Yes, it looks bad, and as I suspected there is something different about Kat. This wouldn't have happened normally. Uninfected people don't turn like that after the bite. I've never known it. Never."

"Well, I'll take comfort from that. Thanks," he replied dryly.

She appeared to make a sudden decision and turned to the trolley beside her. "I'm putting up a unit of blood. See what that does. And … "

"And?"

"And I want to try something, but you need to agree."

He didn't move or say anything.

"I'm going to give you a double dose of Anti-HVV. I don't know what will happen. It's a risk, Beckett and you need to make the call."

"Do it. Do it now." He closed his eyes.

She wasted no more time on talk, reaching for a loaded syringe, and pumped its contents into his arm. She leaned into him, listening to his heartbeat, erratic and weak then pounding. Then silent.

"Beckett! Beckett, don't you dare!"

She listened intently, her own hearing far more reliable than any heart monitor. There was nothing. Beckett's heart had stopped. For an instant she considered full resuscitation and then instinctively knew that this was the nature of the virus in the final stages of the turning. If Beckett was brought back then, she didn't know what he would come back as. And she remembered her promise to him. She felt a pain deep inside, the pain of grief that she had tried so hard to avoid over the centuries by not allowing any human into her heart. She allowed herself this moment of pain; for Beckett. Then, as suddenly as the silence within him had come, there was a faint flutter, then another, then – miraculously - a heartbeat. And another. Then another.

His eyes opened slowly. The glint of life in them was unmistakeable.

"Beckett? Thank God, Handsome. Thank God." He was back, and the whys and wherefores didn't matter to her.

"Don't thank him. You did it, not God. I told you before; he and I don't get on any more."

"Whatever, Beckett. But you should know that not many survive a single dose, let alone twice that. And look at you! Goddamn it, I don't understand it."

"So, what now?"

"Now, we wait and see. I'm going to look at your blood again. I'll be right back.

He hadn't even noticed her collecting the sample. His mind was racing, pictures of Kat and Andrei tearing through him, searing into his thoughts and emotions. He clenched his fist and banged it into the bed. Lane looked up at him, ready to react to his sudden aggression.

"Don't worry; I'm not going to do anything. But you need to know that I'm feeling scarily better."

Lane didn't answer him as she left with his blood.

Beckett's mind seemed on fire, and he began perspiring. There was a yearning for something he couldn't quite reach, a need for something he didn't recognise. He fought it, determined to wait for Lane. He needed her now like he never had.

As if in answer to his racing thoughts, she appeared. She seemed to walk with a lighter step and there was a new light in her eyes. He read relief in them.

"It's too soon to be sure. But there are no new vampire cells and no more red cell loss. I think it worked, Handsome. I really think it worked."

"Of course it did. I could've told you that. Just wanted to be certain."

"I said I wasn't sure yet. Don't get too excited."

His answer was to step off the bed and hug her.

"Beckett, get back on that bed. You have to rest."

"I'll rest when I'm dead. Which thanks to you, doesn't seem to be any time soon. Let's go, Legs. You can tell me about that damn Anti-HVV as we go".

He grabbed her arm and headed for the door. Lane shook her head in disbelief; he should be dead, or at least as near to it as wouldn't make a difference to the Devil. "Where? Where are we going?"

"Greece," he said grimly. "Get your passport, Doc."

CHAPTER THIRTY-FOUR

Santorini and Nik had arrived at Thessaloniki and booked into the Presidential Apartment of Les Lazaristes, a luxury hotel just ten miles from the centre of the city and directly opposite the Moni Lazaristoni, housing the State Museum of Contemporary Art. Santorini relished the proximity of the culture, and the taste of the cultured.

The hotel manager had been deferential and personally attended to them, dismissing footmen with a wave and escorting them in the private elevator direct to the apartment, where a butler waited to greet them. Nik frowned. He knew that Santorini had obvious wealth, but the Presidential Apartment? He had quickly noticed that it was not listed on the accommodation list in the lobby. It wasn't let to just anyone who had the cash, you had to be known. And the apartment itself was something that Nik had never dreamed of. His life had become surreal, being catapulted from an angry young vampire on the periphery of the vampire world to companion of Santorini, the silken-masked vampire who held prominence and dominance in that society, despite his young age compared to others of his kind. Nik guessed he must have been in his mid-twenties when he had become one of the Undead. Santorini had chosen to mentor him and bring him to his father, the reasons for which were now apparent. Nik was a pawn in a dangerous game, but pawns did not have to be sacrificed to reach the king, if he played the game with Santorini until he had taken from him all that was available, he would watch for the opportunity that would free him to find his father on his own.

Nik had been quiet throughout the journey, brooding on his immediate future. What would his father be like?

Would he, Nik, disappoint him? What plans did his father have for him? Did he even know he was on his way?

Santorini had allowed him to dwell on these things, reading him, inwardly amused at the boy's remaining doubts about his potential, unsurprised by his plans to leave his protection and seek his own destiny. The arrogance of the boy. There would be time to bring out in him that which would make his father grateful for his care and teaching. For now, the boy was hungry. He sensed it, not yet was he able to subdue the ravenous sensations that would only be satisfied by one thing. He had done well, bringing Nik to a peak and now the pleasure of the polishing would fall on his father, and that would earn him extra credit in his eyes. And there was his added bonus. The Anti-HVV didn't work. Not in the way Nik's father Gregori, wanted it to but it had properties that would propel Santorini to his rightful place on the Council.

Each time it had been tried, it had failed dramatically, usually killing the victim within an hour. Gregori didn't know that. But he would soon enough. When it was too late. And then he, Santorini, would take his place; with a weapon such as the Anti-HVV, no vampire would be able to stand in his way. Gregori wanted the Anti-HVV to use for the good of the vampire world, to help them to integrate with humans and live side by side. Santorini despised him for this. Humans were their food and nothing else. What Gregori proposed was blasphemy. It demeaned the power of the vampire and reduced them to weak copies of their full potential. But he, Santorini, would use the Anti-HVV to rid the vampire world of the half-bloods, the Latents. Surely such a race as the Vampire deserved to be kept pure, its weaknesses eliminated. If Gregori was too old and blind to see that, then he had no right to wield the power that the Anti-HVV would bring him.

Nik brought him from the depths of his obsession to the present moment.

"When do we leave for Parthavos? I'm anxious to meet my father. When?" he demanded.

"Soon. I have already told you. There are still some basic skills that you need to master before I take you to him. I will not give you to him without completing the foundation of your education. We are here in Thessaloniki because I can't bear the thought of staying in the kind of places that Larissa has to offer. We are farther away, but it is worth the delay. "

"Then let's get on with it. How much more can there be? I know how to feed and not kill. I know how feed and take the life. I know how to …"

Santorini cut him off. "I am aware that you know these things. Thanks to me. Remember, without me, you would still be a young punk cruising the club for the occasional meal and eventually fall foul of Andrei. He would have enjoyed you, Nik. He likes a challenge. Just as he has enjoyed your Mother."

"Don't keep calling her that." Nik spat the words from his mouth as if poisoned. "She is not my Mother. She is nothing more than a whore. He is welcome to her. I want nothing more to do with her or even to discuss her. I hope she rots in Hell."

"Oh I doubt she will be doing that. When I saw her last, she looked radiant, quite the most beautiful vampire I have seen in a very long time. Those eyes, and her smile, they will take her far in our world. It is a great pity about the remnants of compassion that still linger, but that will change. In time. And Nik, time is one thing that she now has in abundance." He laughed; amused at Nik's obvious surprise at the fact that he knew so much of Kat.

"Oh yes, Nik. She has fed, and turned, and belongs to Andrei. For now. I doubt if he will be able to keep her when her full potential is reached. She's quite something. In fact I intend to bring about a reunion. Mummy and Daddy, together again. How touching that will be, do you not think so?" His face darkened at the look of rebellion from Nik.

"What do you mean 'reunion'?"

I mean Nik that I intend to take her from Andrei. I intend to take a double gift to Gregori. His son and his bride. I do so love a wedding, don't you?"

"You're mad," Nik said quietly.

Santorini was on him in an instant, no longer the benevolent mentor. The whites of his eyes flooded crimson, his canine teeth elongated and treacherous in a heartbeat. "Listen to me, and listen well. You have no say in what happens to you until I hand you over to your father. Do you understand? It was never my intention to bother with her; I thought she would be a distraction, that it would somehow dilute the gift that I would bring to Gregori in you. But now I see it differently. Now I see it as being twice the gift. And as I said, it will be a touching family reunion. Now sit down and hear what I have to say. There are things you need to know. Things that are about to change our world."

He waited for Nik to sit next to him.

"Centuries ago there was no Vampire Council, just random pockets of our kind. Then the virus began to mutate and there were others, like us but not like us. Latents, born of humans but somehow carrying the dormant gene. Half breeds that had the ability to turn when bitten and allowed to consume the blood of their sire. It weakened us, made us vulnerable. The Born, or the pure blood vampires, rose up against them and what ensued was a bloody war that brought about the deaths of thousands of our kind and theirs too. The result was the formation of the Code and the Council to administer and police it, allowing the vampire community to live alongside the humans. For centuries it has been a weakening force on the Born and now they are ready to fight again. This time they will not stop until there are no half bloods left. And that would include you, my friend, and your mother, and, unfortunately me. Except for one thing. Gregori.

Gregori is as near to the original of our kind that there is, a direct descendant of the source, just as you are a direct descendant of Gregori. Not one of us knows his true age, but he is considered one of the Ancient Ones. The only one left. He commands too much respect for you to be in any danger. Without his protection, you will eventually be wiped out. And without my protection you will get nowhere near him. So, you see, we have a mutually beneficial effect on each other. My price to Gregori for your return is a place within the Curia, and protection from the cleansing that is threatened."

He carried on, telling the boy of dark times and bloody wars that no side won. He painted word pictures of such carnage and death that Nik sat motionless, shocked at the imagery.

"If the wars were so bloody why doesn't anyone talk about them? I never heard of vampire wars, and as far as I know they are in no history book."

"They took place so long ago Nik; predating written history, they only live on in the memories of the oldest of the vampire houses, families if you like. The powerful ones anyway. They remain alive by oral tradition."

"So why go there again?" he asked.

"Because this time we have something that will make the need for the spilling of all that pure blood unnecessary. This time there is a weapon. And I have it. And I intend to do what is always done with an item of value. I intend to sell it."

Not for the first time did Santorini's sanity become doubtful in Nik's eyes.

"Sell it to who?"

"Sell it to whom, Nik. To whom. Why, to your father of course."

Nik ignored the jibe at his lack of refinement and education. "Why would he want it and why do you know that you have access to him if he's so important? "

"You don't need to worry your pretty head about that,

233

Nik. Trust me. He will want it." He hesitated, pondering whether or not to tell Nik the truth of his relationship with Gregori, then made a sudden decision.

"I have access to Gregori quite simply because he was the vampire that made me. Along with your mother, he is my sire. Now, enough. There is an attractive young couple in the bar across the road, and you must be hungry. I know I am. Come, let's feed."

Nik's head swam with new concepts and dark images that only served to fuel his hunger. He closed his eyes and allowed his senses to travel to the taverna opposite, seeking out the prey that Santorini had already condemned. His inner sight came to rest on a young couple, oblivious to all but each other, as it should be with all honeymooners. He smiled, the energy of the prey already taking hold of his consciousness; love and lust and dreams of a happy ending that would never be. He would take their love and taint it, twist it back on itself until its narcissistic tendrils found their way into his own being and their lust, unfettered by the emotion of love would fuel his desire for the unsuspecting nymph on whom he would feed. He moved towards the door.

Santorini held up a hand. "Wait Nik, I believe you are ready for your next lesson. They are sitting in a very public place, and to take them from there would lead to unwanted attention. So what do we do?"

"Call to them? Plant a suggestion that they leave?"

"Yes, it's possible. But we are going to go in and take them from there without being seen."

"Become invisible? How?"

"To the human eye, yes. In truth, our movements will be so quick that a human eye can not track them. It means taking the couple out at the same speed. To other human eyes, one moment they will be there, the next – gone."

"How is that possible?"

"By listening to me. Are you ready?"

"Oh yes," said Nik.

"Now, I am going to the lobby and you will join me. You must connect with your musculature and know that you can move faster than the human eye can detect. It takes time but time you do not have if I am to take you to your father tomorrow."

"Tomorrow?" Nik's mood soared. He could do this. If Santorini could do it and believed that he could do it too, then do it he would. He turned his consciousness inward and reached to his vampire musculature, sensing the connections and the synapses as his nervous system went into overdrive, then by concentration and every atom of his being he felt his body respond to his inner commands. Corridors and elevator blurred and passed in fractions of seconds and when the whirlwind of his movements stopped and his consciousness returned, he was standing next to Santorini.

"What kept you?" he asked Nik. "Not bad, but the old lady over there in the armchair saw you appear from nowhere. You have to tidy the settling better. It looked to her as though you materialised from thin air. You have to learn to cloak yourself as your body stills. I have blanked her mind and now she just thinks she had another 'episode'. But this time you will get it right. Shall we?"

They walked to the front door and Santorini was inside the mind of the doorman instantly. He would not remember the salute to the guest in the Presidential Apartment and his young friend. He would not remember the hefty tip that Santorini pressed into his hand as he clouded the curious mind.

"Are you ready?"

In tune with Santorini's cue they settled at the side of the young couple who were still exchanging whispered endearments and promises. Momentarily the young girl looked up and shivered; someone had walked over her grave, she thought. In that instant her mind disconnected from her new husband as Santorini entered her conscious mind and paralysed it of all thought. He nodded to Nik.

"Take her," he said. "Just grab her and take her. I will deal with the man."

In less than a second Nik had grabbed the girl around the waist and taken her outside the taverna and across the road to the front of the hotel. He stopped and smiled to himself. He looked up and concentrated on the light in the window of the apartment. He thought of the balcony and began to rise into the air as Santorini had previously shown him, only this time he took his prey with him. He landed on the balcony with a soft thump. An instant later Santorini was behind him, the young bridegroom limp in his arms.

They fed on the blood of the innocents and drained their bodies, Nik devouring the girl's life blood without pause. His hunger was raging out of control and the blood wasn't going to be enough to satisfy him. His eyes betrayed the lust that boiled within him and he knew that it wouldn't be the last time that he fed that night.

Santorini knew it too. He put a restraining hand on the boy's arm. "Be careful Nik. All things that a vampire has to learn come easily to you, but it makes you careless. Remember, we are not truly immortal. We can die, and in this country that knows about our race we cannot afford carelessness. Go and roam the back streets of the city if you will, but leave no trace of yourself." He nodded to the inert and bloodless bodies at his feet. "I'll take care of this. We leave tomorrow for Parthavos."

Nik left the apartment with a nod. There had been a young waitress in the lobby earlier who had smiled at Nik; he was about to become better acquainted.

Santorini pushed the call button for the butler who appeared silently after only a minute or two and bowed in deference to him.

Santorini prodded the body of the young man with his foot. "Alexi, will you clean this up please?"

"Of course, sir. Perhaps you would make yourself comfortable in the salon whilst I dispose of it for you. It will only take a moment. I have brought the laundry cart in anticipation of your needs. Is there anything else I can do for you?"

"Ah, Alexi, you always make my stay here so much more enjoyable. It's good to know that I can rely on you. You will, of course, be amply rewarded."

Alexi bowed again, "It is enough to serve your house, sir." He returned to the corridor and wheeled a large laundry cart into the apartment and deftly placed the bodies inside it, covering them with a sheet. A glance around told him that further clean-up was unnecessary. As was always the case with Santorini, he savoured his prey and spilled nothing, but the boy, he had been certain, would have been careless - but he had obviously been too hungry to waste a drop. Satisfied that there was nothing further required of him, he left as quickly and silently as he had arrived.

CHAPTER THIRTY-FIVE

Michael Rabb held the telephone in his hands for several minutes before deciding to dial the Prelate's cell number. It would be easy to reach him telepathically but that would mean opening his own consciousness to a vampire that he didn't quite trust.

He wasted no time with irrelevancies and spoke out as soon as he heard the Prelate's voice. "Prelate, I thought I would reassure you that the matter of the Patriarch has been dealt with. It would appear that there are to be some changes within the Council. I believe it would be in your interests if you can come up with the Anti-HVV that you have long promised us."

"Michael, so nice to hear from you. The Anti-HVV is in fact ready, but there is one more test I wish to carry out before I hand it over to you."

"Prelate, the Born are uneasy and there are rumours of another war. I cannot stress the importance of this to you. You know that the Anti-HVV will ensure my position as the new Patriarch, and you have my assurances of your own position once that is confirmed. As allies, we will command the balance of power within the Council, and I am certain that I need not explain what will happen if you double cross me now. The Anti-HVV, Prelate, I want it within the week. Or our alliance is cancelled and I will assume that you prefer to be considered a threat rather than my eventual successor."

"I am sorry, Michael. But the final test is crucial; you wouldn't want to hang your banner on the promise of Anti-HVV that doesn't work? I will get the Anti-HVV to you in one week."

"Good, I wouldn't want to have to discount you as a

friend, Prelate. There is too much at stake. With the Patriarch and his outdated principles and codes no longer obstacles to us, it is time to take the places on the Council."

The Prelate frowned but did not hesitate in his reply. "I assure you Michael, you have my full support and I know that I can persuade many others to stand behind you. The Anti-HVV will be in your hands in one week. It is an honour to be able to assist you, Patriarch."

"Thank you, but a little early to address me that way. Have a caution, Prelate, that your enthusiasm for rebellion and change doesn't bring our plans to the attention of those who would thwart them. In one week, then."

Michael Rabb cut off the call before the Prelate could reply. He still didn't trust him and once he had the Anti-HVV safely in his hands, the Prelate's short and illustrious career on the Council would be brought to a swift conclusion. He didn't have a taste for constantly watching his back, and he sensed that would be the outcome of allowing the Prelate further power and his support.

Rabb frowned as he filtered the information that his senses relayed to him. The Prelate was not in the country. Images of the remote monastery screened themselves on his inner eye. He was going to Gregori.

***

Lane and Beckett left the Sanctuary in grim silence, neither of them underestimating the enormity of what was to come. If they found Kat in time, it was unlikely they could do anything to save her from the fate of what she had become and it was highly likely that Andrei would still be with her. There would be plenty more blood spilled before the nightmare was over, and the chances of it being their own were high.

Lane had left her car discretely out of sight of the Sanctuary and, as they approached it, Beckett groaned. She followed his line of vision.

"Shit!" she yelled. Every one of her tyres had been slashed. This was no time to be victim to vandals. They would have to waste time calling a taxi to take them to the airport.

"Care for a lift?" Darius stepped from out of the shadows.

"You little bastard. You do this?" demanded Beckett.

"I'll pay for new tyres when we get back. That is, if we get back. You didn't think you were going without me now did you? Nice job Doc. I thought he was a goner for sure. How'd you do that? Or maybe it's best if I don't know."

"Shut up, Darius. Before I forget it was you that called me in time to help him. It's a stupid and dangerous game that you're playing, but I believe we are going to need all the help we can get from here on in. Are you up to it? Is there a slayer in you after all? Because if not, stay away, you're likely to get yourself killed. Or worse."

"I deserved that I suppose. But I've already told Beckett; maybe not as a career move, but I intend to kill Andrei. Then I'll see. Meanwhile we're wasting precious time standing here arguing. My car's just here, engine running and there's a flight to Athens in four hours and I have three tickets waiting at the airport."

Lane frowned. "That's good but unnecessary. I made a call to a friend. His private plane is waiting for us in Cardiff. They have a lead on us that needs shortening." She looked thoughtful. "If you're really up to it, you can come with us. If not, as I said, stay away. We can't afford any more liabilities."

Beckett's face relaxed and almost made it to a smile. "Okay slayer, let's go."

"Do you think you could stop calling me that? It sounds kinda stupid."

"Look kid, you're no Van Helsing, we all know that, but you'd better get your head around this if you intend getting on that plane. There is a high probability that you won't be coming back. In fact, none of us may get back."

Darius opened the car door, his expression grave. "So, what are we waiting for?"

They remained mostly silent throughout the drive to South Wales Airport. Each of them contemplating what may or may not lie ahead. Darius's thoughts were on Andrei and how he may possibly succeed against him. Beckett's head was full of Kat; her kiss and the promise it once would have held, a million years ago. Lane's mind was flitting between the black silk-masked vampire and the ancient one that awaited them. She knew that eventually Santorini would lead her to him.

All of them knew it may come to the ultimate sacrifice; that they may have to pay the highest price.

A uniformed pilot awaited them at the airport door; he took their passports and ushered them towards a VIP lounge. The turboprop jet was ready for them at the gate with a thirty minute window for take-off.

Beckett turned to Darius, "Last chance, Slayer. No one will think any less of you if you walk. It even crossed my mind briefly. So, as I have said so many times in my previous life, 'Speak now, or forever hold your peace'. We can't afford for you to get in the way when things get rough. And they will. One way or the other, there's going to be death. So, if you come, you're in it to the end. If you can't do that, then leave now. No harm, no foul."

Beckett's voice had been hardly a whisper, his face remained impassive but the stormy grey eyes had turned to granite.

Darius took in a deep breath and turned away from Beckett, his eyes closed, then almost immediately swung round to face him. His face had hardened to his accepted role and Beckett could see determination in his eyes.

And something else. Something dark.

Darius didn't speak, and the nod of his head was imperceptible, but for a fragment of time he locked his eyes into Beckett's and the understanding was clear. They would stand together.

Then, something was wrong. A fleeting feeling of unease, leaving Beckett shaken. Then it was gone. As quickly as it had arrived, the feeling vanished, but it left behind a legacy. He began to perspire and tremble and his vision blurred. There was a high pitched whine in his ears. He grabbed at Lane a moment too late to prevent himself crashing to the floor.

Reaction was immediate. People backed away, an alarm sounded in the distance and running footsteps brought two burley security guards on top of them. A sign of the times.

Darius knelt at his side as Lane yanked at his shirt, ripping off buttons as she fought to get him more air. Her fingers searched for his pulse. It was there -, weak, but there. She blanched as she noted his heart rate. Not only was his pulse getting weaker, it was also slowing down, beating less than twenty times a minute. Her stomach tightened, she had to get him out of there.

Beckett opened his eyes and walls carouselled around him as the sensation of being pulled out of his body through his stomach overwhelmed him. Lane grabbed on to him and squeezed his arm so hard the pain allowed him to focus on her momentarily.

The security guards were talking into radios and the empty space around them had grown, and thankfully, someone had killed the alarm. Lane looked at the guards to discover which of them would be the most difficult to influence. One still had his back to her, radio to his face; the other, a youngish man with the physique of a Welsh prop forward was looking directly at her, waiting for answers. She had no choice. Her eyes met his and grabbed the root of his consciousness. She had to be quick.

Clouds formed in his mind and drifted around his head. He hadn't even felt the moment when his will had been relinquished to her control. *It's all right. He'll be fine. He's diabetic, I'm his doctor. He just needs some space and an insulin injection.*

The other guard turned around, his radio at his side. "There's an ambulance on its way, madam. In the meantime, may I see your boarding cards?"

Prop Forward touched his arm. "No need for that, Jo. This lady's his doctor. He's diabetic and needs an injection.""

His partner appeared to be going to say something, then changed his mind. His shift was almost over and he had a long awaited and hard gained date with the girl of his dreams from the information desk, and getting involved in any 'incident' that would require lengthy paperwork in triplicate before he could leave held little appeal.

"You sure?"

Prop Forward nodded. "Yeah, sure. See you later."

"Madam?" he persisted.

Lane smiled at him. She knew how to work her womanhood when necessary. "It really is okay. But he needs his injection right now."

She tried implanting the thoughts that they should both just leave them alone but Beckett's condition alarmed her and she became disconnected.

Still appearing doubtful, he gave in. "If you're sure …", he nodded at his partner. "Okay, see you later."

Lane didn't have the luxury of feeling relief as he walked away. She knew what Beckett's problem was; the virus had taken hold again. She made a grab at her bag and pulled out a case holding a syringe and a small vial. Beckett's only chance was another shot of the Anti-HVV. Without ceremony but with extreme precision, she jammed the needle into his arm and pushed hard on the plunger of the syringe. Her vampire senses heard his heart rate steady before any physical signs were apparent, then imperceptibly his colour returned and the thready pulse began to strengthen. She allowed herself to breathe again.

She brushed back the stray silver hair that clung to his forehead in the film of perspiration that coated his face.

His eyes were moving back and forth at a tremendous rate beneath his closed eyelids, and his breathing was erratic. Flashing thoughts of Beckett's history and images of the night she had sat with him, watching his sister rise from the dead, a vampire with the most horrendous of potential, and the subsequent beheading and removal of her heart. The night he had stopped being a priest and turned his back on his God.

Beckett, you poor sod. You don't deserve any of this. What did you do to piss off the Fates, this much? She was stroking his forehead when he opened his eyes at last.

Her breath came out in one long exhalation of relief.

The uniformed guard turned to his radio and reassured the security centre that all was well; the diabetic man that had collapsed had responded quickly to his insulin shot, and at Lane's insistence he cancelled the ambulance.

Beckett tried to stand and found it harder than he expected, losing his balance as the walls still swam around him even though he felt stronger with each minute that passed. The shaking and sweating had stopped and the whine in his ears was down to a tolerable buzz.

The pilot was at Lane's elbow in that moment and steered her and Beckett to his left. Darius strode ahead.

"We can board straight away; our slot has been brought forward." He handed runway passes to the security guard and before he could question Beckett's condition, they were out of the side door and heading towards the aeroplane.

Half way up the steps, Beckett's legs began to shake again. His look to Lane said *'It didn't work.'*

The interior of the plane was luxurious and Lane pushed Beckett down onto a plush leather sofa as once again he slipped into unconsciousness. Feeling for his pulse, her eyes betrayed her alarm. His heart rate was so fast she could hardly count it and every now and then there was a long pause between beats as his heart muscle seized.

She was losing him.

Darius remained pale and quiet, his eyes haunted by memories of his own family experience now being played out in front of him in Beckett. His brother, Andrei, was going to pay dearly, whatever the cost. Because he knew he couldn't face a future without putting an end to the horror that had kept him from sleeping for the past ten years. He knew there were others, and that there would always be, but he knew his soul would never rest while Andrei walked.

Lane's eyes had never left Beckett's face. He was still with her, but his heart continued to beat at an unsustainable pace. He would have a heart attack very soon unless it slowed down. There was nothing else she could do. She didn't dare to give him any more Anti-HVV; there was no way he would stand up to it. What she had given him would either work or it wouldn't. She paled as the thought fixed in her mind, '*Oh God, please don't let me have killed him.*'

As if in response to her panic, Beckett opened his eyes again and Lane noticed his pulse rate slowing by the second. 200 -160 – 140 – 120 – and settled at around 90. Lane shook her head. With all he'd been through in the last thirty-six hours, Beckett should not have survived.

He stirred and lifted his hand onto hers. "S'okay Legs. I'll be all right."

Lane shook her head and struggled with her emotions. "Beckett, I don't know how long this will last. If the first time is anything to go by, only hours. I doubled the dose … I had no choice … so maybe a bit longer. I don't know if your body will withstand another."

"I was dead if you hadn't, I know it. Maybe I should be. I don't know anymore."

"Second guessing God?" she asked quietly.

Beckett closed his eyes. "We've been through this a hundred times. Our fate is our own, there's no God, no heaven and no forgiveness. We do what we do and pay the price. Here and now."

Lane sighed. "Okay, Beckett. I just meant that … well, maybe it's time to stop blaming yourself for Grace."

"So, what's in this magic Anti-HVV then?" He snapped, ignoring her comment.

Lane shook her head. "I don't know. I don't even know if it works, I only came by it a week ago. I know it has been developed by one of our own kind. Its aim is to prevent the latent turning. I know you weren't a latent, Beckett, but it was a last chance. Nothing else was working. Did I do wrong?"

"*I* don't know. *Did* you?" He was exasperated. "Hell, I'm sorry, Legs. It's been kind of rough."

"Tell me about it. You think you can sit up? Your pulse is almost normal and you've got a good colour. How're you feeling?"

"A bit of deja vu, I think. Like the first time, all of a sudden I feel okay. A bit tired maybe, but that's all." He looked intently at Lane. "So, what do you think that means, doctor?"

"I don't know Beckett. And I'm not going to try and guess."

Darius stood up and began prowling around the compartment. He had a wild look in his eyes, when he turned on Beckett. "Well, if you want to know what I think. I think the damn stuff not only isn't working, it's having the opposite effect! I think you're turning."

"Well, as it happens we don't want to know what you think. You're here under sufferance and because we both think you need keeping an eye on. For your own safety of course. So sit down, and shut up," said Beckett, dryly.

Lane put her hand on Darius' shoulder. "I think maybe you should sit down. Get some rest. I have no idea what is waiting for us over there."

He appeared about to protest, but thought better of it. The glint in Lane's eye belied her softened tone.

Lane smoked continually during the remainder of the

journey.

"Hate to tell you this, Legs, but it's illegal to do that anymore. He nodded at her cigarette.

"So, sue me."

None of them spoke further until the small plane landed at Kozani airport. Andrei and Kat had all flown into Thessaloniki, restricted by commercial airlines and flights, whereas Lane and Beckett had made up for their lost time by landing at Kozani and now had a chance of catching up with them.

Kat's transformation had been rapid. There was no denying now the vampire within. Her only hope remained with Beckett and Lane and that the Anti-HVV may have the same positive effect on her as it had with Beckett.

Andrei had watched her carefully, admiring her beauty which was enhanced in every way, but aware of a defiant streak that he would have to curtail in her before he took her to the Ancient One. The final part of her transformation had been the ultra-rapid healing process and so the livid weals of purple and red that had covered her face had faded within an hour and her swollen and split lips had returned to their ruby fullness in only moments. Andrei alone would know of the beating that she had received at his hands for defying him and challenging his authority over her.

She was subdued and sullen during the journey to Greece and Andrei had made it clear to the stewardess in the first class compartment that they didn't want to be disturbed and that they would want no food or drink during the flight. Kat spoke to Andrei only when he spoke to her. She was sullen and not about to forgive him easily for the rough treatment but at the same time she knew that she needed him and she resented that fact.

It was late in the afternoon when they landed at Thessaloniki airport and Kat's heart had soared as she saw the familiar Byzantine church spires as they came in to land. The euphoria was only temporary though, as she was suddenly filled with a dread that bit into her soul. The reality of her condition and its origin hit her like an icy shower. Long buried memories, only recently awakened by Lane, flooded her. Images of an ancient vampire entombed in silver, and erotic scenes that sent shivers through her entire body.

Andrei tuned into the thoughts that tumbled around in her head. He frowned as he struggled to subdue his slowly rising anger and resentment at having to part with Kat. She fascinated him and enchanted him in a way that no other female had ever done, human or vampire. Perhaps the Old One would tire of her and she would return to him. They would make a powerful pair.

CHAPTER THIRTY-SIX

Santorini stood at a distance from the monastery of Agios Georgios watching the late afternoon sunshine reflecting in the upper windows creating the illusion of fire. He sensed the activity within, the anticipation and the general business that spoke of visitors. The following day was the first of the two feasts of Agios Georgios, the patron saint of the region, whose uncorrupted body lay in its silver shrine in the chapel of the monastery. It was the day that the people from the region came to pay their respects to their saint whose body had not decayed in death because of his goodness in life, or so they believed. It was the day that the silver padlocks were removed and the silver bolts drawn back and the heavily ornate silver side of the shrine lowered to reveal the uncorrupted corpse of Agios Georgios, better known in the vampire community as Gregori.

The people came from the surrounding countryside with their gifts and their offerings of fruit, bread, coins and wine as they had on that day each year for hundreds of years. And on that day Gregori awoke and rose from his self-imposed slumber and feasted not on their fruit or loaves but on the blood of his chosen innocent.

Sister Maria sat in vigil, as she had done for the last twenty nine years, tied to the monastery by her vows of obedience and the knowledge that her destiny lay there for good or ill. She prayed daily that it was for good.

She was uneasy that night, the air in the chapel seemed glacial and she was chilled to the bone. All day there had been a pervasive feeling of anxiety, reaching its peak with the arrival of a distinguished guest. And from the crumbs of information she had gleaned, there were more expected.

She was overcome with a sense of deep brooding from within the silver shrine, a faint movement, as if he was waking early. Her hands automatically went to her rosary and her lips began to move silently in their ancient prayers. She prayed to the Madonna for protection and for something else. She asked for the strength to do what had to be done, whatever that may be.

A light appeared in the gloom of the corridor and shuffling feet announced the arrival of Sister Agnes. She was the oldest nun at the monastery although Maria had never known her age. Her ancient face was etched with deep lines that made her appear timeless and in the twenty-three years that Maria had been at the monastery Agnes had never missed a single vigil. It was they alone that held the Ancient One in his self appointed containment, confined in silver. In all of those years it had always been Agnes that had unlocked the padlocks and allowed the heavy sides and top of the coffin to slide down and reveal their saint, Agnes that held the vigil on his feast days, and Agnes that locked the chapel doors when he had chosen the one who would provide the young blood that would give him sustenance for the following six months.

It was also Agnes that had cared for the donor, whose constant supply of blood over the previous thirty years had allowed Gregori to lay dormant, only waking on the two feast days. The donor was old and infirm and on the few occasions that Maria had accompanied Agnes to his tiny cell she had doubted he would survive much longer. He could barely lift his cadaverous frame from the mattress and doubts rose in her and wormed their way into her being. Her vows within the Order prevented her from questioning what was told to her as the will of God, albeit as interpreted by Sister Angelique. It was hard to always understand what God wanted from her.

The old nun's step seemed heavier, and she moving even more slowly than usual. Maria stood to greet her old companion and to offer her arm. Sister Agnes shrugged her away without looking at her and didn't speak as she moved painfully towards the stark wooden chair. After she had eased her stiff old frame into as comfortable a position as the chair would allow she looked up into Maria's cornflower blue eyes and beckoned to her.

The younger nun bent low in order to hear the old woman's frail voice that was no more than a whisper and reminded her somehow of cobwebs.

"It is your time now, dear. I have merely come to give you these."

She handed a bunch of ornate silver keys to Maria with a sigh. Maria was silent as she reached out with a wavering hand. Her heart was doing crazy things inside her ribcage and her mouth was suddenly dry.

"I don't understand Sister; they are in your sacred charge. It is for me only to sit vigil and say the prayers whilst you rest. I am not ready for the burden."

"Ready or not, the burden is yours now. I have borne it these past seventy years and can carry it no longer. You have witnessed the events of tomorrow many times now. You are ready. You have to be, I'm afraid I will not be here tomorrow, thank my Saviour."

"Don't talk that way. You're tired, that's all. Let me help you back to your bed and then I'll get Sister Angelique."

The old nun shook her head. "He must not be left unattended. Especially tonight."

"Tonight?"

"He is awake. Surely you can sense that. He waits for something. Something that has been many years in coming."

Maria bowed her head and lowered her voice.

"I sensed he was awake. And restless."

"He's impatient. My time is over; it's up to you now. So, take these."

She closed Maria's hand around the keys. "Now, help me up and God be with you."

She struggled up from the chair with Maria's help and shuffled towards the chapel door. Sister Maria stood motionless, looking at the keys that lay biting into her hand like shards of ice as frozen dread roared through her like an unstoppable avalanche. Eventually she returned to the chair at the side of the tomb, hung the keys from her belt next to the wooden cross, and began fingering the beads of her rosary again. Ancient and endless prayers fell from her lips as she battled for the peace that she would never know again.

Several hours passed and the atmosphere thickened as the litany of supplications hung in the air. From somewhere deep inside the monastery a bell tolled. Three single tones that announced the passing of one of the sisters. A tear welled in her eye then fell silently down her cheek and dripped onto her ever-moving fingers. She knew for whom the bell tolled. The old woman had said her goodbyes and handed her the mantle of responsibility that bore the weight of centuries. Sister Agnes was dead.

Santorini had heard the mournful tolling of the bell as he had stood watching the evening descend on the old monastery. He smiled. So the old witch was dead, and her white magic with her. He doubted the one he had seen so often at her side was up to the challenge; it was going to be easier than he had dared to hope for. In all of the years he had been back and forth to Gregori's side, the old nun had watched him with hawk-like eyes, protected by Gregori she dared to challenge him and in so doing had become the only human that he had ever backed away from. And now she was gone.

He returned to the road where Nik waited patiently for him in the shadows.

"I was worried. You've been gone for hours," said Nik.

Santorini sighed, "Why are the young so obsessed by time? You will soon realise that time, and your place in it, are eternal. Many of us possess neither watch nor calendar for that reason. I have been communing with Gregori. He is awake."

"Awake?"

Santorini sighed. He never ceased to wonder at Gregori. "For one who holds such power, he chooses to lock himself into a tomb and emerge only twice a year to feed and then return to his self-imposed exile of deep hibernation, surviving by the constant drip feeding by a donor. It happens often with the ones of us that are weary of life. Only once in the last twenty years has he broken with the tradition, on the night that your mother came to the monastery; the night you were conceived. You, Nik, are one of the Born. Although your mother was a Latent, you are the son of one of the original vampire seed. I have watched both you and your mother for years now, on his behalf. I was his eyes and ears as you grew into your heritage and now he wants to acknowledge you are his heir."

Nik looked confused. "Heir to what? He lives in a coffin!"

"A shrine, Nik, there is a subtle difference."

Whatever that difference was, it was lost on Nik. He was getting weary of all the talk of how great his father was. Well, if he was so great, why did he sleep his vampire life away? And why was he interested in Nik after half a lifetime? He'd survived this far by his own wits and resented the idea that he needed the old vampire for anything and he was anxious to tell him just that.

"Patience, Nik. It's almost time."

"What for?"

"For your mother. She is on her way here as we speak, and I intend to present her to Gregori too. Andrei is a thug. A sophisticated, talented thug, but a thug none the less. He thinks that he will give her as a gift to Gregori and receive the reward he thinks he'll get from the Old One. He is wrong."

Nik's face was stony. "She's coming here?"

"I suspect she has no choice in the matter. She is still

under Andrei's control. Remember Nik, she is newly turned and doesn't have your abilities as yet. He will be dominating her completely."

"So, what do you want me to say? That I feel sorry for her? Forget it. I told you, she is nothing to me."

"But you are something to her Nik, and when she knows you are here she will come looking for you."

Nik shook his head in disbelief. "So I'm to be the bait? Is that it? That's cheap."

Santorini smiled. "Cheap perhaps, but effective."

Nik was thoughtful. "So tell me about the Anti-HVV."

Santorini narrowed his eyes momentarily, then relaxed and smiled at the boy.

"So, you know about the Anti-HVV. I see your telepathic abilities are increasing, I had no idea you had been reading me."

"You developed it? Why? Surely you have no interest in seeing the reduction of our numbers. Why develop something that has the power to kill us?"

"That isn't how it started out. Originally I was looking for something that would prevent the Latent from turning to keep the integrity of our race. We are fast becoming akin to a pack of mongrels."

"And now?"

"Now, I realise that the Anti-HVV is more than that; it is a weapon that can be used to great effect in any future war against the Created. "

"You've developed a weapon that will kill your own kind?"

"Insurance. I have developed the Anti-HVV and I will control its future production. If there is another war, The Born will hopefully be grateful to me and protect their future supplies of the Anti-HVV."

"But you're prepared to kill you own kind." Nik's voice had an edge that startled his mentor.

"It's about survival. Survival of the fittest: it's a law of nature. I'm a survivor, Nik. And I hardly think you are in a position to find a conscience. I have seen you satisfy your hunger. That too, is about survival."

Nik was quiet. He couldn't deny that his new nature had turned him into a killer, but there was something else going on deep in his psyche that he couldn't quite cling on to and understand, something that had only started to make itself heard since he'd been in that place. He shook his head as if to clear the jumbled thoughts.

Santorini read him. "It's a confusing time for you. But later, when you meet your true father, you'll find a new perspective. In the meantime I want you to reach out with your mind and tell me what you sense.

The boy seemed about to protest then obviously thought better of it. He closed his eyes and concentrated, reaching out, searching for whatever it was that Santorini was tuning in to.

He heard the occasional chatter in the few remote homes dotted around the hillside. He heard the movement of animals settling down for the night. Reaching further he sensed the grief of the nuns in the monastery as they mourned Sister Agnes. He sensed the building fear in one of them as she tried to find peace with her maker and draw courage from the incessant prayers and clicking of her rosary.

Then, before he could relay all this to Santorini he felt something else, something closer.

"She's here," he said. My mother is here, and so is Marinescu."

Santorini nodded. "You are indeed ready for presentation to your father. But first, we have to take care of Andrei. Cloak your mind from him, Nik. We must not give any warning of our intentions."

"What are you going to do?"

"First, I'm going to get them to oblige me by stopping. Then I will take care of Andrei and you will restrain your mother. You may use any method and any force you think necessary."

A vehicle was approaching and Nik sensed their presence immediately. A mixture of old grudges and pent up anger blended into a heady cocktail of resentment. If he was to be used as bait, then he would have the pleasure of seeing them punished. *Any force necessary* gave him a whole lot of flexibility in how he administered that punishment.

CHAPTER THIRTY-SEVEN

Beckett and Darius had closed themselves off from Lane, neither knowing exactly what they faced but both aware of the enormity of their situation and each driven by personal pain that screamed for revenge.

It suited her, as her mind raced between possible scenarios and keeping a watchful, if silent, eye on Beckett. Although he hadn't shown any further signs of relapse, she didn't know if his body could take any further attacks or another dose of the Anti-HVV. The whole Anti-HVV thing bothered her. It was being developed to stop the Latents from turning, but if given to a Created it caused a painful death. And then what happened to the Latent? Would they spend the remainder of their lives suffering, as Kat had? It had been her last resort with Beckett and miraculously it had worked, though she didn't know why. What was different about Beckett? She'd never sensed the Latent in him, yet after being bitten by Kat he displayed all the early signs of turning, effectively joining the ranks of the Created. So, why didn't he die? Whatever the reason, she thanked God for it. Thoughts of Kat brought her back into focus. Kat was going to be a problem. If it came down to it, could Beckett stand by and let Lane deal with her? She doubted it.

They travelled the last miles in palpable unease, exchanging monosyllabic conversation only when necessary. Finally, the monastery came into view in a valley, its white walls standing out against the twilight and the dusty olive groves. She pulled onto the side of the winding road and got out of their hired jeep.

She was leaning against the bonnet lighting a cigarette, frowning and clicking her fingernails while she stared at the monastery below when Beckett joined her,

He stood at her side without speaking for several minutes then in unison they broke the silence.

"Beckett…"

"Lane…"

They both relaxed and allowed themselves a smile.

"You first," said Beckett.

"Okay," she replied. "I'm worried about you, Beckett. I've been thinking that perhaps you shouldn't go down there."

Beckett stood away from the jeep and faced her square on. "Now just you hang on a minute. First of all, I'm fine, you can see that. Second, if Kat is down there and in trouble, then I'm going down there to do something about it. And third, what the hell gives you the right to stop me?"

Lane sighed; she'd known it would come to a fight. "Beckett, listen to me. You've been through a living hell these past few days, I don't know if you are going to be physically up to whatever's going to go on down there. It isn't going to be pretty, that's for sure."

"That's not all of it, I know you, Lane."

"All right, Handsome. I'm worried that if it comes to the ultimate with Kat, I don't want you getting in the way. There, I've said it. I'm sorry Beckett, but you know how it is. If it comes to it and I hesitate, even for a second, well …"

His face was ashen and anger was etched into every pore. The tell-tale twitching muscle in his cheek warned Lane that she had crossed the line.

He inhaled deeply. "You don't have to worry about that. I don't intend to let her down like I did Grace. Besides, it won't come to that."

"You *see*, Beckett. You've already decided that everything's going to be all right and there's going to be a happy ending to the fairy-tale. But Handsome, in my experience, it doesn't tend to happen that way. I'm sorry."

He was furious. "And *you* seem to have made your

mind up to the opposite. How are you going to be objective? How are you going to be able to give her a chance?"

"And I need to know that if it comes to it, that you will take care of me. Do what has to be done. Can you, Beckett?"

They fell into a deep silence. Mistrust had never before entered into their relationship and it was an unpleasant feeling. And one that had to be eradicated if they were going to face the next hours together.

Darius stepped out of the jeep looking grim. He turned on Lane.

"This can't happen, you two. If we are to have any chance of coming out of this in one piece we have to do it together. Your words, not mine. We've all got our own reasons for being here: Beckett because of Kat; you because of Santorini and whoever else is down there; and me because of Andrei. So it would be better if you could both put this crap away and we get on with it."

He didn't wait for a reply; he simply walked away and climbed back into the jeep and slammed the door.

Beckett looked sheepish. "He's right. I'm sorry, Legs."

Lane grinned at him. "Me too. So let's do this, Beckett. Let's end this now; for all of us."

Without further words, they got back into the jeep and set off down the winding road.

CHAPTER THIRTY-EIGHT

Santorini moved so fast that even Nik wasn't able to track him. Then a noise on the dusty hillside above him made him look up. His mentor was standing beside a massive boulder, contemplating the road below. Nik picked his thoughts up instantly. He was going to push the boulder down the hillside and aim it at a white poplar on the side of the road. If it hit the target, the road would be effectively blocked.

It happened in the blink of an eye. Dust and small debris filled the air, dislodged by the rapidly descending rock which hit the tree dead centre, its own momentum giving it enough rebound to lie centrally in the road.

Santorini was back at his side, flicking dust from his thousand dollar suit. He reached inside the jacket and brought out his black silk mask.

Nik looked puzzled. "I thought it was for amusement only? What's going on?"

"Theatre Nik, just theatre. Humour me."

There was no time to argue further as Andrei and Kat drove onto the scene. In the seconds that it took Andrei to brake before hitting the boulder, Santorini and Nik were on them. Kat was easier to restrain than he'd thought she would be now that she'd fully turned and had vampire strength and abilities. But Santorini had been right, Kat's adrenaline rush had been centred on seeing her son again and not on her flight or fight mechanism. He had her in an arm lock around her throat and an arm twisted behind her back in the same easy way that he had done the first time that they had met.

Andrei on the other hand was in full fight mode. It was vampire against vampire. Sophistication against brute force. And from where Nik was standing, it looked as though brute force was getting the upper hand.

Santorini had been injured but was fighting on. Then from nowhere came the deafening roar of an animal in agony. The noise both deafened and chilled. Nik felt Kat go slack in his grip as she too was caught up in the sound of death.

Both vampires stood locked together as though in a lover's embrace and Nik couldn't see which of them was going to walk away.

Then as suddenly as it had begun, Santorini took a step backwards as Andrei slumped to the floor like a sack of grain. There was no movement from him and Nik couldn't pick up on his heartbeat, however slow.

He daren't release his grip on Kat who leaned against him, bewildered at the swiftness of the attack and the brutality of the ensuing fight. Santorini turned his back on them and knelt over Andrei.

Kat struggled against Nik's hold but got nowhere, his strength containing her with ease. She tried in vain to pull free but with each movement Nik tightened his grip on her arm sending waves of familiar agony searing into her brain. She was no match for him.

Santorini stood up and remained standing over Andrei's lifeless body for several moments before returning to Nik and Kat.

He reached forward and opened his clenched fist. Inside was what appeared to be a small silver pen. Nik stared at it, unable to process what he was seeing.

"It's an injector that was loaded with Anti-HVV, Nik. I managed to get it over his carotid artery and give him the lethal dose." As an afterthought he said, "I'm disappointed, I thought he'd be a more worthy opponent. What about you, Katerini? Will I need to sacrifice the reward I may get for you, if you aren't compliant?"

Kat was staring at the cruel mouth that seemed to be mocking her. It was the last thing she saw before he took control of her mind and she slipped into unconsciousness.

Nik held on to her, unsure of Santorini's intention. He was answered by a nod from his mentor.

"Throw her in the back, Nik. She'll be out for a while."

Nik tossed Kat into the rear of the car that Andrei had driven, while Santorini moved the boulder from the road like a small pebble.

"Now, Nik, you are going to meet your father." Then, almost as an after thought, "Finish him off. I don't want blood on my suit."

"But I thought you said it was a lethal dose."

"It was, but he's one of the Undead Nik. Finish him off or he will eventually repair himself. And that would be a nuisance."

With a deft movement he drew an ornate dagger from the small of his back where it had been tucked into the waistband of his trousers.

"Its blade is Toledo steel, so we won't have the undignified hacking off of his head. Don't take too long," he said.

Nik took the dagger from Santorini and knew instinctively that the blade was sharper than any surgical scalpel. He paused. He'd killed before, in hunger, in pleasure and in rage, but this was different. This time he felt unsure of himself.

Santorini sensed his uncertainty and turned on him. Before he knew what was happening Santorini had grabbed the dagger from him, leaving a red trail of blood from the rapidly closing wound across his palm. He knelt behind Andrei's head and pulled his chin backwards. With two deep slashes he separated the head from the shoulders and tossed it to one side, where it rolled into the bushes lining the road. He glared at Nik, who paled under its influence.

Santorini threw the dagger at his feet.

"*Now* finish him."

In silence Nik picked up the dagger and knelt at

Andrei's side. He sensed the location of the heart and began the grisly task of removing it from the body.

When he eventually stood up, his hands were a gory mess. He looked at his mentor for approval. Instead Santorini's mouth twisted into a mocking smile before giving way to harsh laughter that cut into the boy as deep as any Toledo blade.

Santorini had never hidden his true agenda from Nik, and recently he told the boy that he was also using him as bait to get his hands on Kat. What else did he expect?

CHAPTER THIRTY-NINE

Sister Maria stopped praying, her hands lay still on her rosary. There was a voice in her head.

For years she had prayed that God would speak to her, tell her what he wanted of her, for years she had waited to hear that voice. Now the voice in her head was insistent and commanding, but it was not the voice of God.

She felt Gregori stirring in the tomb, and felt the temperature drop even further. She could see her own breath in front of her now. The oppression she had felt all day and evening deepened and constricted around her chest, making it hard for her to breathe.

Her hands strayed to the silver keys that she had hung from her belt only hours before, although it felt as though she had carried them forever, unhooking them and selecting them one by one, and opening silver padlocks, one by one. The locks were open as she reached out with trembling hands to lower the side of the tomb. Always, at this moment, she had held her breath as Sister Agnes had performed this duty, always unsure of what to expect. And always, it had been the same: Gregori lying inside, awake and ready to rise. A miracle. But never had the shrine been opened on the night before his feast day. Not knowing what drove her and not wanting to, she responded only as her saint instructed her.

She bowed her head and moved away from the tomb to stand in the shadows at the rear of the chapel.

There was movement in the corridors and she desperately wanted to look up and see who approached, but she dare not. She heard Gregori leave the tomb and walk towards the approaching figure, his long frock coat swishing against his high leather boots.

And she was afraid.

Through the silver lit gloom she heard Gregori speak. Never before had she been in his presence outside of his tomb. The voice that answered him was from Sister Angelique.

"He has returned, and he has your son with him. I left them in my rooms until I knew where you wanted to meet with them."

Gregori didn't answer her. Instead he paced the corridor as if searching for something. Then he stopped directly in front of Sister Angelique. "She is here too. Why didn't you say so?"

The nun bowed her head. "I wasn't sure how you would react. It wasn't what you expected."

Gregori nodded in dismissal and Sister Angelique turned and disappeared into the rear gloom of the corridor.

Maria shrank further back into the shadows, her mind racing, her heart aching. This was no miracle. This was dark and somehow tainted. She pushed herself back against the icy wall as if it would engulf her and keep her hidden, keep her safe, even though she knew they were impossible hopes.

Gregori was pacing the chapel now, his footsteps firmer and heavier with every stride as he regained his strength after his six month hibernation.

None of it made any sense to Maria who had unquestioningly accepted the words of Sister Angelique, that the saint they guarded had fallen victim in death to a vampire, and that it was their duty to protect him while he slept and provide for him to feed when he awoke. That they would house his donor who would give his blood each and every day to keep Agios Georgios alive while he slept in his tomb for half a year, and it would be drip fed through a tubing system into his tomb. They would open their doors twice a year for the people of the surrounding villages to come and pray at his open shrine and they would turn away as an innocent became the true feast. It was their duty to look after their saint and to do his bidding. It was the will of God, she said.

But what of right and wrong? Where had God's will come into that equation? It was surely wrong to ignore the taking of life, for rarely did the chosen one survive. And if this was indeed a Holy man, a saint, why would he have such disregard for the life he took?

Maria's head felt as if it would split open. Years of conditioning and doctrine melded into a hotchpotch of fragments among the dawn of understanding. This was wrong.

She closed her eyes and tilted her head upwards, seeking solace from an image of the Blessed Virgin. None came.

Voices came again, one familiar, one not.

"Gregori, I have kept my promise to you. This is your son, Nikolos."

Nik blanched. *Nik*, he wanted to shout, *Nik*.

Gregori moved into the silver reflections and candlelight and Nik saw his father's face for the first time.

He didn't know what he was expecting, but he was ill prepared for the silver haired, sharp-eyed man that towered in front of him. Nik was no midget, but Gregori, at full height, owed him at least five inches. Nik was left in no misapprehension that he was being inspected.

Gregori was obviously satisfied with his appraisal, as the soft leathery face broke into a refined smile. He stepped forwards suddenly and embraced Nik tightly before he could back away. His son, his own flesh and blood, after so many centuries.

Gregori turned to Santorini. "You did well. I will reward you, as I promised. For now, I must feed. You two will wait for me in Angelique's room. Are you hungry? Help yourself." He laughed as he waived an arm in a gesture of hospitality.

Santorini nodded briefly in thanks. He knew when to

speak and when to keep his mouth shut. Gregori led the way down the dark corridor and, when she was certain that they were gone, Maria fled.

At first she just ran blindly, tears of regret and shame on her face. All those years that she had spent in the belief that she was doing God's will. All those years she had been harbouring a vampire. Her beloved convent was nothing more than a vampire's lair.

She stopped and leaned against a dark wall. Looking around she realised that she was in the guest corridor. Even though they were a closed order, the nuns always had rooms ready for travellers and infrequent visitors to the monastery. She laughed as she thought of those who had come seeking sanctuary over the years. Some sanctuary! She didn't even know if those poor wretches had ever made it out of there.

A small noise from the room behind her made her spin around. She listened. It was there again. There was someone in the room.

Maria leaned against the door, listening intently. Reaching far back into her memory, back nineteen years, to the time when she had pressed a silver crucifix into a young girl's hand and later prayed for her as she raised her arms in blessing when she departed. Why was she remembering this? She knew the answer.

Sister Maria opened the door to the tiny cell and stood in the doorway, her eyes fixed on the woman who lay on the bed, talking and tossing her head in delirium. She would have recognised the amethyst eyes in any circumstances. She had looked into a similar pair many times over the years she had been understudy to Sister Agnes.

CHAPTER FORTY

She stepped into the gloomy cell, lit only by a candle at the side of the bed. Kat struggled to focus on Sister Maria.

"I know you … Oh, my God, it's you. You're still here."

Maria smiled down at Kat. "Of course I'm still here. Where else would I go? Let me help you. Can you stand?"

Kat struggled to sit on the edge of the tiny bed. She sat there for a moment, steeling herself to stand and pull away from the restraints that Santorini had planted in her head.

"Why have you come back here? I believed that you were safe. I thought when you left here that you would be all right," said Maria.

Kat shook her head. "I'm one of them now. Oh, don't be afraid," she said, "I won't hurt you. I remember your kindness back then. I'm here because I had to come. They've brought my son here. To meet his father."

For a moment Maria looked puzzled, then her brow cleared suddenly as she understood, probably for the first time, what was happening at the monastery.

She took Kat's arm, "Come with me, there's something you need to see."

Kat followed her, gaining her strength back with every step. By the time they had reached the end of the corridor her vampire senses were at full height.

Maria stopped outside a cell door. "I'll wait outside," was all she said.

Kat approached the door, sensing a presence inside, human not vampire, but weak to the point of death; the heartbeat as weak as a butterfly's wing. Whoever was inside was in lingering torment.

She opened the door gingerly and went inside.

Her vampire sight cut right through the darkness to the skeletal form on the bed. He was not much more than skin and bone, with thin, straggly white hair and beard. His eyes were closed and his breathing so shallow it was barely perceptible.

She crossed over to the bed and put a hand on his shoulder, blanching at the cadaverous appearance, his cheekbones scarily prominent and his eye sockets sunken like a corpse.

She cast around the tiny room for evidence of who the man was and her eyes came to rest on a small wooden table opposite the bed. On it were all the trappings of transfusion kits and collecting vessels. This was Gregori's donor.

Her heart went out to him. Is this what happened to donor's? Surely this wasn't the picture painted by Lane at the Sanctuary. The poor man was almost bled dry. She wondered how long he had been there, draining away his life force to keep Gregori alive.

He stirred under her touch.

"Hello," she said.

The voice was weak but the words were unmistakeable. "Katerini? Is that you? "

She was startled and went to pull away, but a bony hand grabbed her wrist.

Then he opened his eyes.

Everything stopped for Kat. Time, space, sound, feelings, emotions – everything, - stopped for an instant, as she looked down into a copy of her own amethyst eyes. These were clouded now with age and his obvious condition, but she knew.

"Father?"

A tear formed at the corner of his eye but didn't have the strength to make it down his cheek; it just lay there pooled under his eyelid.

Emotions collided inside her then, rage, pity, despair, and love.

She put her arm under his head gently and tried to lift him. He put his bony claw back on her arm.

"No, Katerini, it's too late. I can't leave. There is only one way out for me now. Please, Katerini, help me. Help me to leave."

She tried again to lift him gently, but again, the claw. He gave a feeble shake of his head. "Please Katerini, I'm begging you. Release me." The pleading in his eyes burned into her soul and she knew that she would do it.

She gathered herself into a central focus and wiped his tear away. "I will help you, father. But first, tell me how you come to be here. They told me you were dead."

"I was dead to you all. It had to be that way. I made a bargain that I would keep him fed and alive if he left you alone. I came here because he was going to take you. I brought you here one feast day, you and your mother. We came as we always did to bring our gifts to Agios Georgios, then when we were leaving, an old nun came to us and asked us to go back inside. Your mother wouldn't go back. She was afraid, and she tried to stop me going back with you. But I went and I took you with me. You were holding my hand really tightly. Even then I did not suspect what was about to happen.

The old nun told me that the Saint had chosen you to remain at the monastery, to become one of the nuns. I told her that you were too young, that if you wanted to do that when you were older I would bring you myself.

I grabbed you to me and tried to make it to the door, but before I could get half way across the chapel, he was there, in front of me. Agios Georgios, alive, and standing in my way. You were crying by then and he put his hand on your face. I tried to pull you away from him but he was stronger than me. I tried to stop you crying, to calm you, thinking that it would anger him and put you in more danger but there was no calming you."

He paused for breath, his voice weakening with each moment.

"I don't remember that. Why can't I remember that? I remember coming home one day and mother was crying. Father was dead, she said. Later they told me you had died from tuberculosis."

He struggled to speak again. "A memory that he left you with. Anyway, I begged him to leave you alone. I would give him anything I had if he left you alone. He kept looking at you, and then suddenly he agreed. You could go, if I stayed behind and become his donor. You ran outside to your mother and that is the last I saw of you. Until now. I would know you anywhere, Katerini."

Kat was sobbing; all those years she had believed him dead. Then, in an instant, a bitter thought came right into focus. When she had been there with Greg that night, her father had been there too; feeding Gregori with his life blood to keep her from harm. It was too much.

She turned to leave; there was more than a score to settle now.

"Katerini … you promised."

She stopped dead in her tracks. The truth of it was plain: he was dying. She knew he was past help now and without her keeping her promise to him he would lay there in that limbo of existence until Gregori had drained him dry.

She went back to the bed and took his bony hand in hers.

"You know, don't you?"

He sighed. "Yes, I know. I have since the night you were here all those years ago. Gregori enjoyed telling me how he had gone to you and taken you. I've lived with that pain since then, but I knew that one day you would come back, because of the boy."

"You know about Nik?"

He nodded. "Please, Katerini. Help me leave this place."

Kat didn't speak. She simply bent down low over him and kissed him on the forehead. Memories of Beckett and what she had done to him came to her. Once again she would suck the blood from someone she loved. This time she wouldn't stop until it was over and his torment at an end.

It didn't take long to drain the old man past the point of death and she was careful not to allow a single drop to touch him. She straightened up again and gently closed the amethyst eyes that could no longer see.

Turning quickly, she was out of the room in a heartbeat. Maria had been true to her word and was waiting for her. She looked at Kat and at the tell-tale spot of blood at the corner of her mouth.

"He's at peace now," was all Kat could say.

Sister Maria nodded. "What now?"

"Now, I'm going to find them all and make them pay, even if I die trying."

"You should know that others are here; he is not alone."

Kat knew her own limitations. Well, if she died trying so be it, but she was going to take at least one of them with her.

"Who are they?"

"I don't know some of them. One of them I know well; he has been coming back here for many years. Agios Georgios has taught him all and he returns to visit often. The one in the mask."

"You should stop calling him that. His name isn't Agios Georgios, it's Gregori and he's probably the oldest vampire alive on earth right now. And the nuns in your order have been keeping him alive and fed since God knows when. Who else is here?"

Maria bowed her head. When she looked up, the fear was gone and she appeared calm. "There are three other men and a woman. I don't know who they are. One of the men arrived yesterday and has spent much time with Agi … Gregori. He seems important because Sister Angelique is always making sure he has what he needs. I think she is afraid of him."

"Is one of them called Andrei?"

Maria shook her head. So, Santorini had done for him – well, that was one she didn't have to worry about. Her main objective was to find Nik and get him out of there. If she could do some damage to Gregori on the way, well that would be a bonus.

"I think you need to get the Sisters away from here. And stay away yourself, you've done enough already," Kat said.

CHAPTER FORTY-ONE

Lane stopped the jeep a hundred yards from the monastery gate.

She turned to Darius. "You've made your decision to do this, but I warn you: don't you dare put either of us in danger by wimping out at the last minute. It's going to be bloody and there is going to be death. So if you aren't up to it, stay here."

He was pale but the glint in his eye told of his determination to see it through, whatever the cost. He swallowed hard.

"I've done my running. I'm coming with you. And don't worry; I won't get in your way."

"What have you got in the way of weapons? Or do you intend to be the sacrifice?"

She'd read him well.

"No, but I would make good bait. Andrei won't miss the chance to finish the job he started."

"As I thought, the sacrifice. Well, sorry, but that isn't the way it's going to be. If you come, we stand together. So you'd better get yourself something to fight with. What have you got for him, Beckett?"

"Me? Only what I always bring."

Lane glared at him. "One of these days Beckett, you're going to wake up in the real vampire world and get yourself some decent stuff." She leaned forward and pulled a razor-sharp dagger in its sheath from the side of her boot. "Here, Darius, take this. Hopefully you won't get close enough to use it, but if you do, don't hesitate. And I want it back, it's two hundred years old and it's priceless."

"I won't hesitate," he replied stonily.

They walked in silence to the outer wall of the

monastery and Lane was up and over it in seconds. She pulled the gate open and they were inside.

All the doors and windows were shut and bolted.

"Wait here," Lane snapped. "I'm going in through the bell tower. I'll come back and open the door for you. If I haven't shown up in three minutes, raise hell."

She was up the outside wall so fast that neither of them was able to track her. They saw her disappear into the bell tower at the top of the roof. In less than two minutes she was back at the front entrance, holding it open.

Beckett and Darius followed her into the cold gloom of the monastery and, despite the frosty atmosphere, beads of perspiration formed on Beckett's brow. He felt clammy and his pulse rate was rising. This was not the time for a relapse. He said nothing, hoping that it was nothing more than anxiety.

Lane stopped and turned to Darius. "You need to know that Andrei isn't here."

"You're sure? How can we have been so wrong?" He looked at Beckett, meaning 'How could *you* have been so wrong?'

"Listen, if she says he's not here, then he's not here. And I don't believe I was wrong. Maybe he just hasn't got here yet?" He looked to Lane.

She shook her head. "No, I can't sense him at all, but, Beckett, Kat is here. And I think Santorini and another two besides Gregori, though one is too well cloaked for me to see him properly."

Kat was there, that was all Beckett needed to know. He pushed past Lane and strode into the interior of the monastery. Lane was with him in an instant and Darius only a second behind her as they made for the chapel.

As they entered a large inner hallway Sister Angelique appeared before them.

"You have no business here," she began, but could say no more as Lane leaped forwards and knocked her out cold. They stepped over her inert body and moved forwards. Lane pulled a small revolver from her hip. It had a pearl handle and was unmistakeably made many years previously.

"You can shoot them?" asked Darius, in surprise.

"They're flesh and blood, or most of them are. They won't die with ordinary bullets; that's why mine aren't ordinary."

"Don't tell me, they're silver bullets, I thought that was Hollywood."

"Close, although pure silver bullets are most effective on werewolves. These bullets carry a small charge and they explode on impact, carrying the Anti-HVV and silver nitrate inside the body. Same principle as a tranquilizer gun; it will bring them down long enough for this. From her other boot she drew the hilt of what appeared to be another dagger, but when she pressed the ornate hilt, a blade shot out, the length of her lower leg, effectively turning it into a sword.

Darius whistled. "You sure your name isn't Van Helsing?"

"Shut up," snapped Beckett. "Or get out. We've got work to do."

Darius bridled momentarily, then common sense kicked in and he apologised.

Lane was already on the move and scanning the entire building as she moved at such a speed that only her own would see her.

"They're not in the chapel." She stopped and sniffed the air. "There's been a death."

Beckett paled.

Lane shook her head, "It's not her. The others are together, we have to be quick; they'll already know we're here. Move."

Before they could obey her, Santorini appeared in front of them. His canines were down and ready, he hissed and launched himself at Lane who had no time to fire the gun.

Santorini took her down and raised his hand to strike.

His fingertips glowed in the half light. On each fingertip he wore a gold sheath with a lancet in the end and he prepared to put an end to Lane. Darius came from nowhere and threw himself onto Santorini's back, clasping him around the neck. The masked vampire roared with rage and flung the boy off like a feather, kicking him with savage intensity in the side of the head. Darius lost consciousness as Beckett was propelling himself into Santorini from the front. The gold lancet tips caught his throat, but didn't bite deep. Beckett felt the warm blood trickle down behind his collar. He turned on Santorini again as Lane caught him from behind.

Before she could act further, Nik and Gregori were on the scene. She turned and fired blindly as Beckett lost his grip on the wooden stake he held. It clattered to the floor and Santorini took the opportunity to grab Beckett by the throat and hurl him against the wall. Santorini's eyes were black caverns in the silk mask as he gave vent to his true nature and his fury.

Two of Lane's random bullets had found a home and Nik was sliding to the floor with a stunned expression. Gregori roared in wild rage and leaped at Lane. "That's my son and you'll pay for that!"

He grabbed at her and twisted her around, pinning her to him, as he grabbed the blade from her and held it to her own throat.

There was a shrill keening noise that came from Kat as she arrived to see Nik lying on the floor in a widening pool of blood. Mistaking his assailant, she snatched the stake from the floor and rammed it home into Gregori's back.

He arched his back and momentarily relaxed his grip on Lane, but it was long enough for her to pull free. He spun around to face Kat and grabbed her by the hair, pulling her to him in an easy gesture. Beckett ploughed towards Gregori who was still dragging Kat by the hair and with the stake protruding from his back as if it was a toothpick.

"Ah, shit," spat Beckett, as Santorini lunged at him again deflecting his contact with Gregori.

Lane reached inside her jacket but Beckett couldn't see what it was that she pulled out. In less than a second she was flying towards Santorini, her arm raised. She brought it crashing down into the side of his neck, then Beckett saw that it was a syringe. She rammed the plunger home and jumped back to watch as Santorini's face beneath the mask suffused red as his blood vessels dilated and reacted to his own Anti-HVV. Santorini was dying.

As he stepped back, Lane snatched the mask from his face and looked at him for the first time. He fell to the floor and began writhing and screaming in agony as his death throes took hold.

Lane paused long enough to give a significant glance at Beckett. That had been the last of the Anti-HVV. If Beckett needed more, he was going to be out of luck. He understood her unspoken message. He was in deep shit.

A gasp from behind her made her spin around. Gregori had released Kat and was lunging at Beckett. Lane screamed at him and made a dive forwards, hoping to deflect Gregori's attention from Beckett. The ancient vampire reacted in milliseconds and moved in a heartbeat to once more take hold of Kat. Lane wasn't quick enough; even with the stake in his back Gregori was faster than she was. In his hand was her own long blade and he sent it home with deadly accuracy into Kat's chest.

It had been enough to stop Beckett in his tracks. Everything was going wrong; they were not going to win this one and he'd failed again. But this time at least he would have the satisfaction of watching Grace's killer die from his own Anti-HVV and he would die avenging Kat. There was to be some payback in his own death.

In the seconds it took to process the thought, he started to shake, and the pain in his chest sent him crashing to the floor. Gregori was on him in an instant, dragging him to his feet and holding him upright in a vice-like grip.

"Take one step forwards," Gregori said to Lane, "And his throat will be open in an instant."

Lane knew that he was serious and would take Beckett's life without thought or remorse. She didn't move.

In the surreal minutes that followed, footsteps announced the arrival of another. Michael Rabb, born Mihai Rabinescu in Prague at the turn of the fourteenth century, was standing before them.

Kat had fallen to the floor and was clutching the blade that protruded from her chest; blood was trickling from the corner of her mouth. Lane was beside her in an instant.

"Mihai, old friend," said Gregori amiably, as if he was welcoming the Proconsul to a party.

Lane was stunned. "You," she whispered. "I knew it. How could you betray the Council? Have you any idea what you've done? You've effectively sanctioned the deaths of thousands of the Created. Why?"

"Call it a cleansing, if you like. We intend to eradicate the weakest part of the vampire race so that we can once again hold power. Gregori and I have been working together for years now, supporting Santorini in his work on the Anti-HVV."

"He's not Santorini," gasped Kat.

All eyes were on her.

"His name is Greg Randall," she whispered.

CHAPTER FORTY-TWO

"It seems that Gregori had more than one meal that night, eighteen years ago," Lane said. "It makes sense now, his super-fast rise to Consultant Haematologist. And of course his research into AIDS was a cover for his real work – the Anti-HVV."

Beckett looked up at the face that had haunted Kat for so many years. "Sonofabitch," he gasped.

Further talk was halted as Kat coughed and spluttered.

Michael Rabb bent over her and pulled the blade from her chest, and then, turning to Gregori who still had a tight hold on Beckett, said, "May I?" He pointed at Beckett.

"Be my guest."

The Proconsul stood between Lane and Beckett. She closed her eyes as she heard the thud and breaking ribs followed by the soft thump of the body hitting the deck and sounds that she was all too familiar with. The sounds of decapitation. She allowed herself to fall back, holding an open wound in her chest.

Before thoughts of approaching death had gelled in Beckett's brain, he felt a surge of energy and in that same moment Michael Rabb brought the dagger plunging forwards. He closed his eyes, preparing for the strike that never came.

The blade had gone straight past him and into Gregori's heart.

The ancient vampire threw back his head and screamed into eternity, releasing Beckett from his grip. Rabb withdrew the blade and had sliced off Gregori's head before the scream had died into the night. The oldest vampire on earth was no more.

The next thing that Kat was aware of was a hand

underneath her neck and someone trying to lift her. She opened her eyes and his face swam in and out of focus.

"Beckett? What have I dragged you into?"

"Shh, don't talk."

Kat coughed again and more blood appeared at the corner of her mouth. She closed her eyes.

Beckett turned on Rabb. "Why isn't she healing? What can we do? Help me *do* something, dammit."

Lane shook her head. "Beckett, that blade was coated in silver nitrate and the Anti-HVV, the same cocktail that was in the bullets. The blade hit her so close to the heart the poison on it is effectively preventing regeneration. We have to wait and see. She's strong, let's hope it's enough."

"Well, she can't stay here like this. I'm going to take her to a bed or something. She's going to be fine," he said defiantly.

Beckett lifted her in his arms and turned to Lane who was bending low over Nik. "How's he doing?"

She looked up from Nik, his head cradled in her lap, and shook her head, "Go and take care of her, Beckett. There's nothing you can do here."

"Is he …?"

She nodded in reply and bent over him again.

Beckett strode to the end of the corridor and kicked open the first door he came to. In the corner was the usual spartan bed. He laid Kat carefully on it and covered her with a blanket. She was even paler than usual and she was still bleeding.

She opened her eyes again momentarily. "I need you to do what has to be done, Beckett; for my soul's sake. I know, because Lane told me."

"Don't waste your energy talking. You're going to be fine."

"Promise me that you'll do that, Beckett."

He felt suddenly weak and perspiration ran down his spine and the walls began to swim around him. He fought to stay in control.

"Please, Beckett, please promise me."

He held her hand, "I promise," he said. "Now rest."

She seemed to relax then and her breathing steadied. Good, he thought, rest would help her regenerate.

A noise from behind made him turn around. Sister Maria stood in the doorway.

"How is she," the nun asked. "How can I help?"

"You can stay with her while I check on the others. Call me if there's any change. But if you can, leave her rest, it's what she needs."

"Is she a vampire?"

"Yes, but she's a good guy, so don't get any ideas about that."

Before she could reply, there was a sickening roar from the corridor. Lane let out a cry of anguish and Michael Rabb was shouting. Beckett tried to run but found his legs weak and unsteady, he held on to the wall and pushed himself forwards in time to see Rabb disappear towards the chapel. Lane was picking herself up from the floor, an ugly wound on her forehead already closing.

"What the hell …?"

Lane looked at him, despair and disbelief etched on her face.

"It's Nik," she said, "He rose. Rabb has gone after him. Jesus, Beckett, he's one of the Undead."

She looked at him more intently. "Beckett? You don't look so good."

"Won't bore you with the details, but short version, I think I may be turning. So how's that for the kicker, eh?"

Lane looked crushed. He held up a hand. "Not now, it's not the time. I'm going after Rabb."

"Beckett," she whispered as he turned for the door, "It's okay, do what you have to do. It has to be that way."

As he reached the door, Sister Maria appeared in front of him.

"I think you should come," she said.

Beckett pushed past her and down the corridor,

holding the wall as he went. Inside the cell, Kat was lying in a widening pool of blood; her fledgling vampire cells were losing the battle for regeneration.

He took her hand, feeling helpless. She read him and tried to squeeze his hand. "It's okay Beckett; I think I always knew it was going to end this way. But you know what I need you to do for me now. If you don't, my soul can't return to the source. Only you can do it, Beckett. Only you."

Beckett knew what she wanted of him and he couldn't do it. Kat wanted him to pray for her soul as it departed her body. If someone who truly believed in the all-powerful divine, prayed for her soul to be saved as she died, her vampire existence would be over and her soul would be free. But he didn't believe. Not anymore. Not since Grace. And not now.

There was a subtle change in her breathing and he couldn't feel a pulse at all as she slipped from him. The weight in his heart was too much.

"I can't!" he yelled. "I can't do it." He lay across her as if she would give him comfort.

"Father, you must pray for her," whispered Maria.

"Why do you call me that? I'm not a priest."

"But you are. You just lost your way, that's all. It happens. This is the way back."

He lay quiet and still. "And who am I supposed to pray to?"

"To God of course, whoever or whatever you perceive the Creator to be. It doesn't matter. You have to connect yourself back to the source and pray for her."

He stood up, pale and dishevelled, deepening dark shadows around his dark grey eyes. "I've got a better idea," he said thickly, "You pray for her."

He moved painfully towards the door.

"But you made her a promise. I heard you," she said.

Beckett stopped dead. It was true, he had made a promise to her, but it had been a promise he never dreamed he would have to make good on. He looked down at Kat, the mask of death apparent already. 'Beckett, you promised me," she seemed to say.

He fell to his knees and punched his fists into his temples.

Maria moved silently to his side. "Sometimes things happen just the way they are supposed to. We can't change it and we can't just blame God all the time. Sometimes, that's just the way it is. Who are we to question what the divine has planned for us? We just have to do the best we can with it. Pray for her Father, I will stay with you."

She knelt by his side and began fingering her rosary as she had for all of her life. Her prayers and concentration weredeep and yet her face was an image of serenity.

He felt her peace transferring itself to him and with it a strength that he hadn't known before. Everything seemed surreal. Distant and out there. It wasn't happening to him.

A warmth that began somewhere above his solar plexus spread throughout his body and the air suddenly seemed rarefied. His head was full of ancient prayers that he had recited a thousand times before but now they were sharp and clear in his mind. Now he understood their true meaning. He realised then, in an instant of understanding, that all prayers ended up at the same destination. Prayers to God, Jesus, Buddha, Allah, Mother Mary, The Great Mother, The Goddess; all faces that mankind had put on the faceless in an effort to understand the divine; all externalisations of the truth. That we all contain God in our own being and our endless search for the divine would always be fruitless while we looked outside. A departing soul needed words and ritual, especially a soul that had been lost and needed to find its redemption. He knew the words to say. He crossed himself slowly and tears formed in the corner of his eyes. He had come home.

"In the name of the Father, Mother, and of the Son and of the Holy Spirit. I beseech you, God, in your mercy, to have pity on the soul of your daughter Katerini, who you have freed from the perils of this mortal life, restore to her everlasting salvation. Amen".

He lifted his head and looked at Kat. There was an unmistakeable air of peace about her. Maria's rosary was still clicking as she silently invoked Christ and his Mother.

What had he been expecting? A fanfare? A vision of light? A welcome back?

Outwardly nothing was different; there was no holy vision in front of him, just the open door to the corridor.

He put his hand on Maria's shoulder. "We need to leave," he said.

He had needed no audio visual confirmation, no sensory bombardment of returning religion. He knew this time, at the level of his soul; he knew the truth. And he believed. Perhaps he was a priest after all.

Unashamed tears of sadness, regret and love fell down his face as he traced the cross on her forehead. "Goodbye, Kat. I'm so sorry I let you down, but I couldn't bring myself to see what was in front of me. Requiescat in Pace, Rest in Peace, I reckon you deserve it."

Sister Maria rose with him and followed him into the corridor.

"Father ..."

"Beckett," he interrupted, "Just, Beckett."

"Father Beckett," she persisted," Isn't there something else you have to do for her?"

Beckett knew what he had to do, but first he needed to find Lane.

"It can wait. You should leave now."

Maria protested but he took a firm grip on her arm. "When I say - you should leave, you *really* should leave."

She allowed him to propel her to the corridor and towards the front door. He turned on his heel and strode with rapidly increasing strength towards the chapel.

Nik was on his back under Rabb, struggling to match the strength of the Proconsul when Beckett entered. As they tumbled across the chapel floor he picked up the dagger that had been Kats undoing. Without hesitation he strode across to them and kicked Rabb under the chin, knocking him away, then with one clean slash, opened up Nik's throat. The second cut severed his head from his convulsing body. He threw it into the tomb and turned, blood spattered, to Rabb.

"Which side are you on Rabb? I'm still not sure."

"My friends call me, Mihai," he said gently. "Your side, Beckett. For many years I have known of the unrest and the cruelty within our race. There is no place for it in this world. I had to allow them to think I was with them so that I could monitor their actions and schemes more easily. When you don't know who to trust, you trust no-one."

"But you killed the Patriarch. I heard you admit to that."

"He is not dead, Beckett. I would never do that. Santorini was happy to believe that I had done so, but the Patriarch has decided to step down. I have been elected by the Council to take his place. The Code really does need revision, but not in the way that Santorini and the others wanted. We need to tighten up on everything for the sake of our race and the safety of the humans who we share this earth with. It won't be easy, but then I've got plenty of time to do it in. There are vacancies on the Council that need filling. Perhaps you would care to join us? She doesn't know it yet, but Lane is to be the next Proconsul and I think you would make an excellent Tribune."

"I don't really know what that is."

"Call it a bad vampire catcher and dispatcher, that's pretty much it. From what I've seen, you're already doing the job. You may as well hold the title."

Lane moved into the chapel so fast they were only just able to track her. She scanned the place for Nik and her eyes came to rest on Gregori's tomb. She jumped up into it in one easy leap to see for herself the bloody remains of the boy. She looked at Beckett. He nodded briefly. It was over.

"Kat?" she asked.

Beckett lowered his head, took a deep breath in and couldn't reply.

She came to his side in an instant and her arm was around him. "Oh, God, Beckett, I'm so very sorry. I would have done anything to prevent this."

He nodded his understanding.

"I have to leave this place," said Mihai. "I can't be found here."

"No-one is going to be found here," Beckett's voice was choked with emotion and exhaustion. "You go, I'll see to it. Take her with you," he nodded at Lane. "Take the boy too, he looks in bad shape. His name's Darius, look after him will you?"

Mihai nodded and leaped into the tomb and put a hand on Lane's shoulder; his vast age and experience controlling her and willing her to follow him.

"Come with me, Proconsul, we need to talk."

CHAPTER FORTY-THREE

Beckett found his way to the monastery's small kitchen. Once inside, he pulled the ancient stove away from the wall and yanked the gas pipe from its connection, opening the valve to its maximum.

He left the room immediately and returned to Kat. He picked her body up effortlessly and strode towards the front door. In the hallway he stopped and laid her down. "Be right back, honey."

The corridors were bare but in the chapel he had seen what he needed. The drapes in there were ancient and heavy and the tapestries, although threadbare, were huge. He yanked them down and threw one of them into the tomb, then climbed onto it with one of the vigil candles in his hand. The dusty material ignited immediately and the flames soon took hold of Nik's clothing and the silk lining of the tomb. Despite the amount of silver, the fire spread quickly, feeding on ancient timbers.

Beckett plucked one that was newly alight from the edge of the growing fire and marched back down the corridor.

"This might help."

He spun around. Lane was standing there holding a large container.

"Petrol," she said, "From the jeep."

He took the container from her, understanding unspoken.

Together they walked the corridors, dribbling petrol onto the floor as they went. They stopped short of the kitchen where the hiss of the escaping gas could just be heard.

"How fast can you run?" she asked.

"We're about to find out."

"Hold on to me," she said.

He understood and put his arm around her. She was at the front door, with him still holding on to her, in a fraction of a second.

Lane reached into her pocket and took out her slim gold lighter and flicked it into life. She threw it down onto the nearest puddle of petrol.

The flames were immediate, taking on a life of their own and engulfing the corridor. Beckett stooped and picked up Kat's lifeless body.

"You have to leave her here, Beckett. The fire will do what has to be done."

He looked at her, pain lighting his eyes, but he knew she was right. He put Kat down carefully. Then they both leaped for the outside.

Mihai was at the gate with the jeep.

"Get in, Beckett; it's going to be tight."

Darius still lay unconscious across the back seat, so he and Lane jumped into the front together. The engine roared and they were heading back up the valley as the explosion ripped into the night.

Mihai stopped the jeep. The flames licked into the darkness and from the middle of the fire, the monastery bell sounded for the last time.

None of them spoke; they just sat watching the flames sweeping into the night.

A figure stood at the edge of the flames, arms raised in a blessing. Sister Maria.

Beckett turned to Mihai, but there was no sign of him and Darius was no longer on the back seat. He leaned back onto the headrest. "I hate it when that happens," he said.

"Get used to it," she replied.

"Meaning?"

"I mean, I can sense you Beckett. You were right, my dearest friend. I sense in you the turning. I can only assume it isn't so violent with you because of the Anti-

HVV. You know there is no more?"

He nodded.

"What the hell have you done to deserve all this, Handsome?"

"I should have been there for her."

"Don't do this, Beckett. I am so very sorry about Kat but there really was nothing you could have done. We are what we are. I don't understand why you have turned, I really don't. The only thing I can think of is that in swallowing Kat's blood it has reacted with the Anti-HVV to bring this about."

"So where do we go from here?"

"We go on, Beckett. Wherever that might be. But we go on together. You're going to need me."

"I think I've always needed you, Lane."

"Yes, well, from what Mihai has told me, we're going to be pretty busy from here on in." She was silent for several minutes, then said in almost a whisper, "Did you pray for her?"

He nodded. "Yes," he said, "Suddenly, I knew. I understood the meaning of it all. I found my way back. I won't go back to the Church, though. They don't quite have a handle on it, you know? There are other ways to serve God. And I can't think of anyone else I'd rather do it with."

Lane was silent and thoughtful as she laid her hand on his arm, her heart leaping at what after all may be possible.

"I do have a more immediate problem though," he said. "I'm hungry."

Beckett's adventures continue in *Lycan*.

If you would like to be notified when the next book is released, be sure to sign up to my newsletter at:

janmcdonaldemailsign-up.gr8.com.

THANK YOU!

To my Reader:

Many thanks for downloading and reading *Midnight Wine*, I hope you enjoyed reading it.

If you did enjoy, please post a review on Amazon or your favourite social media site and let your friends know about *Midnight Wine*.

I hope that this has whetted your appetite to read the novels in the Beckett trilogy. You can find details of these in the next few pages.

And don't forget to sign up for my newsletter for details of my latest books and a FREE exclusive short story!

Happy Reading!
All the best
Jan

ALSO BY JAN MCDONALD

Mike Travis Paranormal Investigations
The Crowsmoor Curse getBook.at/Crowsmoorcurse

Long Shadows getBook.at/longshadows

The Sacred Ark getBook.at/sacredark

The Haunted Diary of Victoria Little getBook.at/haunteddiary

The Merlin Manuscript getBook.at/merlin

The Sin Eater coming 2015

Mike Travis short stories
Beginnings getBook.at/Beginnings

Halloween getBook.at/halloween

The Beckett Vampire Trilogy
Lycan getBook.at/lycan

Part 3 coming 2015

ABOUT JAN MCDONALD

Jan lives close to the Welsh borders which have their own mystical quality and provide endless resources in the way of legends and folklore surrounding paranormal experiences. She loves all things paranormal and has read the best: Dennis Wheatley, Stephen King, Edgar Allan Poe, Bram Stoker and all those authors that excel in the creepy or downright scary world of paranormal events.

When she embarked on the Mike Travis series, she realised that the field of paranormal investigation is more than we see on the popular TV programmes. So in order to provide compelling ghost hunting tales but with the greatest accuracy, Jan trained as a Paranormal Investigator and has studied parapsychology.

CONTACT DETAILS

Visit the authors website:
jan-mcdonald.co.uk

Follow on Twitter:
@janmcdonald1

Like on Facebook:
www.facebook.com/pages/Jan-McDonald-Author/

Cover designed by www.StunningBookCovers.com
Cover art: © fotogestoeber - Fotolia.com

Published by: Raven Crest Books
ravencrestbooks.com

Like us on Facebook:
facebook.com/ravencrestbooksclub

www.ingramcontent.com/pod-product-compliance
Lightning Source LLC
Chambersburg PA
CBHW070725280626
47159CB00023B/2711